BACK TO RESOLUTION

Book 1 of the Resolution Series

ROSE DEE

HOLE IN THE WIND PUBLISHING

Formatting by: Wild Seas Formatting (RikHall.com)

ISBN EBook:978 – 0 – 9944011 – 3 – 7

ISBN Print: 978 – 0 – 9944011 – 4 – 4

Hole in the Wind Publishing

ACKNOWLEDGEMENTS

First and foremost, I thank my Heavenly Father, who answered my prayer and guided me in what He had planned for my life. It's never too late; Ask and you shall receive.

This book is dedicated to my TJ's. My son, Tully, for his tolerance in having a 'writing mum'. And in memory of my late husband, Terry who loved us, as well as my dad, Tom, who gave me the love of writing.

FOR MY TJ'S

CHAPTER 1

Bay was lost. She had known this day was coming. Why did she feel so numb, so helpless, so alone?

"Ashes to ashes, dust to dust." The preacher's words were familiar, yet she had never given them any thought. She hadn't given this moment any thought, and now her mother was dead. The cancer she had been diagnosed with only six months ago had taken her life.

She should be relieved that Mum's suffering was over. It had been a painful illness that had borne a heavy toll. Bay had witnessed the ravages of the disease as her mother transformed from model-thin to emaciated. Her bones jutted out sharply, and her skin fell loosely over her wasted frame. The beautiful face that had been sculptured with such sophistication by the surgeon's knife lost its impact under a yellow complexion.

Forty-four was too young to die. Bay knew her mother had given up the day she had been diagnosed. She recalled how fervently she had tried to urge her to fight the disease. "You have to at least try, Kate. The doctors give you a good chance of surviving this."

Her mother had been indignant. "What is there for me to fight for? You're all grown up. You have your own life, and no time for your mother." She had sighed. "And, let's face it, Peter will be happy to be rid of me. Then he can marry that tart he's seeing."

Her stepfather's dalliances with younger women were no secret. Bay was aware that her mother and stepfather had a long-standing agreement regarding their marriage. Peter agreed to be discreet in his affairs, whilst giving Kate every material thing she desired and keeping up the appearance of a perfect marriage. The agreement had functioned successfully until Kate's diagnosis. Now Peter openly paraded every conquest to the world. The situation was unacceptable to Kate; appearances were everything to her.

Bay looked around as they lowered the coffin into the ground. Kate would have been horrified at the meager turnout to her funeral. Bay. Tasha, her roommate. Richard, her boss. Peter. Maria, her mother's maid. And two old friends, one of whom had spent most of her time flirting with Peter.

Where were the rest of Kate's society friends? At the very least, where were the representatives of the charities Kate had supported?

While it was true that her mother was not as popular as she would have liked to believe, she did have regular friendships and social connections. They must have been more acquaintances than friends, because none had seen fit to attend her funeral.

The preacher finished his spiel and Richard turned and hugged her. He was her boss, mentor, and father figure. She needed his support and strength now more than ever. Bay broke away to look up into his face. His kind eyes echoed his fatherly affection for her.

Richard threw an arm around her shoulders. "You'll be alright, my girl. You're strong. You just need direction, strength and the love that only comes from one place. I know you'll find it."

Find it where? Direction, strength, and love felt far out of her reach. She covered her confusion by hugging him back.

"Thank you, Richard. Your friendship means the world to me." Fresh tears sprang to her eyes. Bay swallowed the lump in her throat before turning to accept an air-kiss from Tasha. Her flat mate had been restless during the short service, glancing at her watch several times. Bay could tell she was in a rush to get away.

"I'm so sorry for your loss." The lack of emotion in Tasha's voice made the statement sound insincere. Tasha's presence was all about self-preservation—she shared Bay's apartment at a greatly reduced rate. The apartment was in a great location. Modern and spacious, with ocean views. Tasha was protecting her position.

Bay gave her a tight smile.

"I had organized a wake back at the house, but I really don't think it's necessary. What do you think, Peter?" She turned to her stepfather. He hadn't tried to hide his discomfort during the service, and Bay almost felt sorry for him. With his rugged jaw line and dimpled chin, he would have been stunning in his immaculate tailored suit had he not been sweating so profusely.

"No, you're right. We should give it a miss." His deep voice carried a sense of relief as he wiped his forehead with a handkerchief.

Her mother's friends came to give their condolences and say goodbye. The one Bay recognized as Kate's tennis partner was sincere when she said she would miss her mother. The other was there for show. She gave Bay a quick semi-hug and air-kiss before returning her attention to Peter.

The only other person to cry at the funeral was Kate's maid. Maria had always been a support to Bay, especially through her teenage years. She had helped her cope with the lack of affection and parental guidance in her own life.

"It was good of you to come, Maria. Thank you for all that you did for my mother." Maria wrapped ample arms around her. Her Mexican accent was even harder to understand when muffled by tears. "Is ok. Sometime I hate her, but sometime I love her."

Just like me. How could two different people have such a similar relationship with Kate?

"Would you like me to drive you back, love?" Richard placed his hand in the small of her back as a silent support.

"Peter can see me home, thank you. We came together."

Bay looked at her stepfather for confirmation. He nodded and averted his eyes. Bay was sure his lack of composure was due to a guilty conscience.

You deserve to be uncomfortable.

They thanked the preacher and attendants and made their way to the limousine.

"Thank God. Air conditioning," Peter exclaimed as they settled into their seats. "I'm glad I had the forethought to tell the man to keep it running." One look at him told Bay that climate control wasn't the only relief Peter was feeling. His whole body slumped into the seat as he undid his tie and removed his jacket.

Bay looked at her stepfather. It was obvious Peter didn't love her mother. However, he had spared no expense when it came to her medical treatment and comfort, accommodating every outlandish demand Kate had made during her hospital stay. Unfortunately, his overcompensation in the material department didn't make up for his absence. Peter had only visited Kate's bedside twice since she had been diagnosed.

"Peter, I know you and Kate weren't the best of friends in recent times, so I want you to know how much I appreciate you looking after her the way you did." Bay paused. "Actually, the way you looked after both of us."

He looked up at her. Bay was sure she spotted a hint of remorse in his eyes. A frown creased his forehead. "I'm sorry, Bay. It all got too hard, and when she told me she was dying . . . well. At first I thought it was another trick."

He wrung the handkerchief in his hands. Bay had never seen her stepfather so distraught. Even in his fights with her mother, he was the calm, cool opponent, always in control.

"Before I knew it, they were phoning to tell me she'd died. I never believed it would be so quick. I thought Kate was dramatizing the situation for her own benefit."

He stopped twisting the handkerchief. "Look. I know I haven't always been there for you. I know I've been a bad father, but I have no intention of cutting you off. Anything you need, you only have to ask. Money is no object, and I'll increase your allowance. You'll need it now that your job's finished." He gave her a thin smile as he reached for the bottled water, handing one to her.

"Thanks, Peter."

Money is no object. Does he treat everyone the same? Peter's solution to any problem was to throw money at it. He'd never been intuitive when it came to emotions or empathy. His material solution to everything meant he never had to commit to anyone. As long as he was paying, he owned the right to withdraw from any unpleasant relationship, any unpleasant situation.

As transparent as it was, Bay wasn't about to turn down his offer. She was unemployed. She'd need his money if she was going to survive while she looked for a job. The task of having to drag herself off to interviews so soon after burying her mother was daunting.

Bay helped herself to a bottle of water and sat back. She gazed out of the window as the LA traffic sped by. She couldn't believe how much her life was changing. She had been Richard's assistant and protégé for over three years. It had been a shock to find out that he was closing up his photographic studio and taking a job at National Geographic.

She distinctly remembered the excitement in his eyes over the prospect of the challenge.

"I'm going to do it, Bay. It will be my last assignment. I'm not getting any younger, and I wanted to retire years ago, but I needed to keep busy." He had glanced away for a second before turning back to her.

"I'm so sorry. There's no way I can take you with me. It's too dangerous. The military have stated they can't guarantee my safety, and travelling with a woman in that country is impossible for obvious reasons." He had reached across the desk to take her hand. "I don't want to leave you behind. Not now. But I can't take you with me. People aren't your subject, Bay. You've learned as much from me as you can. You need to spread your wings." Bay recalled his genuine smile and the regret written all over his face.

Working with Richard had provided Bay with an invaluable breadth of experience, photographing the homeless of LA to Hollywood superstars. She had met many popular actors and celebrities, and had become the envy of her friends. Regardless of the opportunities, Bay was happiest photographing nature, not people. For her, nature was far more unpredictable and spectacular than a face. Even Richard would get excited over the candid moments in time she captured in her lens.

He had been a great influence. The way he communicated with people from all walks of life, not judging or condemning anyone, was a new experience. She learned to emulate his communication skills and wanted to be like him. It was hard to imagine life without Richard.

He had also made her contemplate spirituality. God didn't exist in the world Bay had been raised in, but Richard shared his spiritual journey with her, his honest thoughts and feelings about his Christian faith. Spirituality and faith had never been far from her mind over these last weeks with her mother. *Is there more? Do we go somewhere when we died? Surely this can't be it?*

So many questions and Richard had been there to answer every one. However, instead of putting her mind at ease, his answers had raised more questions. *Is there a God?* Bay felt a stirring that refused to go away, that refused to be extinguished by science or human reason. Now he was leaving, she was alone in her confusion. Bay felt as though she was losing both her mother and her father at the same time.

Her relationship with her boss had filled a huge gap in her life, the desire for a father. She had no memory of her real father. She had daydreams all through her childhood about who he was, and where he might be.

Her earliest memory was standing on a beach looking across the water at an island not far from the shore, feeling the sun on her skin and a large hand engulfing her small one. She was sure the hand had belonged to her father.

According to her mother, he'd run off when she told him she was pregnant. The only other reference Kate had ever made to him was being forced to explain to a teacher why her daughter preferred to be called by her nickname, Bay, instead of her given name, Jane. "She won't answer to it." Her mother had been exasperated. "Jane is such a lovely name, but she insists on a nickname. She's stubborn, like her father."

Any further questions about her father had been shut down by her mother. Bay had given up asking and resigned herself to never knowing. Then, only last week, Kate had dropped her bombshell.

It was the last time she had spoken with her mother. The memory was so clear. Bay had been sitting by her mother's bedside and had taken Kate's hand in hers. She had felt a deep compassion she never expected for her frail, dying mother.

Kate stirred and awoke. Bay gently squeezed her skeletal hand.

"My lovely daughter." Kate's voice was frail and disjointed.

"I'm here. Don't try to speak. You need to save your strength." Bay patted her hand.

Kate shook her head slowly. "No, I have to tell you. I'll be gone soon. I haven't done right by you." Her voice was barely a whisper.

What? Kate admitting fault was unheard of. Bay knew she should tell her mother to rest, but curiosity made her bend forward towards the bed as Kate spoke again.

"Your father didn't run off." She paused, closing her eyes.

Bay thought perhaps the painkillers had made her pass out, but she opened her eyes to continue.

"I left him." Kate took a small, frail breath.

The revelation shouldn't have surprised Bay, but it did. What should she feel? She sat, shocked, confused, dumbfounded. She stared, willing Kate to overcome her pride, to continue.

"He was a good man, Bay. He loved you very much. He just couldn't give me what I wanted." Kate tilted her head back and closed her eyes for a moment.

So many questions. She didn't know which to

ask first.

"I tried my best, but it wouldn't work. It had to be his way. His time. I needed more."

Bay shook her head, trying to come to grips with her mother's words.

It didn't surprise Bay that Kate had wanted more. More, more, more. It was the motto of her mother's life. More money, more jewelry, more prestige, more real estate, more designer clothes, more attention.

Had Kate's pursuit of more cost Bay her father? It was too much. She dropped her mother's hand back onto the bed.

Is it ok to be this angry at someone who is dying?

She took several deep breaths, rubbing her palm across her eyebrow and attempting to process the information.

The sound of the door opening drew her attention and a nurse entered the room. "I'm sorry, but I need to take your mother down to x-ray," she said. "She will need her rest when she gets back." It was a nice way of saying that Bay had to leave, and the timing couldn't be worse. There were so many questions.

Bay hadn't seen her mother awake again. Hours later, she had suffered a massive stroke and never recovered. All Bay's questions regarding her father remained unanswered. The only family she had left in the world was a disinterested stepfather.

Bay looked across at Peter, who had downed his water.

Could he fill in the gaps that Kate left? No time like the present to broach the subject.

"Peter, before Kate died she told me a few things about my real father. I still have a lot of unanswered questions. Did she ever said anything to you about him?"

Peter reached out to pour himself a glass of scotch before answering her. "I wondered if she'd tell you about him. She probably thought I'd spill the beans after she died. Kate hated to be trumped." He raised one side of his mouth. "I can't say I know much about him, but we did meet once."

Bay straightened in her seat. "When was that?"

Peter swirled the liquid in his glass. "Well, when I met your mother, she told me the same story she told you and everyone else. That he ran off when she was pregnant. Believe it or not, I was once very much in love with her. I think I fancied myself her knight in shining armor. At least she made me feel like that. We met in Cairns. I was in Australia, looking into the viability of purchasing a chain of hotels."

Peter's family fortune was in the hotel business, starting with his grandfather, father and now continuing with Peter. Kate was born and raised in Australia. She was the only child of aged parents who had both died before Bay was born. Bay was her only child, and had also been born in Australia. They both left to live with Peter in the States not long after Bay's fourth birthday.

"I thought you met in Sydney?" Bay was confused. Her mother loved telling the story of how they had met at the Sydney Opera House at a society gala. Cairns was a coastal city located at the top end of Queensland, a long way from Sydney.

"I never bothered to correct that lie. Kate loved

to rewrite history. It was easier to ignore most of the mistruths." He shrugged. "No, we met in a hotel bar in Cairns. I was there on business and she was visiting a friend. She gave me the sob story of her life. Parents dead, boyfriend run off, no prospects . . . Over the week I fell desperately in love with her, and she managed to convince me to bring you and her back to the States with me. We married less than three weeks after we met." Peter paused to give a low chuckle. "I think I did it quickly to spite my father. He hated the idea. His disapproval made me love it."

He took a long swig of his drink. "We were happy for a while. Kate was involved in the business. That's where I went wrong, involving her in every aspect of my life. If I'd kept the business from her, I wouldn't have had to live a lie for so long."

Bay frowned, confused. She couldn't remember her mother being involved in the business.

Peter saw her expression. "At the time I was involved with a bit of a rough crowd. I was doing some ah …" He paused, clearly searching for the words. "Some special favors for an organized crime mob. My father didn't know about it and Kate was involved in certain aspects of the scheme. It provided us with some cold hard cash, and bought us some expensive toys. Kate loved to have money."

It sounded harsh, but his statement was truthful. Her mother did love money, and all the material things it could buy for her.

"Your father turned up at my office, looking for you when you were about eight. It was more than a bit of a shock. Kate and I had been married four years. He made it clear that he didn't want anything to do with Kate. He just wanted to see you. He also told me the real story." Peter moved in his seat, finding a more comfortable position before continuing.

"He proposed marriage when Kate fell pregnant with you, but she kept putting off the date, saying they had to make their fortune first. That was Kate. Eyes always on the finer things. He was about fifteen years older than her and, from what I could gather, he was more than capable of providing for you both. He told me he had a home and money he'd saved from working an opal mine. Kate emptied the bank account when she ran off with me. She left him with no money, and no clue as to where she'd gone."

Bay was in shock. It would have been hard to believe if she wasn't so accustomed to her mother's manipulation and deceit. But Peter had nothing to lose by telling the truth now, and Bay knew from personal experience how Kate loved to scheme. Peter's story sounded plausible.

Peter gave her a moment to digest the information then continued his story. "It took him the four years to raise the funds and mount his own investigation into where you were, and to get over here. He told me he didn't care about the money Kate had taken. He just wanted to see you."

Bay looked at him, lost for words. Her father had come all the way from Australia, tracked her down and had wanted to see her? "Why didn't he see me?" The question was thick with hurt and betrayal.

Peter looked out the window of the limousine. The silence was deafening. When he finally spoke, his voice was soft and slow. "I failed you that day,

Bay. I should have told him where to find you. I should have . . ." His voice trailed off and he sighed, long and deep.

A lone tear trailed its way down her face. *Is it even possible for me to have tears left today?*

Peter turned to look at her and, seeing the tear, pulled a tissue from the box and handed it to her.

"When I confronted Kate with the lies, she threatened that if I gave him any information about you, she'd go to the authorities and my father with evidence linking me to the mob. There was no evidence of her involvement, but she had accumulated plenty on mine. Even before that, I knew our marriage wouldn't last. Kate was driven, and I was just a pawn in her plan. She wouldn't divorce me, so the best alternative was to keep up the pretense of a marriage, but lead separate lives."

Peter slumped back in the leather seat. "Of course, this made all of us incredibly unhappy, even Kate. I haven't been able to live with it. I want a life of my own. Free of lies and free of Kate."

Bay looked away from him as a volcanic-sized swell formed in her stomach. They were as bad as each other. Selfish, scheming, manipulative.

You want a life of your own, and you're happy to destroy others' lives to get it! She was so angry she could feel her jaw clenching.

Her mother was a piece of work, but Peter couldn't even pretend to be her husband to make her last days on earth happy. She pushed down the rage within. It would do her no good to blow up now. She needed more information.

"Can you tell me my father's name or where I can

contact him?" She hoped at least he could give her a starting point.

"I'm sorry. After that first encounter, Kate forced me to take action against him in order to keep him from seeing you. "

"What sort of action?" she pushed.

"Do you remember the vacation you and Kate took to Hawaii?"

She did remember. Kate pulled her out of school for two months of travelling around from one five-star resort to another. Her mother spent her time drinking at the bars while Bay swam in the hotel pools. Even at age eight, two months was way too long to spend in the company of her mother.

"Apart from getting you out of LA, she also hired bodyguards to shield me against any further contact with him, as well as a private investigator to shadow his every move. I felt it was overkill, but she was determined to keep him from you. Eventually he ran out of money. He spent two weeks on the streets then boarded a plane back to Australia." He reached over to pour himself another glass of Scotch.

"I don't understand. Why didn't she want him to see me? Was he abusive or something?" Perhaps there was good reason for her mother's behavior.

Peter took a long swig of scotch before answering. "I thought that too, but when I asked her she said he wasn't. Not at all. He was a loving man. He just couldn't give her all she wanted. She said that you were the only person who would love her unconditionally, and she needed that in her life. She wasn't prepared to share you with him."

Self-centered . . . Bay regretted the thought. Even

if her mother deserved it, she was dead now and no good was going to come of hating her. That road led to nowhere.

She turned her attention back to Peter. "So you know nothing about him? Not one detail?" She was hoping for any piece of information. Any lead he could give her.

"Sorry, no. He left and I never saw or heard from him again. Some years ago I went through your mother's office in an attempt to locate the evidence she claimed she had on me, but I found nothing. Kate would have something up her sleeve, so I put off plans to force a divorce. I didn't find a scrap of information on your father. Not even a photo or copy of your birth certificate, only passports. She covered her steps well."

"Can you at least tell me what he looks like?"

Peter thought for a moment. "Well, as I said, he was older than your mother, but it was fourteen years ago. He's probably changed now. From what little I can recall, he had blonde hair, like yours, and your pre-surgery nose." Peter gave her an unkind smirk.

At the age of thirteen Kate had all but forced her daughter to have a nose job. In the land of 'beautiful people' it was unacceptable that her attractiveness was being hampered by such an obvious blemish. Bay hadn't seen the need for surgery. Her thick wavy blonde hair, well-proportioned body, and dark green eyes more than made up for her oversized nose. Kate wouldn't give an inch, calling in her plastic surgeon. An operation was performed in a matter of weeks. *Another example of Kate's vanity.*

"Is that all you can remember?" Bay let out a heavy sigh. "You can't tell me anything else?"

"Well . . ." Peter frowned hard. "He did have a slight accent. German or something. That's all I remember. Sorry." Peter sat back, and turned his attention to the surroundings as the gates to his driveway opened.

"So I have nothing to go by." Bay thought out loud. All hope of finding her father was slipping away, and she realized she didn't have the strength or confidence to do anything about it. Certainly not in the near future. Just getting through each day would be a struggle.

The limousine pulled into his mansion and Peter turned to her. "The driver can drop you home. Remember what I said. Anything you need . . ." The chauffeur opened his door and he was gone.

The car started up again to take Bay back to her apartment. She poured a glass of Whiskey.

CHAPTER 2

Bay's mind was still reeling from her conversation with Peter when she walked through her door. She wanted to know her real father, especially now that her mother was gone. Unfortunately, she had no clue on how or where to start her search.

She poured another glass of Whisky and walked out onto the small balcony, taking a seat on one of the deck chairs, and enjoying the cool ocean breeze that filtered through the palms lining the deck.

The sound of the front door opening and closing distracted her for a second before she blocked it out again.

"Bay, are you home? You must be. I can see your camera case at the door." A shrill voice rang out. Tasha.

Since beginning an internship with a stylist, Tasha had made it her full-time occupation to emulate the fashion and celebrity set. Her voice had changed to the distinct whine that was classic speech for LA party girls, indicative of their general displeasure with everything.

"There you are." She walked onto the patio and took the seat opposite Bay.

"I don't want to add to the stress of your day but I feel the need to tell you something." Tasha had a mischievous smirk on her face and was looking anywhere but at her.

Bay deliberately didn't reply, just glanced at

Tasha before she launched into her gossip driven rant.

"It's about Tiffany Russell. You know that model your stepdad's seeing?"

Usually Bay was happy to let Tasha prattle on about who did or said what, but today it cut a little close to home.

"I'm not interested in my stepfather's women. I don't care."

Tasha pouted. She obviously had some juicy gossip. Bay had a change of heart. It may be good to know what her stepfather was up to. "Go ahead then. It might take my mind off things." Her day couldn't get much worse.

"She came into the shop this morning like she owned the place, and demanded to be waited on. She was wearing boyfriend jeans. Taaaacky. So last year."

Bay rolled her eyes. It looked as if she was going to get details.

"She spent the next two hours buying up, and got those cool lime green pumps. You know, the ones with the pink trim I told you about. Love them. So wasted on her. I've never seen such ugly feet. Truly hideous." Tasha came up for air and plunged back in. "She spent huge, and put it all on Peter's credit card. Then when I said she was lucky to have a boyfriend who spent so much on her she said, and I quote, 'He's not my boyfriend, he's my fiancé.'"

This day could get worse. Bay closed her eyes.

"That's not all. She said they've been engaged for over three months." When she had a story to tell Tasha held nothing back. "She had a diamond ring on her finger. Massive. Like a zillion carats. Can you believe it? He buried his wife today. What a jerk."

Yes, he is. Anger welled up inside her.

Tasha was on a roll, and not prepared to end there. "I bet he's got no idea you've found out about it. You should call him right now and let him know what you think of him." Tasha feigned indignant displeasure, sweeping her fringe back from her eyes.

"I can't let this get to me, Tash. Kate knew what Peter was like. She knew he'd marry his mistress as soon as she was out of the picture." Saying it out loud was hard.

"I'm so sorry, Bay. Here I am prattling on about Peter when you're grieving." She dropped her bottom lip in an attempt to feign sympathy.

"It's okay. It's best I know what Peter's up to. I like to be prepared when it comes to him."

Tasha gave her a sympathetic frown. "I'm here if you ever need to talk." She then walked back inside. Clattering noises in the kitchen suggested she was searching for dinner.

So much for the shoulder to cry on. Although she and Tasha had grown up together and had once been inseparable—had even spent a year touring Europe together— they'd grown apart in the last two years. Once back in LA, Tasha had gravitated towards the world of fashion, and Bay had pursued her photography. Then, with Richard as a mentor, she had grown to detest the lack of substance in the world Tasha thrived in.

Not that she could be too judgmental of LA excesses and the exclusivity of fashion and popularity. Kate had furnished her with every luxury from the latest in must-have technology to a wardrobe of designer clothes and accessories. Kate had even set Bay up in her apartment with its ocean views, and given her a BMW convertible once she had acquired her driver's license. *I've been as much a trophy as everything else in her world.*

Bay sighed at the thought. She had to concede that she had always taken full advantage of Kate's wealth. She allowed the society she kept and the must-haves of her generation to dictate who she was as much as Kate had. Lately, she had questioned the worth of it all.

Her mother's dead body had been a shock. It was nothing but a shell. Where had her mother gone? She was no longer there, and all the beautiful jewelry she had spent her life acquiring lay perfect on a lifeless corpse. Bay had realized money and things didn't make a person. They didn't comfort her now that her mother was gone. They didn't replace not having a family. They didn't make her a better person. No matter how much she had, it didn't fill the aching, gaping hole that was inside her.

What would fill that?

Bay stretched and listened to the waves roll onto the beach beyond. She would never have questioned what was missing in her life if it hadn't been for Richard. Richard had told her his lifelong faith had faltered when his wife and daughter were killed by a drunk driver ten years prior. "How could he take away the two most important things in my life, Bay? I was angry at him," he had said.

Bay had been taken aback by the statement. Richard sounded as though he was talking about a friend, not God. As honest as the statement had been, Bay felt uncomfortable with the subject matter. Up until that point she had never really thought much about the place God might play in her life. She had often admired the awesome beauty in nature and wondered if maybe a higher being did have a hand in its making. It seemed implausible that it all happened due to a scientific accident.

She just never felt God was relevant to her. She had everything she wanted, and had never been without. And why would God want to know her? She'd never done anything for Him. But one thing was clear: material things were not enough.

Seeing Richard off at the airport was hard. They stood hugging as the flight was called. She felt secure in his embrace. Loved. His face held a multitude of emotions: concern, sadness and a fatherly protectiveness she would never forget. She was sure her face held one emotion — fear.

He hugged her tight before gently holding her shoulders. "I hope someday you'll understand my decision to move on. All my life I prided myself on being in God's plan. When June and Amy died, I lost all faith in God and His plan. My anger overtook my desire to please Him. But I worked through the anger long ago and realized that, although I still don't understand losing my girls, I know they are with Him, and He can turn any situation around for our good."

Richard paused, his kind eyes searching hers. "Look at what he's done for me in the last few years.

Having you in my life has given me back so much that I'd lost. You've let me be like a father again, and to love another person as my own. He can turn your hurts and losses around for good, if you let Him. All you need to do is ask, and believe."

It was so simple a solution Bay almost laughed. Kate had always said, 'seeing is believing.' How could she believe in a God she couldn't see?

Richard continued. "I know this is bad timing, and it feels like I'm deserting you. It even feels like that to me, but I know that my leaving is in God's plan. He's given me time to heal, and time to love again. Don't ever forget that I love you, Bay, but He loves you more."

Richard reached into his satchel and pulled out a clumsily wrapped gift. He handed it to her. "Don't open it until I'm gone."

With that he kissed her forehead and made his way through the gate, turning to give her a smile and a wave. Bay stood at the gate until the plane left the holding area, hoping for a miracle that would see Richard disembark from the aircraft and remain in her life. As the plane taxied down the runway Bay slowly opened the present he had given her. It was a red leather Bible. The dedication on the inside of the front cover read: *'For my Bay. May this gift help you to find your way home. Love, Richard'*. The words confused her. *Home where?* As she turned the book over in her hand she noticed that Richard had marked many places throughout. Bay tucked the Bible in her bag and made her way out of the airport.

Bay hadn't opened the Bible Richard had given her since he left. Instead, she tried to fill the gap left by her mentor by partying, shopping, and living the high life. Until it become apparent that her lifestyle of self-destruction wasn't working.

The room spun as she opened her eyes. Bay recognized the familiar feeling of sickness in her stomach. She moaned as she rolled over and closed her eyes again. The faint light that poured in from the slight opening in her curtains cut through the darkness, and made it impossible to enjoy the sanctuary of the dark room. A slight touch on her bare stomach startled her and she sat up in bed.

What was that? Next to her, lying amongst the pillows, was her ex-boyfriend, Darren. *No way. What the hell was I thinking?* Regret filtered through every fiber of her being. She blinked her eyes again to make sure the vision was real. It was real, and lying comatose in her bed.

Bay covered her face with her hands willing it all to go away. *Of all men, why him?* As soon as she asked herself the question, she realized she knew why. Darren had been making it clear he wanted her back, and would go to any lengths to make it happen.

Ever since her mother's funeral, Bay had been on a roller coaster of excess. The generous allowance from Peter meant she didn't need to work, and Tasha had reintroduced her to the LA social scene. Her life consisted of partying all night and spending most of the day at coffee houses recovering from a hangover.

This wasn't the first time in recent weeks she had woken up sick. She was the life of the party and Darren, who had never left the scene, had latched onto her newfound sense of fun and all things self-destructive. She had been bombarded with text messages, phone calls, flowers . . . all the wooing techniques.

His interest was most likely sparked by seeing her with other guys. She had had no lack of attention the last couple of months, but this was the first time she had woken up with someone. Why did it have to be him?

She got out of bed pulling the sheet with her, and wrapping it around her semi-naked body. The movement on the bed woke Darren up. He looked up at her. A smirk filled his smug face.

"Hi there." He sat up slowly, rubbing a manicured hand through streaked blonde hair.

Bay looked at him. She was disgusted with herself. This had to be one of her lowest points.

"Did we ...?" She couldn't finish the question. The thought made her sick. Sicker than the hangover, anyway.

"You were great, baby." Darren gave her the triumphant look of a satisfied man.

Her whole body slumped and Bay threw her head back, drawing her arms around herself.

"Hey. Hey. It's okay. Look, nothing happened. We tried but you were sick. It all got a bit messy. We slept together in a purely literal sense. That's it." Relief spread throughout her body, and she recognized the bad taste in her mouth. She moved to the bathroom in search of a toothbrush.

The bathroom smelled as bad as her mouth felt. At least it looked like she had made it to the toilet. She brushed her teeth and mouth with so much force she probably scrubbed the enamel off her teeth. The pressure pack of air freshener made short work of the lingering sickly smell.

Bay found her dressing gown hanging on a hook in the bathroom and put it on. She paused to look in the mirror before moving back to face Darren. She looked hideous. Her hair was a mess, and last night's make-up clung to her face. She grabbed a brush and ran it through her hair. A face wipe got rid of most of the old make-up.

Slightly better.

Darren was out of bed and putting on his clothes when she returned.

"I can't remember much from last night." Bay didn't really trust Darren's version of events. He was known to get creative with the truth, but the last thing she remembered was dancing in one of the nightclubs uptown.

He smiled at her as he grabbed his shirt from the floor. "You were certainly on fire last night. I don't think I've ever seen you like that before. It really turned me on."

"Seen me like what?"

What did I do? Bay didn't know if the sick feeling in her stomach was from the alcohol or regret of the unknown. She sat on the bed and gave him her undivided attention.

Although she wasn't sure she wanted to know.

"You really don't remember, do you?"

Bay shook her head.

"We were all having a great time. You were pretty wasted. Then Peter and his blonde bimbo walked in." Darren's degrading reference to Tiffany was no surprise. He had little respect for women in general.

"You went over to them and started yelling and screaming at Peter about being a jerk to you and your mom. When the bimbo stepped between the two of you, you slapped her across the face. Then you went for him with a closed fist, although you didn't get there."

Bay covered her face with her hands. It was worse than she thought.

"But, I have to say, my personal favorite moment of the confrontation was when you told her that she was little more than a whore, and would be replaced when she outlasted her usefulness." A slow chuckle escaped from deep down in his throat. "That was a shock. You used to be such a sweet thing, Bay, apart from dumping me. That was a mistake."

Yeah. Sure. Big mistake.

"Peter was livid. After we got you under control, he told me to take you home. You were useless. You must have been sick five or more times. What were you drinking?"

From what she could remember, anything she could get her hands on. It didn't surprise her that she had lost it with Peter. It had been building for some time — perhaps all her life.

She took a moment to digest the information. *Oh, well. Nothing I can do about it now.* But there would be repercussions. She'd probably be cut off. She sighed. Then she remembered the leech was still there. *Time for you to leave.*

"Thanks for getting me home." She stood up. Darren had other ideas.

"Want to get some breakfast? Something nice and greasy for my fallen angel? We can go to that place we used to go to back when we were dating."

Bay resented being his anything. Darren may have been her one long-term relationship, but she hadn't forgotten his womanizing, or his sense of entitlement when they were together.

"No, thanks. I just want to go back to bed." *Alone. And maybe die.*

"Come on. Some greasy food is what you need to soak up the alcohol. I'm sure you've got nothing left in your stomach after last night."

It wasn't going to be easy getting rid of him.

"Thanks, but I really need to be alone at the moment." She moved towards the door and out into the hallway. She reached the kitchen and poured herself a necessary glass of water.

Darren followed her and made himself comfortable on a kitchen stool. "Can I have one of those?"

No. Go away. Bay rolled her eyes as she turned to open the refrigerator. It would be best not to be rude. After all, he did get her home, even if he made it clear that if she had been capable of giving him what he had wanted, he would have taken it, regardless of the state she was in.

She poured a second glass and set it in front of him. He took a long drink, looking at her through the glass.

The sound of an incoming text message rang out from the cell phone in his pocket. He fumbled around for the phone and read the message.

"I have to go," he said, as if it was his idea to

leave and she would be heartbroken by the news. He put the phone back in his pocket. "We can catch up later for coffee."

Bay gave no response.

He tried another tactic. "Actually, scrap that. I'll call you. Maybe I can clear my schedule for dinner."

Not a chance. "I'm not sure what I'm doing." There was no way she was extending this encounter.

He looked at her for a second. She stared back, hands firmly on the kitchen counter. Finally he resigned himself to the fact that he wasn't going to get anywhere and turned to go.

"Playing hard to get again? Okay. Well, I'll see you round. No doubt in a club. Happy hangover."

Bay breathed a sigh of relief when the door closed behind him.

"Is he gone?" Tasha dragged herself into the kitchen from the vicinity of her bedroom.

"Yep. Gone for good," Bay said with certainty. She took another drink of water and wished she had been drinking it last night.

Tasha looked up through her long blonde fringe. "I wouldn't be so sure about that. He's pretty persistent. After last night, you might be stuck with him."

"Nothing happened. I was too sick."

"You know, he's still pretty cute." Tasha had supported her friend when she had dumped Darren before, but she had the philosophy that all men cheat and was pathetically forgiving in her dysfunctional relationships.

"I'm not interested in Darren. I've made enough problems for myself. I don't need him hanging around." Bay gulped her water.

Tasha took the seat vacated by Darren. "I wondered if you'd remember what happened last night."

"I didn't. He filled me in. I kind of wish he hadn't. Was it as bad as he said?" Bay knew Tasha would be honest with her.

Tasha poured herself some water. "Probably worse. What got into you? I mean, apart from the alcohol. You were like a woman possessed."

"I don't know. I guess it's been building up for a while, and seeing them together brought it all to the surface. Not to mention the false courage." Brief flashes of memory were coming back, and they weren't good.

This was a new low. Peter wouldn't let this go, especially as the incident took place in a public arena. For sure he would change their agreement. Perhaps it would be for the better. She may not be able to move on by herself.

It took two days for Peter to contact her. Bay knew he was letting her sweat it out for a bit, extending the time in order to highlight his displeasure. She was surprised by how little she cared, despite knowing her entire wellbeing rested upon his charity. She'd received no inheritance from her mother — everything went to Peter. The partying was her way of numbing the pain of losing both her mother and Richard at the same time. It gave her some direction in life — a destructive one, but at least she was occupied.

Her cell phone rang.

Time to face the music. "Hello, Peter." Her voice conveyed a confidence she didn't feel.

"Bay, how are you? Recovered, I hope?" There was no concern, only sarcasm.

"Yes, thank you." Bay had vowed not to apologize. He'd had it coming for a long time, although she was a little remorseful about attacking his fiancé. "I hope Tiffany didn't suffer too badly. I can't imagine I did much damage considering the state I was in."

"She's fine apart from wounded pride. You've put me in a very difficult position, you know."

She could tell he was struggling. "What position is that?"

"Apart from the humiliation I've suffered, I now have to deal with an angry and vindictive fiancé."

So not all was right with the lovely Tiffany.

"She wants me to cut you out of my life."

It wasn't any surprise to Bay. She knew what he really meant was to cut her off financially. There was no other way she was in his life.

"I have a proposal for you."

This should be good.

Peter continued. "I still have some contacts in Australia. One of them is the owner of an exclusive five-star hotel in the Daintree. That's the forest north of Cairns."

Bay was familiar with the area. Since Peter revealed where he'd met her mother, she'd looked up the area on the internet and spent hours poring over various towns, wondering if one of them was where her father still lived.

"He's agreed to take you on as a photographer for a few months. Apparently, he has guests who will pay good money for a professional to take pictures of their wedding. He also needs new material for an updated media campaign."

It didn't sound too bad.

"I will continue to pay your allowance, so long as you go. If you decide to stay in LA, I'll be forced to cut you off."

Bay knew he wouldn't be forced to do anything. This was his way of getting rid of her. He may even feel guilty about continuing with his marriage plans with her around.

"You do know, Peter, that Australia has stopped being the place to send undesirables." Even though the trip sounded exactly what she needed she couldn't resist the sarcastic comment.

"I'm well aware you're not a convict, but the move is for your own good."

Move? The word rang warning bells. It all became clear. Peter was paying her to leave for good. "Are you suggesting that my going to Australia would be a permanent arrangement?" She needed to get this straight.

"I certainly don't want to see you back here any time soon. With the social events surrounding the buildup to the wedding, we're certain to cross paths with you. I don't want a repeat of the other night. When the assignment in the Daintree ends you may like to do some sightseeing. Maybe settle somewhere appealing."

Bay couldn't believe the audacity of the man. "I guess I can't expect an invitation to the wedding then?"

He ignored the question. "There are other reasons why I want you to leave. You've gone from having a serious career to being a useless society party girl. I thought you were past that. It will do you good to get away from the bad influences."

He sounded like a parent—something he certainly wasn't and never had been. She resented it, but let him continue to sell the move.

"You have an opportunity to get a good look at the country of your birth. Who knows? Maybe you'll find some information that could lead to your father."

She knew Peter couldn't care less about her finding her father. It was just another convenient carrot to dangle in front of her.

Bay tossed up the positives and negatives. All the things he had said were true. She needed to get out of the LA scene before it destroyed her. It would also be convenient to escape Darren. She hadn't picked up her camera for a while. It would do her the world of good to get back into photography. She could always come back to LA, minus the allowance, if she wanted.

"Okay, I'll go." It actually sounded like a great adventure, but Bay was careful not to sound too enthusiastic. She didn't want to praise him for the suggestion.

"Good. I'll make the arrangements."

The phone went dead. Bay pressed the disconnect button and looked out the window. The Pacific Ocean was wild today. White caps broke out to sea, and large waves rolled onto the beach. This was the same ocean she would travel across to reach her new home.

She felt a flutter of anticipation in her stomach. What would await her?

CHAPTER 3

The color was so intense it was blinding. Even after three weeks, it was still overwhelming. Bay had never seen so many versions of green before, each one a distinct and vital part of the most awesome canvas of nature. She marveled at the many vibrant colors and un-touched beauty. Nothing could ever have prepared her for the Daintree. It amazed her that every shot she had taken was lovely, yet not one had done the views justice. Bay stood still, as if any movement would break the moment of tranquility.

The slow coo of a rainforest pigeon echoed in the air. Its delicate tones broke the never-ending tinkling of running water, and croaking of green frogs. The lush rainforest canopy provided a constant twilight, and the occasional stream of sunlight that broke through the umbrella of branches above was like sparkling gold suspended in air.

A rustling noise drew her attention. She looked to her right to see a small creature scampering along the ground and into the hollow of a log. The only visual evidence of its existence was the straight tail hanging out of its home. She recognized the small rodent-like animal as a bandicoot. She readjusted her camera and wished she'd had it poised to capture the sweet-looking creature, but she had been mesmerized by an enormous fern that stood as master of its domain.

She had tried different times of day in order to

capture the magnificence of the plant. Each attempt had evoked its own version of light, but she had yet to achieve a satisfying portrait. Bay positioned herself against a boulder, sensing this was the moment she had been waiting for. She hesitated a second, then began shooting. The hesitation paid off. As if by cue a cool breeze drifted off the tiny waterfall, and a slight mist enveloped the fern, catching the light and creating glistening diamonds on the leaves.

Bay smiled and put her camera back into its case without taking another shot. Instinct told her that was the picture she craved. She took one last look at the little waterfall that breathed life into the area. This was the last time she would walk along this particular track. Having captured the photo it offered, she would now concentrate on another area of the forest.

She dragged her heels all the way back to her cabin, reluctant to leave. The fern and the waterfall felt like old friends. The time she had spent there had reduced her anxiety and sadness to a functioning level. She had finally opened her Bible and had begun randomly reading through the passages Richard had marked. The stories of the Old Testament were fascinating, and she had started reading the passages marked for her in the New Testament. She marveled at many of the tales of faith and courage. At times she was so captivated that dusk fell unnoticed.

Her time spent in the Daintree had also been professionally successful. In a few short weeks she had captured some of her best shots, and had found within the forest a release in her spirit. On one of her forest walks she had come across a cassowary, a large bird with a small thick horn on its head. She hid among the foliage and snapped away as the bird moved gracefully through the trees. All of a sudden, a baby arrived, catching up to its mother with great speed. It produced a terrific photo.

Bay had also found kangaroos grazing on the luscious grass shoots, green frogs glistening on rocks, and a huge tree python lying lazily on a branch. The location was a photographer's dream.

Layers of forest foliage cushioned her steps as she made her way along the path. A magnificent blue butterfly met her at the bottom of the steps to her cabin. This resort was more than a five-star getaway. The eco-environment created here ensured guests had an authentic nature experience. Each cabin curved around a huge raintree with stilts holding it up, and boardwalks everywhere allowed the pristine rainforest to remain untouched despite the human intrusion.

A restaurant overlooking one of many waterfalls in the area boasted award-winning à la carte cuisine. A day spa set among the forest ensured guests had a truly relaxing holiday, and the pool bar added to the relaxing feel of the resort.

The Evans family ran the resort. James Evans was an acquaintance of Peter's—they'd met in LA when James was temping as manager of a spa retreat. They were a lovely family: James, Rebecca and their children, ten-year-old Cooper and eight-year-old Claire.

Claire had taken a special interest in Bay. The

child sometimes followed her while she photographed. She had been a valuable source of information on the native flora and fauna. Claire had been full of questions of her own, constantly quizzing Bay about what she was doing.

Bay didn't mind the interruption. Claire didn't tag along often—only when not being home-schooled—and Bay had picked her as a budding photographer.

The little girl now peered at her from the small balcony above. "Did I miss you? Mum said I could go, but I had to finish my report first and I couldn't think of anything to write about. It took me ages." Her big brown eyes looked out from a thick fringe of light brown hair. Her ponytail was so long that it swung over her shoulder as she looked down.

Bay was relieved Claire had missed her. It had been nice to visit her special place one last time on her own. Bay walked up the steep steps and took a seat on the balcony next to her little friend.

"Don't worry. There's always tomorrow. I'm going to do some more shots around the resort. Your Dad told me there's low occupancy, and I want to get some more photos of the buildings."

Claire made a face. "Not the buildings again. I thought you got plenty of pictures of them last week." She loved the adventure, and as long as she was with Bay, she had been allowed to journey deeper into the forest than when on her own.

"I'm hoping for some good light tomorrow. It rained all last week and I think I can get better shots."

Claire rolled her eyes. "I know, I know. Lighting is everything."

Bay had given her many lessons on how to achieve the best lighting, something she was still learning herself. Nature and animal photography were far different from the sort of portraits Richard had favored. It was labor-intensive, and Bay only had herself to complete the task. A permanent assistant would have been preferable. Unfortunately, none of the staff were able to be spared, so she had harnessed the enthusiasm of Claire and put her to work as her assistant.

"If you give me a hand tomorrow, I'll take you on my next walk to the beach," Bay said.

Claire's eyes lit up. "That would be so cool. Can I bring my camera too?"

The little digital camera was her prized possession, and Bay had been teaching her to use it properly.

"We can even go for a swim if you bring your bathers."

Claire raised forehead and shook her head. "No way. I'm not crocodile bait, and neither are you. No swimming."

Bay had forgotten the warning she had received from James when she first arrived. No swimming anywhere but the designated areas. The isolated location meant the population of saltwater crocodiles had increased dramatically in recent years, leading to an increase in attacks and deaths. Last week a crocodile had sprung out of the creek to drag a dog back into the water. The crocs made swimming in the ocean impossible, with so many of them prowling the coast.

Bay was always careful to swim where advised,

in case she ran into one of the prehistoric monsters. "No swimming. I forgot. It's such a shame. The water always looks so inviting." The 'no swimming' rule was frustrating. The beach and the pristine waters that met the coast were a wonderful surprise on her first bushwalk away from the resort. She was strolling along a track when the rainforest canopy gave way to the most magnificent sandy beach and blue green water. Pieces of coral had washed up on the sand, and she had collected the most ornate pieces to take back to her cabin.

Claire picked up a ladybug that was making its way across the decking. "Maybe Mick will take you out to the reef again. I'm sure he would if you asked him. I can tell he really likes you." She gave a sly smile.

Bay shook her head at the young girl. "I like Mick. He's a really nice guy, even if I don't always understand him." She struggled with his accent and his Aussie-isms.

Claire giggled.

The first day she had been introduced to the bronzed, muscular handyman, he had asked if she would like a 'cold one', and handed her a beer. Then he took a deep gulp, and let out an intense "Ahhhhh." He looked at the drink and exclaimed, "Make a peewee fight an emu." Bay giggled at the description even though she had no idea what it meant. When she asked, he explained that a peewee was a very small bird, and the emu a very large one. The beer was so good it could inspire the smaller bird to fight the larger one.

Since then she had become used to Mick's

descriptive Aussie-isms, and the way the Aussies in the resort shortened everything. Breakfast became brekkie. Afternoon became arvo. And for some reason that not even Mick could explain, afternoon snack was called smoko.

Claire twirled a piece of her hair and frowned. "I don't know why you can't understand Australian when you are one."

Bay smiled at the little girl. "Well, I was four when I left here. I grew up in America, but I hold dual citizenship. That means I'm a citizen of both Australia and America."

Claire shrugged. "Mum has that. She was born in New Zealand." She stopped to squash an ant that was making its way towards her leg. "So are you going to ask Mick? I think he really likes you. He took you out to the reef that day, and normally he doesn't take anyone."

Bay had to admire her tenacity and obvious matchmaking skills. Mick would be a catch, if she was interested in a relationship.

When Bay had expressed a desire to go snorkeling, Mick had been more than obliging. He had prepared the boat and taken her out one afternoon. The water had been like glass as they cut through it in the small boat he called a tinny. Thankfully it was equipped with a canopy to protect them from the scorching sun. The reef was far enough away from the mainland to be out of reach of the crocodiles.

If Bay had thought the mainland forest was captivating, the reef under the water was equally awe-inspiring. Where the forest was a symphony of green, the reef was a sensation of color. Every creature looked as though an artist had wielded a rainbow brush and splashed each one across its body.

Mick had tried to point out various creatures to her as they snorkeled, but Bay was so stunned by the variety she had trouble concentrating on just one.

There were the little bright blue and yellow striped fish dashing in and out of the coral fingers. Large orange fish—coral trout, as Mick informed her later—were moving slowly in the shadows. And a small black tipped reef shark circled the shallows in search of prey.

When Bay first saw the shark, she panicked. She swam for the boat, but Mick pulled her back making gestures that everything was alright. She relaxed and drew her attention back to the swaying coral, moving in slow harmony with the ocean current.

It was a day Bay would never forget. Although she would have loved to have re-visited the reef, she needed to move on. She was itching to explore other parts of this country. It would be too easy to stay here and become like so many of the staff members, captives to the beauty of their home.

Bay pulled herself out of the memory of the day to answer Claire. "The reef was magnificent, but my work is almost finished, and your father doesn't want a permanent photographer. He was clear about that when I first arrived."

Claire jutted out her bottom lip. "But you can stay a bit longer, can't you?"

"No. I can't." She gave the little girl a wide smile to soften the blow. "I have other adventures awaiting

significant document from her past was the change of name from her birth surname, Jones—also her mother's maiden name—to Peter's last name, Anders. Any other information was a mystery. Her investigator had asked every solicitor, the Australian equivalent of a lawyer, both in Cairns and the little towns beyond. A search of Jones births had revealed so many options that it would literally take years to investigate each one.

The investigator shook his balding head. "I have tried, but there are way too many hours involved in tracing every Jones. I could do it for you, but with the strict hourly limit you've given me, it's impossible."

Bay slumped further. She had exhausted all her funds, and with the last three payments from Peter not going through into her account, she had been forced to put a halt to the investigation. The shortage of cash had also forced her to move from her luxury accommodation into a cheap motel. An uncomfortable, cheap motel. Bay shifted on the lumpy sofa.

"Thank you for your help. I'm going to have to suspend your services for now. Hopefully, I'll be in touch soon and we can kick it off again." She gave the man her best smile. There were no other private investigators in the small city of Cairns, and she wanted to keep him on side.

"I'll be available as soon as you call."

Bay closed the door on the gentleman and pulled out her new cell phone. She had lost her old one. There had to be some sort of oversight. Peter told her he would pay her allowance as long as she stayed away. She had tried several times to contact him, but her calls had been forwarded to an answering service.

Bay tried Peter once more, only to get the same result. She decided to try his office number. It was a stroke of genius as his secretary, Pam answered.

"Hi, Pam. It's Bay." She was well acquainted with the lady. Her mother had forced Peter to hire the overweight middle-aged woman, who had excellent references and experience, after a series of blonde bombshells were hired primarily as potential mistresses.

"Oh . . . hi. Um . . . how is life Down Under?"

Pam's hesitation and attempt at small talk went completely against the nature of the woman. Bay picked up on the feeling that she was uncomfortable talking to her, and suspected she would be the bearer of bad news.

"It's great. Beautiful country. Is Peter in? I need to talk to him."

There was a slight pause before Pam answered.

"No. And to be completely honest with you, he's asked me not to put any calls from you through to him." Pam sounded genuinely upset. "If you ask me, it's pathetic. The man is an idiot."

Bay was taken aback by the comment. Pam was not prone to outbursts of human emotion. She was the quintessential loyal secretary.

"Did he say why?" She had to know.

"He told me to tell you when you called that, due to recent events, he sees no need to continue his financial support of you," she replied.

Bay was confused. "Did he elaborate on these so-called turn of events?"

"Not a bit. But, I suspect it has something to do with his recent marriage to that social climbing tramp."

That comment wasn't like Pam. "You think he's being influenced by his new wife?" Bay stood to pace the floor.

"I think so. They married last month, and lots of things have changed around here. She has a new position in the company, Head Director of Interiors. She's throwing her weight around, firing and hiring all kinds, and issuing orders like she owns the place."

"Wow." Bay could tell Pam was frustrated.

"I'm so sorry, Bay. It looks like you're another victim of her Majesty's will. Are you going to be okay?"

Bay decided to lie. She could tell the lady was concerned for her welfare. It would do no good to give her further stress. "Yes. I'll be fine. The money was nice but I'll get by. There are plenty of employment opportunities for me here."

There was a slight pause in the conversation. Bay knew Pam didn't believe her.

"Well, if you ever find yourself in a jam, give me a call and I'll talk to that foolish man for you."

The offer was genuine and surprising, considering Pam had always made a point of distancing herself from her employer's private life.

"Thanks, Pam. I appreciate the offer. Maybe I'll talk to you again." Bay put down the phone and stared into space. This was an unfortunate turn of events.

She had to admit, it surprised her that Peter would cut her off just because of a woman's influence. Then Bay recalled how her mother had been able to manipulate her stepfather. Perhaps she could take some consolation from the idea that he had gone from the frying pan into the fire.

She lay down on the bed, wishing for the allowance that afforded her the luxury of a Hilton mattress. Everything about the sub-standard accommodation was uncomfortable.

Better get used to it.

Without Peter's support, her life of privilege was over. Thinking about it, she realized the absence of the finer things didn't upset her as much as losing her last link to family. Peter had been a distant and absent stepfather, but he was the closest thing she had to a family. Deep down, she had hoped they would get to know one another better during her mother's illness, and after her death. The new wife had put a stop to that. Peter had moved on, and she wasn't a part of his life anymore.

Bay was surprised by how much that hurt. She was fully alone in the world. Not a soul to care about her wellbeing, and not one significant person in her life. All of her LA friends had dropped off. Even Tasha had only rung once since she had been in Australia. When Bay called her to let her know she had lost her cell phone, and now had a new number, the phone went straight to an answering service. She didn't bother leaving a message.

Although she had met some lovely people in the Daintree, they were no more than acquaintances. After finding solace and comfort at the resort, she now felt lost with no direction.

She reached over to the table next to her bed,

hoping to put her hands on the phone book. The nerves in her stomach had destroyed any appetite she had, but at least she could order a pizza. Perhaps her favorite food would inspire her to eat. Instead of the phone book, her hand found her Bible.

Thoughts of Richard came back to her. He was certain God was leading him through life. The words he said rang in her head: *"All you need to do is ask and believe in Him."*

Bay searched her emotions. *Do I believe in God? In Jesus?* Her mother had never believed in anything but the power of money. When Bay had asked her about God, at around the age of ten, her mother had replied that if you couldn't see it, it didn't exist.

But lots of things existed that you couldn't see. The wind was invisible, yet you knew it existed by the movement of the trees or the rise and fall of the ocean. Emotions weren't tangible, and yet they existed. The body was a shell — she'd realized that when she saw her mother's body. Her whole being existed inside the shell, independent of flesh and blood and bone. Perhaps that unseen part of a human was the part that connected with God.

The God who was revealed in the Bible stories and passages she had read seemed real. He was nothing like the supreme controlling being she had anticipated. Both He and Jesus had a true and real presence in the lives of those who had written the Bible chapters.

Now she realized the answer was yes. She did believe in God, and in Jesus. What other God had sacrificed for the human race the way Jesus had?

She opened the Bible to the next marked passage.

Perhaps it held some divine direction. The words Jesus spoke jumped out from the page: 'Ask and you shall receive, seek and you shall find. Knock and the door will be opened.'

What are you telling me, Jesus? That answers are as easy as Richard said? I just ask for them? Goosebumps sprung up on her arms. She decided that wherever she ended up, she would start trusting God to lead her in the right direction. After all, He had to have a better idea than she did.

Jesus, I believe in you. Forgive me for the mistakes I've made, and help me to trust in you to show me the way, like I know Richard does.

Cairns airport was so busy that the noise made it hard to think. A group of Korean tourists milled around her, chatting away in their own language. Finally their tour guide gathered them together for a briefing. Bay attempted to find a quieter spot to sit in the small airport. She moved some distance away from the Koreans, only to encounter a group of school children louder than the tourists. They were obviously excited to be embarking upon an adventure. She finally found a secluded corner for herself, unpopulated by enthusiastic travelers. She took a seat to stare out at the tarmac.

After another week of living in limbo, a total of three months in Australia, she decided to make the move back to the States. She didn't want to go, but didn't have much choice. She'd run out of money, spending her last savings on the plane ticket home.

Ideally, she would have loved to have found

work and settled down. Australia was full of warm, welcoming and lively people. It saddened her to be forced to give in to her fears and go back to the country she was more familiar with.

There was nothing of significance to return to. Los Angeles held no attraction for her apart from it being somewhere she knew and she would be able to get work without too much trouble. One of the photographers would take her on as an assistant, and she had enough acquaintances to bunk in with until she found an affordable apartment. There were so many negatives to going back to LA, but in her mind it was the lesser of the two evils.

She sat in the airport witnessing the hustle and bustle of travelers around her. The joyous embraces of arrivals as they were met by friends and family, and the tearful goodbyes of lovers as the boarding gate forced their separation. Everyone had someone. The sadness of failure and an intense loneliness enveloped her.

She sat in mindless silence for a long time, staring at a small spot on the horizon. Suddenly the words she had read came back. *'Ask and you shall receive.'*

Lord, whatever happens from here, please send me to people I can call my own. People who will love me for who I am, like the Bible says you do.

Outside, a private jet taxied to its specified position. Doors opened, and a smartly dressed attendant climbed down the stairs to stand at the bottom, ready to greet her passengers.

A booming voice drew her attention to the right. Negotiating his way through the throng was a man

Bay guessed was about in his sixties from the shock of thick grey hair poking out from under a large cowboy hat. His clothes and his boots gave him away even before he opened his mouth to speak in a broad Texan drawl. He was tall and slim and the embodiment of a successful rancher. Bay could see character in his face and she concentrated her stare, thinking how Richard would have loved him as a subject. He was obviously someone important, and issued orders in a polite way to those around him. Bay turned to watch the progress of the man and his entourage through the departure lounge.

He turned around as he walked out. Bay averted her eyes. After all, it was rude to stare.

"Go-oo-olly! Woo-hoo!"

Bay jumped in her seat and turned to face the whooping noise. The Texan had exploded, throwing his hat in the air like he had won the grand prize at the rodeo.

"I can't believe it!" He started to walk her way during the booming sentence. "I've been halfway across the world looking for you, and when I'm about to leave the country, here you are."

Bay looked to her left and right, and then behind her. *Who is he talking to?*

He crossed the space between them with amazing speed and planted his feet in front of her.

"Boy, did you give me some trouble, little lady." He looked straight at Bay, a playful grin widening his face.

She moved back further into her seat and looked around her again. He was talking to her? She looked back at him. A mixture of fear and trepidation enveloped her.

"I'm sorry. You must have mistaken me for someone else." It was the only explanation.

"Jane Anders. Previously Jane Jones." It was said as a statement of fact, not a question.

Bay sat in astonished silence. *Who are you and how do you know me?*

The thought must have been written all over her face because he backed off slightly as his entourage caught up. He never took his eyes off her. "Or perhaps I should call you Bay. Seems you kept your nickname all these years."

Now she was seriously confused, and a little scared. "I'm sorry. Do I know you?" He didn't look familiar, and she was certain she would have remembered him had they met.

He accepted his hat back from the man who had retrieved it, and took his time to answer. "No, darlin'. You don't know me, but I know you. It's a bit of a long story. Sorry to have scared you like that. I'm a bit excited. Been looking for you for a while, and right when I was about to call it quits, well, here you are."

He extended his hand to her. "Braden Ewing. Pleasure to finally meet you. And for the record, no I don't have a ranch called South Fork."

The reference to the old TV franchise, Dallas, made Bay giggle and she relaxed. She stood to take his hand, and returned the smile he offered.

He gestured towards the other side of the waiting area. "Seems we have a bit to discuss. Would you mind accompanying me to the private lounge? I can explain."

Bay paused for a moment to consider the offer, then nodded. He was obviously not a madman, and regardless of his over-the-top reaction at seeing her, discernment told her he was a genuine character. Besides, her curiosity was exploding. She itched to know what he wanted and how he knew her. The private lounge, although exclusive, remained a very public place. She stood and began collecting her carry-on luggage.

Ewing turned to one of the four men standing with him. "Robert, tell the necessary people we won't be needing the jet after all, and see what you can do about booking us back into the hotel." He paused to adjust his hat. "And we may need an extra suite for Bay here. If she'll agree to be my guest after our little talk, that is."

He looked back at her with such familiarity that she could almost believe they did know each other. He took the small suitcase out of her hand, and they moved off towards the lounge.

"Thank you." Bay accepted the cup of coffee from the waitress and took a sip. She and Braden Ewing had taken a corner of the private lounge while his entourage saw to their needs.

"I don't know where to start." The Texan stretched out his long legs. "At the beginning, I guess. Can you humor an old man while I tell you a story?"

His smile was so kind that Bay smiled back. "Sure."

Braden secured his hat on the vacant chair next

to him, and set about sugaring his coffee before continuing. "Three months ago, I was cruising my yacht in the Whitsundays." He glanced up at her. "That's a group of islands further south from here. More towards the central coast."

Bay nodded. "I've heard of them." She had seen footage of the area over the years. It was a hive of tourism.

"It's a mighty pretty place." Braden sipped his drink, then put it back down on the coffee table between them. "I heard about a group of islands south from there, so I decided to check them out. We made anchor between two deserted islands and I took my little tender out for some personal exploration." He rubbed his hand through his hair. "I spent way too much time out in that thing, and when I ran outta gas I realized I'd travelled a lot further away from the yacht than I thought. I had no cell service, no safety equipment, no oars, and basically no way of getting back. I'd plumb goosed myself."

He stopped to take another long sip of his coffee. Bay felt the bubble of patience inside her burst. "So what did you do?" She couldn't help the prompt.

"I panicked a little." Braden laughed. "Then, when the big storm that had been brewing all day arrived, I panicked a lot." This time, he huffed. "That storm closed in fast, and it was nasty. I was adrift and bailing water in a matter of minutes. It must have been blowing twenty-five knots, and I had no way to let anyone know how much trouble I was in." He shook his head. "After an hour of trying to stay afloat, I braced myself in case the dinghy capsized.

Which it did."

Bay could feel her eyes grow wide. She bit her lip at the man's predicament. "You were in the ocean?"

"I certainly was, for three hours. I thought I was going to die. All I did the whole time was pray. And praise God. He heard me, because just when I knew I couldn't keep my head up anymore I saw a little boat coming towards me." He sighed deep and closed his eyes for a second. "Don't ask me how, but I managed to get a hold of the life jacket that was thrown to me, and my rescuer got me into his little boat. It was a miracle, because the seas were still rough as guts, and the rain and waves made it mighty hard to see."

Bay grinned at the adventure. "What a relief."

"Sure was." Braden fixed his gaze on her. "And my rescuer was your Daddy, Bay.

The world stopped as a prickly sensation washed over her. "My father?"

Braden's forehead wrinkled. "Sure was. A man named Dutch. We got back to the yacht and saw out the storm there. He sure is a brave man. He heard my skipper's emergency call, but he knew it would be hours before anyone would get to me, so he decided to come out for a look himself."

Bay took a sharp breath. "Wasn't that dangerous?"

"He's one fine seaman, your father. He followed the ocean, and it led him right to me. Well, I told him I had to do something to repay him. He wouldn't take any money from me, no matter how hard I tried to give him some." Braden broke off to shake his head and chuckle. "Instead he told me all about you, and asked me to spend that money looking into where you were. The man saved my life, so I made it my priority to find you." Bay couldn't speak, dumbfounded. She struggled to get her head around it, finally asking. "So, you know where my father is?"

"Can't say I know exactly. I don't have an address or anything. But he told me to tell you that you can reach him at the hotel at Kiisay Point. He's there every Friday night without fail." The old cowboy looked at her and smiled. "Don't think he realized how seriously I took his request. I suspect he assumed I would sail off on my yacht never to be seen again. But I've been determined to find you, little lady. I prayed to God every day that He would guide my steps to you. Like the Good Book says, if you ask you will receive."

A shiver ran down Bay's spine. Did God plan all this? It was all too much of a coincidence not to be divine.

"And you sure did lead me on a merry dance. I finally found your stepfather in LA, and he was more than happy to give me your location, and a recent photo of you. Especially after I assured him I'd see to it that you were taken care of."

It all began to drop into place. Braden Ewing was the recent development that inspired Peter to cut her off. Bay had to admit some relief—her stepfather wasn't as mean and uncaring as she thought.

"But then, when I got to the Daintree, you were well gone and the cell phone number they gave me for you wasn't answering. I was one step behind your every move. After you checked out of the motel on the highway, well, I thought I might as well go back to where I began in LA. Then, here you are sitting in the doggone airport." His voice rose, excitement taking hold once again.

Bay smiled. She liked this boisterous Texan. "Do you mind telling me what you know about my father?" She was eager to have his impression.

"We stayed up all night talking about our lives. He had some stories alright. His family emigrated from Holland when he was five. He grew up in Western Queensland. Then there was his time working an opal mine. . ." He laughed as if remembering something amusing. Bay wished he'd share the story.

"But I'd be doing you wrong by telling you. Your father will want to share these things with you himself, and I couldn't do justice to any of the tales. He certainly is a character. And he loves you. Must do, if he treasures you over all the riches I offered him."

Tears sprang to her eyes. She had never felt treasured above riches before in her life. She swallowed the tears down, not wanting Braden to think she was sad at having met him.

He looked at her, placing his hand over hers as it rested on the table. "If you let me . . . that is, if you want to meet with your father, I would be happy to get you to Kiisay Point."

Bay turned her hand upwards in his and gave it a squeeze. "I would like that very much, Mr. Ewing."

CHAPTER 4

The little room was small but comfortable. The best feature was the large balcony that boasted a magnificent view of the beach, ocean, and islands beyond. The Kiisay Point Hotel was old and in need of renovation. The one-story main building housed both a bar and res-taurant, while the accommodation at the side of the building was an extension lacking in modern attractiveness. The furnishings were shabby, and the bathroom pipes screamed when forced to function. Inexplicably, Bay had never felt more at peace.

Braden Ewing had been true to his word, ensuring she had everything she needed. A new cell phone, money for expenses, and although he couldn't produce a five-star hotel, he had made sure she got the best view in the house.

Bay found she cared little for the luxuries money could buy. Not when she was finally preparing to meet her father. That luxury was more precious than anything.

Braden had offered to come with her to the small coastal community of Kiisay Point, and see that she got in touch with her father, but Bay wanted to make the journey on her own. Besides, the Texan had done so much already to reunite them. Bay didn't want to impose upon his goodwill. This was something she needed to do on her own. In any case, he had forced her to take his phone number and contact details and made her promise to contact him at the first sign of any trouble. She felt secure in the knowledge that, come what may, he was a friend and helper.

Braden had even relayed the story of how Bay had come by her nickname. Dutch had started to call her Baby Jane, which he eventually shortened to Bay. She realized that somewhere in her four-year-old mind, she was determined not to lose that connection with her father. Her insistence that her mother call her Bay must have been a resolve not to forget him.

She sat on the small plastic outdoor chair and looked out at the ocean. Today was Friday, and tonight she would go to the bar and hopefully meet with her father. The thought scared and excited her at the same time. Braden had assured her Dutch would be ecstatic to see her, but Bay couldn't settle the butterflies that filled her. Would they get along? Have anything in common? Be able to talk openly to each other? There were so many 'what ifs' that her stomach prickled with nerves.

She had been here in Kiisay Point for two days, thinking the time would be well used, unwinding and taking stock before launching into what would hopefully be a new era of her life. But the spare time had been as much a negative as a positive. Anticipation had built up all kinds of scenarios in her mind. Not getting on with her father had been the main worry, but another was him not wanting to have her as a permanent fixture in his life. Here she was, turning up on his doorstep with nothing and expecting him to take her, a basic stranger, into his life. The more she thought about it, the more it seemed egotistical and desperate.

She had spent some time emailing Richard, filling him in on the miraculous events that had led her to her father's doorstep. She also shared her decision to allow God to take the reins of her life.

By far the best use of the last two days was the time she had spent exploring her newfound faith. The more she prayed and read her Bible, the more she realized Jesus was real. He was a definite presence in the quiet solitude. Closing her eyes and concentrating on really speaking to him had opened up her heart and soul. She had poured out her fears, hurts, anger and bitterness to him, like he was her best friend, and he had listened, giving her a peace inside. She re-read that morning's passage: 'And the peace of God, which transcends all understanding, will guard your hearts and your minds in Christ Jesus.'

She closed her eyes and revisited that peace now in an attempt to settle her stomach and mind from the fear of the upcoming meeting.

Braden had assured her that her father was a man who possessed a quiet faith, and it was obvious that he was steadfast in his trust in God. He had told her that they had shared stories about what great things the Lord had done in both their lives. Failures He had turned into successes, hurts into joy, and the ups, downs, temptations and sacrifices of following Jesus. It amazed Bay that the moment she decided to follow Him, Jesus had surrounded her with others who knew and loved Him — including her father.

She took a few deep breaths, and drew on the confidence she knew came from her newfound faith, then walked back inside her room to prepare for the night.

The bar was packed with an assortment of people from all walks of life. Bay was happy to sit in a darkened corner and watch. For a small community, the local hotel certainly drew a crowd on a Friday night.

Sharing her small corner, adjacent to the main bar, was a group of corporate professionals. Several men who had been wearing suits had taken off their jackets and ties and rolled up the sleeves of their long shirts. The two ladies with them had more appropriate attire. Their short-sleeved fitted blouses and knee-length straight skirts were better suited to the muggy conditions outside. Their bare legs shone without the stockings their city counterparts would have worn.

One of the men was busy in a corner where four poker machines took pride of place. Bay noticed that he played with intensity, never losing interest in the spectacular noise of the machine. He only left his position to exchange more money from the bar, then continued playing.

Beyond them, the bar opened up to a larger area full to the brim with working men. Some wore plain navy work shirts and shorts. Others had heavier shirts striped with high visibility fluorescent colors. The remainder of the patrons looked like locals— men in t-shirts and shorts, and women in light cotton dresses. Apart from her corner, there wasn't a proper shoe in sight. Every foot was adorned with a variety of flip-flop.

The whole room was abuzz. Only the occasional loud laugh sounded above the noise. There was a constant tinkling of glasses as they collided, and the hum of the jukebox that never took a break.

Bay sat back sipping her soda and watching the throng. She had already asked the barmaid twice if she could be so kind as to point out "Dutch" to her, but the girl had insisted he wasn't here. She had been very unfriendly, giving Bay a distinct withering look the first time she had asked, and a definite scowl the second time. She now regretted her decision not to make inquiries concerning her father's whereabouts during the last few days. Maybe she would have gained some more information about him if she had, but she hadn't wanted to answer any questions about why she was looking for him. Their meeting needed to be a surprise. She wanted to form her own first impressions. Braden had been careful not to reveal the smallest amount of information about him. He told her he wanted her to have an open mind and heart towards her father.

She finished her drink and walked up to the bar. One of the businessmen who had been trying to catch her attention the last hour turned now, and looked her up and down.

Bay knew she was overdressed the second she had walked into the bar, and was greatly relieved when the professional group had walked in. They provided her with a bit of camouflage. She had agonized over her choice of clothing for hours, finally settling on her timeless designer little black dress. It was a superb fit, clinging to her figure in all the right places, and falling just above the knee. It was modest, stylish, and knowing how good she looked in it gave her confidence a boost. She had added a pair of classic high-heeled shoes, and purse, which completed her look. Her hair fell in large golden curls down her back.

After having gone to all the trouble with her appearance, she had realized her elegant style meant she stood out in this casual environment. So she had taken the darkest corner and planted herself there, willing her father to appear and be obvious so she didn't have to draw too much attention to herself. Now, three hours later, he still hadn't arrived.

She caught the attention of an older lady behind the bar. Her directions to the younger staff clearly showed she was in a high position. The other bar attendant was an older man who stayed in the main bar area. The lady worked as she moved Bay's way, taking empty glasses off the bar, and wiping the top of a beer tap.

"What can I get you, love?" Her voice was low, husky, and entirely complemented her low cut top and bleached blonde hair piled massively atop her head. Regardless of the rough exterior, her face held softness.

"I'm looking for a man called Dutch. Could you point him out to me?" Bay raised her voice as loud as she dared to be heard over the throng, but kept her request private.

The lady looked at her for a long moment and frowned. "Now what would your business be with him then?"

Bay stood back, not expecting to have to explain

herself. One look at the lady's face told her she wasn't going to get the information she needed without some sort of explanation. How could she put this without giving herself away? The last thing she wanted to do was reveal she was Dutch's long-lost daughter who had come all the way from America to reunite with him. It occurred to her that she didn't even know his full name. Braden had only ever referred to him as Dutch.

"Um . . .," she stammered under the penetrating gaze of the bar attendant. "I have some . . . urgent business . . . I need to see him about." It sounded like a lie, even to her ears.

The woman stared at her for a second then looked down the bar.

Bay sighed. *Why couldn't this have gone smoother?*

The lady looked back at her. "Hold on a minute." She turned and walked to the end of the bar to talk to the man there. When she finished he looked at her with a closed-lip smile, then made a brief comment, before turning his attention back to the patron at the bar.

The woman walked back to Bay. "He's not here. May come in a little later though, if you want to wait around." She gestured towards the man. "Archie says it's not like Dutch to miss a Friday night. Now, what can I get you?" Her tone didn't invite further questions.

Bay sighed again, weighing up her options. "No thanks, I'm okay. I think I'll sit and wait a while."

"Can't stay if you don't drink." The woman put both hands on the bar and gave her a direct look.

"I'll have a Shirley Temple." She requested her

favorite non-alcoholic cocktail. Perhaps having a drink in her hands would help calm her nerves.

"Sorry, we don't do cocktails. It's beer, wine or one of those." She pointed at a fridge filled with an assortment of premixed spirits.

Bay squinted in order to get a better look at the labels, but the fridge was too far away.

The woman sighed in frustration. "Haven't got all night."

Bay frowned. She didn't want to be stranded at the bar while a stream of others were served.

"Just give me something non-alcoholic." At least it wouldn't cloud her thinking. She paid for the candy-pink drink she was handed and retreated to her seat in the corner.

Over the next two hours Bay had three more pink concoctions, and built up the courage to inquire numerous times as to whether Dutch had arrived. Every time the local patrons welcomed a new arrival she caught her breath, only to be told it wasn't him. By the time ten o'clock rolled around she was both bloated, and deflated. Most of the bar had cleared out, with three groups of men left still drinking at different positions in the main area.

Bay moved from her dark corner to take a stool at the bar. The older lady came to clean in front of her.

"You're a stayer. I'll give you that, love." Her blonde hairdo had fallen out of its style during the evening, and it fell in softer strands around her face. "You're not nearly as rude as the other vultures that come looking for Dutch."

Bay had no idea what she was talking about, and

was about to ask her to explain when someone brushed her shoulder as they took the stool next to her.

She turned to find a young man dressed in khaki. He was sandy blonde, with a handsome boyish face, blue eyes, and lashes so long they were completely wasted on a man. His tall, slender frame was muscular, upper arm muscles pulled against the short-sleeved khaki shirt. His mouth tugged into a smile at the corner, and he tilted his head as he stared at her.

"Hi, there. What are you drinking?" His voice was soft and light, complementing his boyish good looks.

"No, thanks. Not for me. I think I've had enough." More soda was not a good idea.

Clearly undeterred from her company, he turned to the bar attendant. "Patty, a beer for me and a glass of water for the lady, please."

She raised her eyebrows at him, then set about pouring the drinks.

He extended his hand to her. "Ashley Chambers." His introduction held the air of regal announcement.

She took his hand in a firm shake. "Bay Anders."

He took a long swig from his beer before speaking. "So what brings you to our neck of the woods?"

What is it with everyone wanting to know my business? This was starting to get frustrating. "I have some business here. What do you do, Ashley?" She turned the conversation back to him.

He put his empty glass on the bar. "Another

please, Patty." He then turned to give her his undivided attention. "I work for the Department of Natural Resources." He motioned to his left pocket where an embroidered logo took pride of place.

"You mean the Department of Counting Possums, don't you?" The comment and laughter that followed came from an old man in a Hawaiian-print shirt. He and his two friends had clearly been listening in to their conversation.

Ashley gave the old man a death stare before turning back to Bay. "Don't mind them. Old men don't like progress. It scares them."

Bay remained silent, picking up on the tension in the room. These men didn't like Ashley, but they were also giving her some nasty looks for no good reason. Perhaps they were just cranky old men too full of drink to behave properly.

"What does the Department of Natural Resources do?" Bay hoped the answer wasn't obvious, and her question hadn't revealed a high level of ignorance on her part. It had to be more than counting possums.

Ashley turned his body on the stool so his torso was facing her, and rested his arm on the bar. "I'm the park ranger in charge of all manner of crawling, furry, hairy, and slippery things." He gave her a charming smile. "Not to mention the exciting trees, bushes and foliage."

His jesting tone downplayed the position, making it sound as though he was above such work.

Bay took a sip of the water before continuing. "Sounds interesting."

"It's a highly respected position. As you can tell."

He looked behind him and narrowed his eyes, staring at the mocking man in the Hawaiian-print shirt, who was now in deep conversation with his friends and no longer interested in them.

"Four years of university and I'm stuck in no-man's-land with this bunch of hobos." He shook his head and screwed his face up at the group.

Bay had to smile. She had no doubt that Ashley was frustrated with the lack of prestige in his job. He oozed unattained ambition.

Bay decided to move the conversation away from his personal failures. "So is there a national park close by?" She had some knowledge of the system due to the World Heritage status of the Daintree.

"Yeah, there are lots of pockets of land that are part of the national park. Plenty of Green Zones as well."

She frowned. "Green Zones?"

"Specified zones of the reef where it's illegal to fish. The government's trying to build sustainable environments, and over-fishing has had a huge negative impact on the reef in recent years," Ashley said.

"You must be kept busy then. Is it a large area to look after?" Bay was more interested in the photo opportunities that existed in the area than in his position. Ashley was bound to know some great spots.

"Over to the Cape, and up as far as the Whitsundays, but I look after Kiisay Point and the surrounding islands." He finished his second beer and signaled the nearest bar attendant for another.

Bay's curiosity was aroused. "How many islands are there off the coast? I can see a few quite close to the mainland."

Ashley tilted his head and squinted at her. "If you don't mind my asking, what has brought a lovely lady like you to this neck of the woods?"

Not this again. Bay racked her mind for a way to avoid the question. She raised one eyebrow, and before she could stop the reaction, rolled her eyes.

Ashley lifted one eyebrow. "Oh, I see. A woman of mystery. Well, that's okay by me. I'm sure your business is top secret." He smiled and winked at her as though they shared an unspoken secret.

The older blonde lady—the one Ashley had called Patty—came to stand in front of him. "Thought you were out chasing those net fishermen tonight?"

He turned to look at her, and then took another swig of his beer, mumbling through the top of the glass. "I am."

Patty pursed her lips and let out a huff. "Might be a bit hard to do with a belly full of booze, don't you think?"

Ashley gave her a smug lip curl, and put the empty glass down. "Three light beers won't touch the sides, Patty." He stood from the stool.

"Duty calls. Lovely to have met you, Bay. I hope we will see more of each other soon." He gave another boyish grin.

He was a charming man. She smiled back. She had no call to dislike Ashley. He may be able to point her in the right direction of some unique photographic opportunities in the future.

She shook the hand he offered. "Nice to have met you too."

Silence fell on the group of men as Ashley passed by them and out of the bar.

Patty maintained her position in front of Bay, hovering as if wanting to say something but not knowing how to go about it.

Finally she spoke. "I don't know what your business is here, but it would be best to have as little to do with that bloke as possible. He's proved to be a bit of a stirrer and . . ." She failed to finish as the barman she spoke to earlier sauntered up beside her.

"Patty, they could do with a hand in the kitchen. Think you could get back there and wash a few pots?" His voice was deep and gruff. He was a tall, but overweight man with the biggest hands Bay had ever seen, and the distinctive feature of one missing finger. Archie looked as though he had had a rough life, and was certainly not someone to question. The stubble on his chin was smattered with grey, though his hair was thick and brown on top.

"No worries." Patty nodded to Bay and made her way out to the kitchen.

Archie leaned over the bar in her direction. "Looks like your man hasn't shown tonight. Must say, it's not like Dutch. He hasn't missed a Friday night for years. I can't say I'm disappointed for you. My bar's no place to conduct any sort of business." The reprimand was issued with a forceful stare.

Bay felt a shiver down her spine. Archie was evidently the owner of the hotel, and most definitely not a man to argue with. She felt the need to vindicate herself.

"Well . . . it's business of a more personal nature really." She tried to explain herself without giving away the details.

"Whatever it is, love, bars are no place to do it. If you want to see Dutch, you best go track him down."

Easier said than done. Tracking him down was proving to be a bit of a challenge. The only information she had was that he was here in the pub on a Friday night. Not to mention the closed community. Bay wondered what she could have done to put these people offside. She decided she may as well push Archie a bit.

"Do you know the best way of getting hold of Dutch?" She hoped the question didn't give away what little she knew.

Archie was thoughtful for a moment. "I suppose you've been trying the phone number and got nowhere. It's been dead for years. I guess your people thought they would send you here to surprise him." Archie lifted his bushy eyebrows and looked at her with squinted eyes.

He was right about the surprise, but how would he know anything about her people, and why was he so suspicious? It didn't make any sense, but she reasoned that if she persevered in her ignorance he might give her the direction she needed.

"Yes, I guess you could say I was going to surprise him. But that looks impossible considering he isn't here." She looked up and down the bar.

"Hmmm," he rubbed the stubble on his chin. "There may be a way you can still surprise Dutch. Get the jump on him so to speak."

His choice of words was unusual to say the least.

Bay wasn't interested in getting the jump on him, whatever that meant. She just wanted to meet him. She couldn't shake the feeling that Archie had her confused with someone else, but she certainly wasn't going to reveal her purpose. It wouldn't be fair to her father to learn his long-lost daughter had come to see him through the local grapevine.

"I would really appreciate it if you could arrange for me to meet with him." Bay put on her sweetest voice in the hope that her womanly wiles would work some miracle on the beast in front of her.

Archie gave her a huge smile, more like the cat that got the cream. "I can organize that for you, love. I can do it right this minute. Wait here and I'll be back."

He moved his bulk to the end of the bar and out into the main drinking area, stopping to talk with a group of men at the end of the room. One was a dark skinned man with a mass of curly hair. As Archie spoke, the men all looked in her direction and laughed. The man just smiled a massive grin, then nodded his head. Archie slapped him on the back, and made his way back to her.

"All organized, love. Amos will take you out to Resolution with him tonight."

Now Bay was genuinely confused, not to mention a bit scared. Go with a man she didn't know to who knew where to meet with a father she didn't know? And where was Resolution?

Her fear must have shown because Archie rushed to assure her.

"Now don't go getting any ideas into your head. I've known Amos for as long as I've been here and you won't find a better man. You can be assured you're in safe hands with him. Safe as houses. He'll get you there alright."

Safe as houses? Must be another Aussie-ism.

"Where exactly is Resolution?" Bay wasn't convinced by his plan. Perhaps it would be better if she stayed and made further inquiries in the morning. There had to be other avenues open to her apart from placing herself in the hands of complete strangers.

"The island's a few miles off the coast. A short boat ride. Ten minutes tops." Archie dismissed it as though it were a walk in the park.

"I don't know if it's such a great idea. Perhaps it's better if I wait until morning."

"Amos is your last chance to get over there for a week or so. Unless you can find someone else to take you out, and I wouldn't recommend that. Lots of transient fishermen are here this time of year. At least Amos is a local, and he knows these waters like the back of his hand. He'll look after you."

Bay looked at the barman. He had obviously jumped to his own conclusions as to why she wanted to meet with Dutch, but she didn't think he would place her in direct danger. She had been watching him all night and he ran the hotel with complete authority. He kept anyone rowdy in line and ensured everyone was being looked after. His friendly camaraderie with the locals was testimony to his being well-liked and respected.

She weighed up her options. Trying to question locals, or officials for that matter, wasn't something she relished. The more questions she asked, the more answers she'd have to provide in return. Having prepared herself emotionally to meet her father, she didn't want to delay the event now. Having time to think about this wasn't a good idea—she was sure to lose the little nerve she had.

Please God, let this be the right decision. And if it isn't, could you please make it right?

"Okay, when do we go?" She sounded much surer than she felt.

Archie smiled as he wiped the bar with a rag. "I'll let Amos know. As soon as he's finished his drink you'll be on your way."

The old pickup truck found every hole in the dirt track as it bumped along, snaking its way around the coastline. A cloud of billowing dirt trailed behind them, and the road ahead was barely visible in the blackness of the night. Bay kept firm hold of the panic bar conveniently placed in front of the passenger seat to keep her from being thrown around the cab. The night was dark, with a sliver of moonlight peeking occasionally through dark clouds. Another sudden hole in the cloud cover offered a glimpse of bright stars which shone through like diamonds.

Bay snuck a look at Amos, his face visible in the lights on the dashboard. She'd seen many pictures of Australian Indigenous people, and had taken some interest in the culture, but what little she could see of the features of this man was different from the pictures. His build was much larger—broad shoulders, unshaven full face and muscular arms expertly maneuvering the wheel of the old pickup. He looked around fifty, but it was hard to tell. Amos wasn't one for talking, so if she was to learn anything about this man or their destination, she was going to have to ask.

"Thanks for taking me out to the island, Amos. How large is the town out there? Do you live there too?"

Amos kept his attention firmly on the road and took so long to answer that Bay thought he had decided to ignore her.

"Not a big town. Only a few people out there." His voice was so soft that Bay had trouble hearing him over the engine noise.

She forged on. "I must admit I don't know much about Resolution Island. It would be great if you could tell me something about it."

Another long pause. "Nice island. Good fishing."

Wow, could this be any harder? She racked her brain for a conversation starter. She was a little stunned when Amos spoke up first, louder than before.

"What you want with Dutch?"

It just got harder. Bay frowned and pondered how to answer.

"I have some personal business to discuss with him." She was deliberately vague.

If you must know, he's my long-lost father, I'm his long-lost daughter and we have some reuniting to do. If you don't mind.

Bay considered telling Amos, and getting it all out in the open. Amos spoke again before she could make up her mind.

"Lots of people want to see Dutch lately. Lots of coming and going."

Bay didn't know what to make of that statement, or how to answer it. She decided to generalize. "How many houses are on the island? Can you tell me the street name and number where Dutch lives?"

"No houses. Just the resort. The main building is where Dutch lives. I'd say he's just got back from a fishing trip. That's why he's not at the pub. Tonight's a bit dark but you'll see his place alright." Amos pulled off the road as he spoke, and Bay sucked in an involuntary sharp breath as the truck stopped short of the bush. He pulled on the handbrake and got out of the pickup.

Should she get out as well? She froze in indecision for a few moments before Amos stuck his head back in the driver's side window, scaring her half to death. "You coming?"

Bay grabbed her purse and exited the vehicle. As she closed the door, she realized negotiating the pitch-black night would take some effort. Five-inch heels combined with ankle-high grass and uneven ground made finding her way around the truck almost impossible.

As she rounded the back of the vehicle, she saw a boat ramp under the illumination of the one road light. There was also what looked like a toilet block across the parking lot, the entrance barely visible. She would have liked to use the facility, but there was no light in the interior, and she didn't relish an encounter with one of the hairy, slippery, or slimy things Ashley had mentioned.

She was unprepared for this. All she had was a

small purse containing some money, her new cell phone, a hairbrush, and lip gloss. What if she had to stay on this island for a few days?

Oh well, I can always call someone to arrange a lift back if needed. She stepped high and slow in case there was a concealed hole in her way. The man in front had no such problems, ambling along in front of her. At times she almost lost him. It was fortunate he was wearing a bright white t-shirt, and there was the distinct flip-flop noise of his shoes on the gravel to follow.

Bay was so intent upon high-stepping through the rough ground that when she looked up she realized they had reached the water's edge. She peered down the long concrete boat ramp. Although she couldn't see the water, she could hear the lapping of soft waves as they collided with the end of the structure. Thick clumps of mangrove trees lined both sides of the ramp.

Amos disappeared down one side of the concrete wall.

Why is he going down there, and not on the ramp?

Bay couldn't see his logic. Why muck through the mangrove when he could walk down the concrete? She could barely hear him negotiating through the mangroves over the wind that whistled through the trees. It was windier down here than up at the hotel.

"Come on. She'll be right." His voice sounded a long way off.

"Will you meet me at the bottom of the ramp?" Bay yelled in the vicinity of the voice.

"Can't use the ramp. Real slippery at the bottom.

It's low tide now." The voice came back.

Bay hesitated. If she couldn't use the ramp, did he expect her to follow him down into the mangroves?

"You follow where I come down," he said, in answer to her unspoken question.

She didn't want to go down there, but what choice did she have? There was a long walk back to the hotel in the pitch dark, and who knew what wild animals or people she would encounter? Bay took a deep breath and stepped onto the dark surface. The heel of her shoe sunk an inch into the soft sand. This didn't seem to be too bad.

Five steps into the journey and her heel was fully sinking, but the rest of her remained upright and stable. She tentatively took another step.

"You might want to hurry. Big croc lives here at the ramp." Amos' voice carried along in the wind.

Bay froze. *Crocodile! Living here!*

A tight prickly feeling ran over her skin, followed by a hot wave of adrenaline. She let out a high pitched "Oh," and quickened her pace to a staggered wobble. She had no idea what was in front of her, but hoped that if she stepped on the crocodile she'd be going fast enough to outrun it.

Several steps later, she took a leap forward and felt herself sinking into soft mud. Her foot was encased in the cold slippery substance up to her ankle.

"Oh no." She paused to retrieve her foot from its sticky captive, took another step, and the same thing happened. A scurrying noise to her right sent hot flushes coursing through her. She pulled her foot and muddy shoe out in record speed to continue down the sloping bank.

She looked up to see Amos and the boat. The promise of an end to the horror propelled her forward. As she took another awkward leap, she found herself slipping in slow motion, slamming onto her bottom, and sinking into the mud. It squelched and coated her as she tried to right herself. Being so close to the stuff, she realized how bad it smelled. And it was everywhere.

She got to the edge of the water and grabbed hold of the side of the boat, which revealed itself to be no more than an aluminum dinghy — or tinny, as the Australians called them. It was smaller than the one she used in the Daintree. She looked up to Amos for a hand over the side. He made no move to help as he sat in silence at the back of the boat, hand resting on the tiller of an outboard. The engine burbled in the water, missing occasionally. The only sign of acknowledgment he offered her was that brilliant smile.

Well, at least you have the decency not to laugh. Bay hitched the skirt of her dress as far as modesty would allow. She did her best to stabilize her balance as she pulled one long leg up over the edge of the boat.

The clunk of her foot on the bottom of the tinny signaled her success, and she wished she had been brave enough to pause and remove her now ruined expensive shoes before attempting to climb the side. The floor felt a bit uneven, but not having time to properly stabilize herself, she pulled her other leg out of the water and swung her leg in, hoping for the best.

She heard a ripping sound as she fell down hard against the aluminum floor of the boat. She righted herself against the bumpy ridges, and found she was sitting in a few inches of water.

Amos's giggles were loud enough to hear over the outboard. "Are you alright?"

If she wasn't so sore, even she may have been able to see the funny side of it all.

"I'm okay." She knew she'd be bruised in the morning, but the worst damage was to her dress. A large rip now went from the bottom all the way up to the top of her thigh. Her shoes squelched with mud as she pulled them off her feet.

Oh well, I won't have the same trouble getting out of the boat. There had to be a bright side.

The tinny skipped over choppy waves as they made their way out of the sheltered water by the ramp and into a larger expanse of black water. The casual attention Amos paid to where he was going amazed her. She couldn't see a thing, and tried to right herself as best she could, sitting up to look over the edge of the boat.

Amos pulled back on the engine, causing the boat to idle. "You better stay down as much as you can. We're going to get a bit wet up here." He gunned the engine again.

Wetter than I already am, sitting in water?

She soon understood what Amos had meant when they rounded the corner of an island to encounter the open sea. Large swells tossed the small boat as Amos negotiated through the ups and downs of the water. Heavy salt spray rained over them as they inched along, the little engine groaning under the weight of the sea. Bay gave up trying to see out of the boat and put her soaking head down, silently praying for their destination to appear.

They rounded another corner to enter better conditions, and she breathed a sigh of relief at the reprieve. The waves were still there, but their intensity had lessened. She was grateful she was accustomed to being on the water. She loved to spend time on her stepfather's yacht, but she'd never had an experience quite like this.

The faint outline of land appeared, and Amos slowed the tinny so it rose and fell in motion with the swell. "You'll have to get out here and swim. Sorry. I can't get up any closer. Swell's too big."

Bay swallowed hard. She could swim, but the beach was at least fifty meters off. What if she was swept away or worse, taken by a shark?

She couldn't see Amos looking at her but he must have picked up on her trepidation because he revved the engine, and turned the boat towards the shore. "Wait a minute. I'll see if I can get you in a bit."

She breathed a sigh of relief.

Seconds later he killed the engine once more. "You'll be able to touch the bottom here. Out you get. Can't hang here or the boat'll get swamped. Go straight up to the main house. I'll wait here till you make it to shore."

Bay scrambled to her feet, shoes and bag in hand, and hitched her skirt up again to jump over the side. The water was warm. He was right—she could touch the bottom. The water reached her waist. But as she made her way to the shore, the waves hit her back and wet her through.

Her feet soon found the shallows and she scrambled out of the water. She took a moment to appreciate still being alive. Amos was long gone, not even a speck in the darkness. Bay wondered where he could be going at this time of night.

She took a moment to compose herself. Her dress was ripped, shoes ruined, cell phone waterlogged, and her hair hung in wet salty clumps down her back. She was sure she looked every bit as bad as she felt. *Just the first impression I wanted to make.* Bay fought the strong urge to sit down and have a good cry. She hoped Dutch could see the humor in the situation, and look past her drowned-rat appearance to appreciate the effort she had gone to. At least the ocean had washed off the smelly mud.

She looked up the beach, making out several small buildings in the darkness. Amos had said to go to the main house. She assumed that was the largest structure, and headed in that direction. At the top of the sand was a section of small prickly nuts that had fallen from the trees that lined the beach. There was no lighting at all, and she stopped to rest on a grassy area beyond the trees.

There was a small paved area with a few concrete tables and chairs outside the door to the main building. As she raised her hand to knock on the door, a slow growl sounded from the side of the courtyard. A dog, head down and eyes fixed firmly on her, crept out from around the corner of the building.

Great. She froze to the spot before looking back at the dog, defiant. "Listen here, dog. I'm wet, sore and completely demoralized, so if you are going to bite me please do it quickly." And she was going mad, talking to a dog.

She put her hand out for the dog to sniff. To her surprise, he did just that, taking in her scent, then wagging his tail and licking her hand. She sent up silent thanks for at least one friendly native.

Considering it worked so well last time, she spoke to the dog again. "Where's your master? Can you tell him I'm here?" The dog looked at her, then turned around and walked back around the dark side of the building.

"I guess I'm on my own," she muttered as she knocked on the door again. No answer. She knocked louder. The homemade sign on the door read, 'Bar Closed'. Several minutes later, there was still no answer. She called out, rapping on the door as loud as she dared. This would be a great reunion, waking her father from a peaceful slumber to find his long-lost daughter disguised as the creature from the swamp.

Still no answer.

Bay tried the door, but it was locked. She considered trying the other buildings, but they looked equally deserted. Tears threatened, and she looked at the chairs, which invited her to sit down. But she knew if she did, there was every possibility she wouldn't get back up again. Dutch would find her there in the morning in an even messier state than she was now.

At least she wasn't cold. The North Queensland summer was hot, humid and generally unpleasant. The temperature was warm, even outdoors at night.

Bay walked to the edge of the building where the

dog had disappeared. It was as good a start as any. She inched forward, holding on to the side of the building for support.

"Ouch, oh, oh, oh." Prickles. She tiptoed her way through, finally finding the end of the prickle bush.

At the end of the building there was another small paved area, and she could see the dog in his bed. He raised his head as she walked past him and knocked on the door. Again, no answer. She rapped louder. *Where is everyone?* Bay wished Amos had stayed with her.

She turned to the dog. "Where are they all, mate?" He immediately got up from his bed to stand by her side, wagging his tail. His friendly gesture made her smile.

She tried the doorknob, and it turned to open. Bay took a cautious step through the doorway. She could just make out the room's layout in the darkness. The entry was a large open-plan kitchen, dining lounge area. She reached around the inside of the door and found the light switch. It didn't work.

"Hello?" Bay called, not wanting to be stuck on the doorstep all night. No answer.

She moved inside and closed the door, tentatively moving through the darkness to what looked like another door at the end of the room. It opened, and what little light the night offered streamed in through a small window. A large bed stood in the middle of the room. A small set of shelves sat on the opposite wall, and a tiny bathroom opened to the right of the bed. The room was empty. If Dutch was on the island, he certainly wasn't at home.

Bay sighed. She would have to rest where she could and see him in the morning, or hope that if he came home during the night, he wouldn't mind her making use of his house.

She fumbled around in the bathroom, wringing out her hair, and toweling off her soaking dress as best she could. She then lay out a towel and settled onto the couch. It wouldn't be fair to lie on the bed, soaking wet. She spent the next hours going through the day's events and feeling more miserable with every disappointing thought.

Please Lord, let tomorrow be better.

Eventually she fell into a restless slumber.

CHAPTER 5

The barking of a dog sounded far away. Bay groaned before remembering where she was. Soft light filtered through the windows and onto her face. Her damp, sticky dress was un-comfortable enough to fully wake her. She would have liked to have taken it off last night and wrapped herself in a blanket to sleep, but didn't want Dutch to return in the middle of the night to find a semi-naked girl in his house.

She sat up on the edge of the sofa, amazed she had slept at all. She had no idea what time it was, but she guessed it must be early in the morning. Looking around, it was apparent the house was poorly maintained. The furnishings were tattered, and the kitchen looked as though it was rarely used. There was no oven, only a small two-burner stove. The floor was covered in a faded linoleum with a floral print. Although the place was shabby, it was clean, and there were signs of life. The sink held several washed coffee cups, and there was a newspaper spread over the table. One entire wall was built of large stones layered upon each other. It was spectacular, like a beautiful piece of art. A two-way radio and small portable record player adorned a shelf above the old wooden dining table. It was the quintessential beach shack.

Bay flicked through the selection of vinyl records on the shelf below. There were around twenty, all

Yacht Rock. She smiled. She was familiar with the beachy music and it certainly fit in with the island atmosphere. Richard had been a dedicated Jimmy Buffett fan—a 'Parrot head', as the fans liked to call themselves.

She moved into the bathroom to look at herself in the small mirror above the sink. Her reflection revealed the extent of the night's disaster. She retrieved her brush from her purse, running it through the messy blonde tangles. A rubber band from one of the rolled up newspapers would do as a hair tie. She washed her face and tried again to sponge more of the dampness out of her dress. Thankfully the front of the dress had almost dried. It was just the back where she had been sleeping that was still wet.

She had no makeup left on her face, and it took some rubbing to remove the black mascara rings from under her eyes. Lastly, she applied some lip gloss. Freshening up made her feel a bit better. Less creature–from-the-swamp, more girl-caught-in-the-rain. She laughed. She was quite literally the girl who came from the swamp. There wasn't a lot she could do about the tear in her dress. Unfortunately it turned classic designer threads into a racy nightclub number. Explaining that would be fun. Not.

A clock on the bedside table showed it was five o'clock in the morning. Bay had always been a morning person but five was early, even for her. She contemplated lying back down on the couch, but dismissed the idea of having to lie on her wet back again.

A tiny photo frame on the other side of the clock

caught her eye. She moved over to get a better look at the picture, sitting down on the bed and taking the frame in her hands.

It was a picture of her. She was about three or four years old, sitting cross-legged on the beach next to a magnificent sandcastle adorned with shells and seaweed. In the background was a small stone cabin and coconut palms. Her curly blonde hair blew untamed in the wind and her singlet top and shorts were faded, even against the age of the photo. She must have been happy, because the smile on her face was huge. Bay wished she had the memory to go with the picture. She smiled at the thought of her father keeping it by his bedside all these years. How often had he looked at it and thought of her?

She moved into the kitchen and opened each cupboard in search of food. The fridge wasn't just empty, it was turned off. *Where does he keep the cold stuff?*

There was clearly no reliable power source on the island, as the lights still didn't work. Bay came across some bottled water in a cupboard under the sink. She giggled at the discovery. Who would have guessed her father didn't have electricity, but kept bottled water.

She stepped outside the cabin to find the dog at the door, wagging his tail at her. She hadn't been able to make out what breed he was last night, only that he was of medium size, but now she could see that he was an Australian blue cattle dog. His age was showing in the occasional grey whisker on his chin. Bay reached down to give him her hand. He sniffed for a second then offered her his head to pat.

"How are you today, mate?" she asked him, smiling down at the friendly creature. Mick had called everyone 'mate' as a term of endearment, and it had rubbed off on her. She looked around the paved area and saw the dog had been left a bucket full of water and some dried dog food in a bowl. Dutch couldn't have been gone for long if the dog still had uneaten food.

She walked out further onto the patio. The view was captivating. The beach was no more than five meters away, and fanned out into a bay of blue-green water. She started to walk out, then remembered the prickles and backtracked to borrow one of the pairs of flip-flops that lined the entry to the cabin. She was sure Dutch wouldn't mind her using a pair.

The slight breeze was a pleasant change from the gusty squalls of last night. She made her way down the beach, then stopped and looked out at the ocean. As she stood taking in the scene, she could feel her heart thrashing in her chest. This was the place in her memory. The first memory of her life — the water, the beach, the island across the bay. The one thing missing was the large hand in hers. This was once her home. She had lived here with her father on Resolution Island.

Bay felt a shiver down her spine and she wrapped her arms around her body, giving herself the cuddle she wished was coming from someone else. She continued along the beach until she found the end of the bay. The open sea lay beyond. Above her was a small stone cottage on a rocky outcrop. She wished she had her camera to capture the light that pierced the walls and highlighted the flash of red ingrained in the rock. Palm trees and coconuts lined the place where the sand met the grass.

She walked back towards the main building. There was nothing between the rock cottage on the peak and the bar, but she did come across what looked to be a swimming pool. An old ladder jutted out over the top of the paved edge. The pool itself was filled, not with water, but with earth. Grass grew lush and green on the surface. It was such a bizarre sight that Bay couldn't help but laugh.

"What happened here?" she asked the dog that had trailed behind her. He cocked his head to the side as if to say, 'don't ask me'. The comical gesture made her laugh out loud.

Back at the main building, she peered into the window. The 'Bar Closed' sign was still there, painted red words on a wooden board strung up with a bit of rope. She could see a small wooden bar decorated with old shoes, stuffed parrots, a skull and crossbones flag, and a Hawaiian hula skirt on the back wall, along with a variety of glasses. There were refrigerators packed with drinks, but she couldn't see if they were on.

There were huge barricaded windows on the beach side of the building. Bay could imagine they lifted out to expose the entire bar to the breeze of the ocean. Beyond the bar was a small paved dining area furnished with terracotta colored tables and chairs. The paved area was shaded by gum trees, eucalyptus, and the occasional palm.

Past Dutch's cottage were four other plain weatherboard cabins. The only one showing any sign of life was the last cabin, which was a little removed from the rest. An old fishing net was draped over a big tin drum on the side wall, and a welcome mat sat at the front door. The paved area outside held outdoor chairs, a table, and portable grill. Bay knocked on the door, but wasn't surprised to find no one there. The place was all locked up with no sign of life.

Past the last cabin was a high rocky point jutting into the sea. A little old pergola perched on the top. It would have a great view.

At the back of the main bar was a huge tin shed, housing what looked like two engines. Another shed stood a few feet off. It was much more decrepit-looking with only two sides, connected by two massive steel drums. Fireplaces sat underneath each drum, but didn't look like they had been used recently.

The entire place was run down, and could hardly be called a resort, but Bay couldn't help but feel the charm and beauty of the surroundings. Beyond the buildings at the back was nothing but bushland and a few walking tracks snaking off into the trees. She itched to follow one—another time, perhaps. When she was dressed more appropriately.

She headed back to the cabin.

The clock ticked onto the next hour. Ten o'clock. She had been awake for five hours and there was still no sign of human life. She had found provisions in Dutch's kitchen. Tins of baked beans, spaghetti, pasta, and packets of chips and nuts, but not much else apart from condiments. She had opened a tin of spaghetti earlier, and finished munching on a packet of chips. She sighed with boredom, having read the last of the newspapers hours ago.

She checked her cell phone again. Still dead. It wasn't recovering from last night's drenching. She had pulled it apart and tried to dry it out, but it was still refusing to work. She was getting worried. Was she marooned here?

The dog barking outside drew her attention and she peered out the window to see a tinny offshore. The man inside the boat dropped the anchor, collected a few things, and jumped overboard, swimming breaststroke to the shore.

As he walked out of the water wearing nothing but board shorts, Bay saw he was far too young to be Dutch. His bare sun-bronzed chest glistened with water, and several large coral trout hung off a belt at his waist, swinging as he walked. He was above average height, perhaps a fraction taller than her, with wild curly brown hair, streaked with natural auburn highlights. It was impossible to gauge his age, as his facial features were hidden under a bushy beard and moustache, also smattered with red.

He planted an anchor firmly in the sand and unhooked the belt, throwing the trout onto the sand. Bay couldn't help but notice his well-toned physique. It would put many gym-going LA men to shame. His muscles were the product of physical labor, not manufactured workouts.

Bay remained in the shelter of the cabin, not sure whether she should make her presence known. The man stood with his hands on his hips, looking around the resort, obviously expecting some sort of welcome.

The dog ran up to him, wagging his tail and barking. He almost turned himself inside out with happy greeting, jumping up and getting his belly rubbed for his efforts.

Bay decided that if the dog knew the stranger that well, he must be a friend of Dutch's. She walked out to meet him.

Flynn stood on the beach wondering where the girl was. He had been fishing for the last twenty-four hours and had little to show for his time. He should have known better. The tide and conditions weren't right, and he'd suspected it would be hard going. He had worked a patch of reef for over five hours before giving up and moving to another spot with no improvement. The water was so clear he could see the fish swimming around the reef ignoring his bait. He had given up in frustration.

He leant down and started unhooking the trout from the belt. They were a good size but he had resorted to spearing them, even though he hated spearfishing. It was dangerous because reef sharks couldn't tell the difference between the fish on his belt and the flesh of his waist.

He had finally headed back in to the island after spearing four, running into Amos on the way. His friend had filled him in on the night's entertainment. Another solicitor had appeared at the pub looking for Dutch, and the blokes had set out to have some fun, scaring her half to death.

Over the last five years, various parties had

employed dirty tactics in their efforts to acquire the island. The entire community was fed up with the intrusion and injustice of it all. Dutch had been here for over forty years, and Flynn had grown up at Kiisay Point. They were locals. The antagonists were not.

Amos had told him the solicitor was a young American girl, a good-looking fancy sort, but not so fancy after he dropped her in the ocean. Flynn shook his head at the thought. It was all well and good for the boys to have their fun, but now he was stuck with her. Dutch had set out on one of his fishing trips over a week ago and Flynn had no idea when he would be returning. He was the sole caretaker of the island and resort until Dutch returned, and the last thing he felt like, after a disappointing fishing trip, was dealing with this solicitor.

He looked up to see the girl making her way down the beach towards him. Amos was right. She was good looking, but Flynn had seen her sort before and a pretty face and good figure wasn't enough to impress him.

She bounded up to him, as happy as the dog had been. "Boy, am I glad to see you! I was starting to wonder if I'd have to swim back to the mainland."

Despite her upbeat tone, he refused to look up in acknowledgement. "It's not that far. You should get there by nightfall if you start now." He wasn't about to play nice with the woman. She could find her own way off the island. The last thing he felt like doing was helping some rich city type.

She didn't reply, so he looked up to gauge her reaction. One eyebrow raised in undisguised indignation. She moved to place her hands on her hips and her skirt opened to reveal a long split working all the way up to the top of her thigh. A very nice thigh. Flynn was aware that he was staring, but he found the exposed flesh hard to ignore.

"Do you mind? You might want to put your eyes back in your head."

He grinned and averted his eyes from her thigh to her face. "If you don't want to be looked at, stop wearing revealing dresses."

"I'll have you know this was a very suitable, very expensive dress until it was ruined by a somewhat hostile local man in an unseaworthy tinny."

"Amos is far from hostile." She was a firecracker.

She let out a loud huff. "How do you know?"

"Because he lives around the corner, and I met him on my way back this morning. He told me you were here."

She reeled back. "Did he tell you he dumped me here? The place was deserted. Just as well I found an open cabin, otherwise I'd have been sleeping under a coconut tree." She waved her hand in the direction of a group of trees as if to further her point.

Flynn smiled. "You wouldn't want to do that!"

Her face screwed up. "Do what?"

"Sleep under a coconut tree. Falling coconuts kill more people per year than shark attacks." As he spoke, he finished unhooking the last fish and came to stand, looking her in the eyes.

"Thanks so much for that useless interesting fact." Her gaze was seething with anger.

"It wasn't useless if you found it interesting." Flynn was enjoying playing with her. It probably wouldn't do him any good to get her more worked up, but the look on her face was priceless and he couldn't help himself.

"Are you always this hostile to complete strangers?" She looked like she was about to explode.

"Only ones I find snooping around my home." There wasn't anything on Resolution worth snooping for, but she didn't know that. And being a solicitor, she would have taken the opportunity to look around.

Her chin jutted out and eyes squinted. "I'll have you know that I am no snoop. Unlike you, I have been taught good manners."

He had to smile. She was certainly a feisty little lady. He knew he was being harsh, and the disappointment and fatigue of the fishing trip was influencing his behavior. But she was at him again before he could make good.

"I wasn't aware I had said anything amusing." She tapped her foot on the sand as though the action would increase her authority.

Flynn couldn't take it anymore. Who did this chick think she was? She was most likely there to cause trouble for Dutch—invading his home, and now insulting him. The temper that went with the red in his hair got the better of him.

"I disagree. There's a whole lot that's funny about you, lady. Did Amos tow you behind the tinny? Or did you set out to look like a drowned rat?"

She let out an incensed, "Oh!", then promptly turned on her heels to stomp up the sand. She lost her footing on every soft patch, swaying comically.

Flynn grinned at her retreating back. Then he

remembered he was responsible for getting her back to the mainland. He cringed, regretting that he had let his temper get the better of him. He'd be forced to seek her out later. Who knew? Perhaps he'd get lucky and she'd call someone to come and pick her up before he had to take her back.

He watched as she walked away from him. He had to admit she looked good from behind as well.

"Insufferable, rude, obnoxious . . . jerk!" Bay raged to the empty cabin. He may be a friend of Dutch's and undoubtedly lived here on the island but he was a complete . . . "Beast!"

She stopped pacing in rage and slumped onto the couch. She took a deep breath and felt her rage morph into despair. A sudden dam burst and tears flowed. She sat crying for a long time, letting the frustration, anger, disappointment and hurts of the last twenty-four hours pour out. When she finished she was surprised to find she felt much better.

Lord, what is happening here? What have I done that all these people hate me on sight? Help me turn this around. Please?

More tears sprung to her eyes. This wasn't the reunion she'd envisaged. Here she was, stuck on an island with no clean clothes, no cell phone, and the goodwill of a hostile stranger the only way of getting back to the mainland. Worst of all, there was no Dutch—her reason for being there in the first place. She felt stranded, body and soul. She lay down on the couch and closed her sore and stinging eyes. She tried some relaxation techniques, breathing deep and trying to release the tension. The wind whistling through the open window was the last thing she heard before falling asleep.

Bay opened her eyes to see the soft afternoon light filtering through the window. How long had she been asleep? She moved into the bedroom and checked the little alarm clock. Just on six o'clock. She checked her reflection in the bathroom mirror. Hideous. The cry may have soothed her emotions, but it had done nothing to improve her appearance. The creature from the swamp was back in full force. Black rings circled puffy red eyes, and a messy pony tail sat atop her head, hair poking out at all angles. She ran her brush through her hair and splashed cold running water from the tap onto her face. The improvement was marginal.

She looked out the kitchen window and saw a fire burning on the beach. Leaning out a little further she spotted the beast sitting a little further down away from the heat. He had put on a t-shirt, and was drinking from a gallon bottle of water. The dog sat next to him, keeping him company. Bay contemplated her next move, and sighed when she realized she didn't have much choice. Dutch hadn't turned up, and righteous indignation wouldn't get her off the island. She was going to have to approach that obnoxious fisherman and ask to be taken back to the mainland. With a big sigh, and a gathering of courage, she stepped out the door and made her way down to the beach.

The dog jumped up to greet her, his happy bark,

wagging tail, and delightful acceptance easing her nerves a bit. Bay bent down to give him a good rub around the ears in appreciation. "How you going there, mate?" The tail wagged faster at the acknowledgement. Bay looked up to find the man looking over his shoulder at her.

"What's his name?" she asked, still patting the dog.

"Mate."

"His name is Mate?"

"That's what I said."

His answer had more than a hint of hostility. This was going to be harder than she thought. "No wonder he let me in last night. I was calling him by name." She moved down closer to where the man was sitting.

"Actually, that's a bit of a surprise. Mate's been known to attack most people he doesn't know. We have to tie him up when there are guests here, until he gets to know them. He's very territorial." He took a swig of the huge bottle.

"Well, you know what they say about dogs and children judging a good character?" She hoped it gave her some recommendation.

One side of his mouth tilted upwards. "Is that what they say?"

Bay tried another tactic. "Look, we obviously got off on the wrong foot." *Even if that wasn't my fault.* She extended her hand in greeting. "Bay Anders."

He stared at her through squinty eyes before finally extending his hand in return. "Flynn McKenna."

He gripped Bay's hand so hard she had to stop

from wincing. "Do you mind if I sit down?"

"Do as you please."

It wasn't a complete snub.

She sat next to him making sure that they had plenty of distance between their bodies. The view was magnificent, even if the company left something to be desired. The day's breeze had died down, leaving a whisper of movement in the palm leaves. The water lapped lazily on the shore in a hypnotic rhythm, and the fading light flashed pink and red streaks in the sky. The island opposite took on an intense blue-green hue. Bay wished she had her camera to capture the moment. Her first sunset on Resolution. She wondered how many more she would get to see.

Come on, Dutch. Where are you?

A stinging sensation on her leg pulled her out of the daydream, and she slapped the mosquito dead, only to discover another landing in its place.

Flynn handed her a can of insect repellent. "You might want to put some of this on."

Bay leaned away and sprayed liberally over her arms, legs, and up the visible split in her dress, which was thankfully on the opposite leg to Flynn. "Thanks." She handed it back.

Time passed and Bay racked her brain for something to say to break the awkward silence. Flynn got there first. "Which firm do you work for?"

What? "I don't work for any firm. I'm a freelance photographer." Bay didn't see any harm in clarifying her occupation. It wasn't giving any important information away.

Flynn frowned. "You're not a solicitor?"

"No way. I'm definitely not a solicitor." Bay laughed. The little she had to do with solicitors when she was in Cairns had proven a waste of time and money.

Flynn shifted his body towards her and raised one bushy eyebrow. "So are you interested in doing some photography here on the island? Is that what you're here for?" The question was direct but by no means intrusive.

Bay considered her answer. "Yes I am. I wish I had my camera now. This sunset is spectacular." It was the complete truth, although it wasn't the main reason for her being there.

His eyes narrowed. "So that's why you were looking for Dutch at the pub? To get over here to take some photos?"

Bay remained silent. If he wanted to jump to that conclusion she wasn't going to correct him. She wasn't ready to reveal her real reason for being there.

He stuck the bottle of water into the sand next to him. "You said you were freelance, but who's commissioned you to take photos of the island?"

Bay shrugged. "No one commissioned me. I heard from a friend who had sailed through here that there were some awesome landscapes." It was the truth. Braden had painted vivid mental pictures of the scenery, and she hadn't been disappointed. It occurred to her that Flynn had been doing all the questioning and her all the explaining. She had a few questions of her own. "Why did you think I was a solicitor?"

"Because that's what Amos told me you were, and we've had a string of them here chasing Dutch over the last few years. They've stepped up their campaign recently. We're all tired of being hassled. Seems you've been mistaken for one of them."

It wasn't an apology, but it did explain a few things. "What campaign?"

"A southern developer wants the island. Dutch owns it under freehold title, so it's perfect to build a flash resort on. Dutch won't sell, so the developer's getting nasty. We don't know who he's paying off, but in the last couple of months we've had an unwarranted drug raid, visits from a string of solicitors, and the National Parks Ranger on our case."

"Oh?" Bay let a handful of sand sift through her fingers.

"Yeah, some bloke named Ashley. He's new to the area and clearly trying to make his mark. We've had trumped up fines, and he's been over-patrolling the area, scaring off the fisherman who come to the resort. Dutch knows the Department would like the island for a national park. All the other islands in this area are already listed."

"I met Ashley last night at the hotel. He was pleasant enough, but I got the impression he wasn't well liked."

Flynn let out a loud huff. "I think the only person the locals like less is a solicitor. When they heard you asking for Dutch last night, they assumed you were one of them, and set out to have some fun with you." He finished his explanation with a lopsided smirk.

Bay rolled her eyes. "I wouldn't say it was fun."

"I don't know. Amos told a great story about you getting chased by an imaginary crocodile," Flynn teased, a big smile visible beneath his hair.

Bay couldn't help but smile back. "Alright, alright. I admit that was probably pretty funny, but I couldn't laugh at the time." But she laughed now at the sight she must have been. "At least the case of mistaken identity explains why everyone hated me on sight. I was starting to think there was something wrong with me, or that everyone hates the American accent."

"No, we welcome all foreigners. But it would be a different story if you were here to secretly photograph the island for the developer."

She was going to have to be more persuasive to convince him she didn't have any underhanded motives.

She turned to face him, and noticed for the first time how piercingly grey his eyes were. She paused, captivated for a second.

"I can assure you that I am here completely for my own benefit. I'm just sorry I've walked into a war." She broke eye contact and looked out to sea.

"You could call it that, I suppose. Or maybe David and Goliath is a better comparison. Dutch has been fighting this for years."

Bay ran another handful of sand through her fingers. "He must be a tenacious man."

Flynn laughed. "You could say that. He certainly won't back away from a fight."

Bay wondered what had made him back away from her mother and stepfather. She felt a little dejected that he had abandoned the most important fight, the one that ended when he gave up on her.

Why did he do that, Lord? When he's such a fighter?

She would get the chance to ask him soon. If he ever surfaced. "Where is Dutch?"

Flynn pointed out to sea. "Out there somewhere. He went fishing over a week ago and hasn't come back yet. To be honest, it's not like him to be gone this long, but Dutch is an old seaman. He can handle anything the ocean would throw at him, and he has all the safety gear." Flynn sounded like he was convincing himself more than her. Bay felt concern for her father.

Please Lord, let him get back soon! She sat looking out to sea, expecting at any moment for a boat carrying him to round the point.

Flynn stood up, sand falling off him as he moved. "If you can stand to be here another night, I can take you back to Kiisay Point tomorrow morning."

Bay smoothed her torn dress. "Thanks, I'd appreciate that. But it would be great if you could bring me back here after I collect my things. I'd love to check into one of the cabins for a short time. Maybe you could point me in the right direction for some good spots to photograph."

She wanted to remain on the island until her father returned, whenever that might be. She didn't want to be stuck on the mainland for weeks, or have a repeat of the night at the hotel.

Flynn stared at her. It was so hard to read his face with the shaggy beard. She could only see his steely grey eyes, so distinct it felt as though they were looking right through her. Bay thought for a moment he was going to deny her request.

"You can stay here if you want, but you've probably noticed that we don't have any power. I'm waiting on spare parts to fix the generators, so you'll have to live on tinned food heated over an open fire." His half smile showed that he expected her to rescind her request.

"I can handle that, if you don't mind sharing the fire with me." Bay wasn't exactly accustomed to roughing it, but if she could survive the last twenty-four hours, she could survive anything. The whole experience had given her a newfound confidence.

He moved away from her to throw a few more pieces of driftwood on the fire. "Suit yourself." He turned over a piece of wrapped foil sitting on the rim of the fire. "I've got some fish on here and a bit of damper in the coals if you're hungry. I can't imagine there was much to eat in Dutch's kitchen."

Bay's stomach grumbled at the suggestion of food. There was no way she was going to look that gift horse in the mouth, or upset the unspoken truce they seemed to have reached. She stood and walked over to him. "That would be sensational, thanks. Can I do anything to help?"

He gave her a cursory glance as she stopped across from the fire. "You could go and get a pair of trousers and a t-shirt out of Dutch's cabin and put them on. That dress is a bit . . . ah . . ." He paused, clearly searching for the right word ". . . impractical. And there's hot water if you want a shower. I've heated the drums in the shed. Gravity feeds water into the pipes." He squatted down to the fire so she couldn't see his face.

So that was what the big drums at the back are for. Bay moved off to do as he requested. She was delighted with the suggestion, now that she had been given the okay to use the facilities.

Getting out of the dress and into a hot shower was pure relief. She scrubbed the remnants of dried salt and mud from her body and washed her hair using some of Dutch's two-in-one shampoo and conditioner till it shone in golden waves down her back. She found an oversized t-shirt and long pants—the t-shirt would be alright, but the pants had no chance of staying up on their own. A search of the room showed no sign of a belt.

She went back out of the cabin onto the paved area. At the right of the door were several pieces of coiled rope. She retrieved a knife from the kitchen and cut a piece off to use as a belt. She smiled to herself. She was already adapting to the Robinson Crusoe way of existence. *If only you could see me now, Kate!* The thought made her laugh out loud.

She made her way back to Flynn and Mate, both relaxing on the beach. Mate thwacked his thick tail on the sand as she approached. Flynn looked up as she sat down, a big smile appearing from behind the facial hair when he saw her outfit.

"What?" She looked sideways at him. "You did tell me to put these on."

He looked away, saying nothing, but grinning broadly.

CHAPTER 6

Flynn watched as Bay walked out of her hotel room with a small bag and a camera case. A much larger suitcase was already in the back of the ute, along with a massive beauty case. She had changed into a pair of linen shorts and a white cotton top, which proved to be completely see-through when she was in the sun. Her lacy bra showed clearly through the material.

Flynn averted his eyes. "Here, let me take that." He threw the bag in the back seat of the dual cab ute. He would have offered to take it from her earlier, but he knew the less contact he had with this woman, the better. She was already getting under his skin.

She had borrowed a pair of his board shorts and a t-shirt to come over on the boat that morning. They were still too big on her slender frame, but they fit better than Dutch's clothes. Even encased in the baggy, nondescript attire she had exuded a sense of class.

Flynn had known women like this before. Most looked down their nose at him, and that was just how he liked it. Expensive, posh, high maintenance women were not his type, no matter how good-looking they were. He had sworn off women for the past year. Relationships meant complications, and something he didn't want in his life. The desire to avoid the wiles of the opposite sex had overridden the physical desire he had for them, and he had picked an easy place to be celibate. Resolution was a fishing destination where plenty of men enjoyed the rugged facilities, but it was hardly an attractive proposition for a woman. Basic accommodation, no restaurant, and no shopping meant the majority of the men were alone.

The only women the island had accommodated over the last two years were two backpackers looking for work. Flynn had enjoyed a casual romance with both of them, much to his regret now. At the time he didn't see any harm in it, but he realized that neither had made any impact on his life. Rather, they were just filling in time. His faith in God had also taken hold, and he had spent the last year exploring that. He had retreated into himself and led a simple life free from relationships. He had become used to being by himself, having no one to worry about, no ties to another person. It was a freedom he had enjoyed.

There were times though, when the suppressed red-blooded maleness in him took hold, and he reasoned that this was one of those times. He would have to push it aside. She wouldn't be on the island for long.

He was taken aback by her decision to stay on Resolution. There was no electricity, and he had to acknowledge the accommodation was barely two stars. There was something different about Bay Anders, something he couldn't put his finger on, and he considered himself a good judge of character.

They slid into the cab together and he started down the road to the boat ramp.

Bay fiddled with her handbag. "Thanks so much for doing this for me. Can I give you some money for the supplies?"

Flynn had spent some time at the local shop after dropping her off, picking up a few necessary items. If he hadn't had to bring her in, and she wasn't intent on staying on the island, he wouldn't have worried. However there was little to eat at the resort except a few tins and some fresh fish. He managed to pick up a gas bottle, so at least they could use the barbecue and wouldn't have to light a fire each night.

"No, it's fine," he said. "Dutch will work out costs with you when you leave." He kept his eyes on the road, intensely aware of her bare legs spread out in the cab in front of him. What was it about this woman? At least he could be thankful for the huge camera case on the seat between them.

He adjusted the case so it wouldn't fall off the seat. "How many cameras do you have? There looks to be more than one in there."

"There are two. One's my regular camera. The other's an underwater one. I haven't had a chance to use it yet. It was a gift from a friend. It used to belong to my old boss. He left LA before I came over here. He's in Afghanistan, on assignment for National Geographic." There was real pride in her voice.

Flynn rested his arm on the open windowsill. "Isn't that a bit of a dangerous place to be?"

Bay tucked a piece of hair behind her ear. "You go where the photos are. Putting yourself in a bit of danger is part of the job. Sometimes it's a necessary evil in order to get the shot."

Flynn lifted his eyebrows at her. "Well, I hope he doesn't get shot. Have you ever had to put yourself in danger?" Flynn surprised himself with the question. Why would he care?

"Several times. I hung over a cliff once to get the shot of an eagle's nest on a ledge below, and I floated over a shipwreck in the Caribbean with a huge shark circling. I was pretty happy to get the shot and get out of there." She smiled.

"Dangerous occupation."

"Sometimes, but for the most part it's thrilling. Being able to capture a moment in time is the best feeling. The danger goes with the territory. Are there any good spots over on Resolution?"

They pulled up to the ramp. "Plenty." Flynn jumped out of the car, grabbing the cases, and heading down to the tinny. He could hear her behind him, scrambling to catch up.

"Aren't you going to lock the truck?" she called.

He kept walking. "Why?" he called back.

"Because someone might steal it." He heard her quicken her pace.

"Why?" He stopped and looked back at her, raising his eyebrows and gesturing towards the ute. "What's to steal?" It was nothing more than a lump of rust on wheels that got them around to the few places they needed to go on the mainland. It certainly wasn't going to last any distance, and there was no point locking it up.

She looked back at the vehicle, then turned to him, giving a shrug and a bright smile. "Point taken." She adjusted her sunglasses as she walked up to him. Her long brown legs went up to forever, gold ponytail swinging behind her, and sun shining through her shirt. He felt his stomach stir.

God, help me get over this. I do not want this kind of

complication. Not with this sort of woman. Please?

Flynn continued his way down the boat, vowing to resist his instincts.

Flynn McKenna was an unusual man. Bay couldn't work him out, and it didn't help that he volunteered no information about himself. She had been on the island three days now and she had thought they were slowly getting to know each other. However, after they had shared a barbecue the previous night, he had said no more than two words to her all day. It confounded her — she wasn't used to being disregarded by a member of the opposite sex.

The one thing she learned about him was that he had lived on the island with Dutch for the last two years. To earn his keep he provided all manner of fresh seafood for the guests, and helped Dutch maintain the island. Other than this, Bay was no more informed about him than when they had first met. Despite this she had found herself constantly thinking about him - who he was, what he thought, what he had done in the past. A million questions raced through her head.

During the last three days she had revealed much about herself - her life growing up in LA, her work and her mother's death. Although, she kept her purpose for being on Resolution to herself. He had a way of putting her at ease and winding her up at the same time. She had given him her portfolio to look at after he had shown an interest in her work, pointing out her favorites, and sharing the story behind each shot. He had given her a tour of the resort and taken her to see an old traditional Indigenous fish trap around the point of the bay.

She had thought they had finally left all sign of hostility behind them when, the night before, he had filled her in on the history of the island. But since then he had gone out of his way to ignore her existence.

The island had apparently taken on the name of the bay, given by a naval captain who sailed through there in the 1800s. The ship needed urgent repairs, and the bay in between the two islands provided a perfect harbor, so he named it Resolution Bay. It was also used by the American Navy during World War Two as a perfect position for ships to anchor.

Bay sat on the beach and looked across to the little stone cabin on the far point. Flynn told her it was the oldest building on the island, having been constructed by the Johnstons, the original landowners, back in the 1930s. It was first used as a processing station for dudgeon meat, and later converted into a pleasure destination. The family had built several stone cabins, but only this one remained standing.

Flynn had told her stories about the Johnston's expeditions to catch the dugong that lived in exclusive areas of the estuary, and process their meat in the same fashion as whaling stations. Amos lived sporadically in a cabin around the point of the bay. His ancestors were brought to the area from the Pacific Islands to work the dugong luggers and plant. Some families settled in the area permanently, and Kiisay Point was named after their settlement, with kiisay meaning moon in island language.

Flynn had promised to take her on some of the bushwalks, which assured sightings of a vast array of wildlife, including kookaburras, koalas and a rare pigmy possum. Bay was enthralled listening to Flynn talk about the area. His passion for the island and the ocean was obvious. His eyes lit with animation when he explained the special traditional places of the indigenous people, the captivating history of the island, and the wonder of the untouched reef a few kilometers offshore. Bay could have listened to him all night. She found it hard to hide her disappointment when he insisted it was time to wrap it up and get some sleep.

She'd awoken that morning feeling excited at the thought of being taken to the reef. She'd dressed in record time in anticipation of the excursion, but instead he had muttered that she would have to get her own breakfast. He had work to do on the generators.

Bay had taken him a drink at eleven o'clock on the chance that he would take a break and have lunch with her, but he had refused the drink, telling her he wasn't thirsty. He'd ignored her for the full five minutes she had stood there. Bay wondered what she had done to inspire the hostility, but couldn't come up with any specific event or comment.

She had taken out her camera and cleaned it, taking some test shots around the resort, but the best light was early in the morning and at sundown, so it was a waiting game until then.

Having changed into her bikini, she sat now on the beach, and relaxed on the towel she had arranged on the sand. If she couldn't work, she may as well enjoy her surroundings. She had already been in the water twice, which was surprisingly cool for such a hot day. Mate had joined her, dog paddling next to her, and surfing in on the waves.

She was nodding off to sleep when a shadow blocked her sun and woke her up. She sat up to see Flynn standing over her.

"I'm going fishing. I'll be gone the rest of the afternoon. Hopefully I'll be back by six. If I'm not, there are leftover sausages in the esky and bread on the kitchen counter. Help yourself." He started to walk away.

No way. Bay scrambled to her feet. "Can I come with you?"

It was direct and pushy, and she knew she should wait for an invitation, but she couldn't stand to spend the rest of the day doing nothing when she had an opportunity to spend some time with him. Besides, the anticipation of Dutch turning up at any minute was getting more than she could handle.

"You won't like it." He turned around and kept walking.

There was no way she was going to let him off that easy. "Please Flynn, I won't be any trouble. I promise." She cringed. *I sound like a begging child. How embarrassing!*

He turned to look at her. There wasn't much lower she could get, short of getting down on her knees. He ran a hand down his beard, something Bay noticed he did when he was frustrated.

"Okay, but get some clothes on. I'll meet you at the boat." He strode off before she could ask what to bring.

Flynn checked his tackle box to make sure he had enough sinkers. What was he doing? He had decided to go fishing to get away from her, and now here he was agreeing to spend hours with her in a confined space. *Am I mad?*

He had decided the attraction he felt was purely physical. Why wouldn't he feel that? He was a red-blooded male, sworn off women for the last year, and here was a beautiful woman in a too-brief bikini. He shook his head to get the image out of his mind.

The problem was he found himself thinking of her in a completely unphysical sense. This morning he had come across a perfect shell washed up on the beach. He picked it up with the thought of giving it to her as an interesting subject to use in a photograph. Thoughts like that were dangerous territory. He resolved to spend less time in her company, which was proving hard to do when they were the only two people on a deserted island.

That situation was another concern. Dutch still hadn't returned, which wasn't like him. He would have run out of food by now. Dutch was more than capable of looking after himself, but Flynn knew from experience that the sea was unpredictable. You never allowed yourself to become complacent, or too much at home on its surface, otherwise you found yourself at its mercy. He sent up a silent prayer for his friend, that he was safe and would return soon.

Flynn had always visited the island from when he was a boy, with his father and brother on regular fishing trips. Dutch had always been here. He was a permanent character of the community, respected and loved by all who came in contact with him. There was the occasional problem—a drunken sailor to get under control, an employee looking to steal from him—but Dutch handled everything with a steely resolve. His unswerving stand against the pressure to sell his home was nothing short of inspirational.

Dutch was a friend. Not only because he had given Flynn a safe place to fall at the lowest point of his life, but because he had introduced him to a faith in Jesus. Like Flynn, Dutch wasn't one for churches, and although they both respected and valued the place a church had in the faith of others, they had both found God in the perfect nature of their island home. Faith had given Flynn back his sense of self, and a worth that came from knowing he was loved and forgiven. His faith had come slowly, creeping up on him in the most unusual way.

He looked up to find Bay waiting for him on the rocks, the only semi-sheltered place to board a tinny without swimming. She was wearing shorts, a singlet top, and a huge wide- brimmed hat, with a tote bag and camera case slung over her shoulders. Big improvement on the bikini. He wasn't taking that out fishing.

They'd go to one of the fringing reefs not far from the island. He didn't want to spend the whole day out, not now he'd been forced into taking her. This would be a quick trip out and back to satisfy his passenger.

He moved in to pick her up, inching the boat up to the edge of the rocks. He left the engine to idle when he was close enough, and reached for her hand.

As she stepped into the boat, a swell hit the side. Flynn gripped her hand as she barreled into the tinny, losing all balance as it swayed under them. He threw his free arm around her, pulling her to him as she fought to regain her balance. They ended up in an intimate dance position, one of his hands still holding hers and the other firmly around her waist.

She moved her hand on his chest, and for a second looked up at him from under the wide brim. Her green eyes were visible through the dark lens of her sunglasses. He caught the scent of her perfume as the breeze blew. He should let her go, but was glued to the spot by some invisible force.

The missing beat of the outboard broke the moment. He dropped his hands like she was a hot piece of coal, and swung around to attend to the seizing engine.

By the time he had stabilized the motor, she had taken the seat at the front. He gunned the engine and the boat took off. Bay's hat went flying off her head and into the water behind them. She threw herself back in an attempt to grab it, but was too late. Flynn laughed at her antics. He turned the boat around and retrieved the hat from the water, passing the soaking mess to her.

She gave him a sheepish look and rolled her eyes. "Probably not the best choice, hey? I was thinking about sun protection."

Flynn retrieved one of the spare caps he kept in a storage unit. "Use this. Adjust it at the back so it fits. You'd better give me that camera to put in here as well." He took the bag off her and tucked it safely into the strong box.

She looked behind at him from her position on the front seat. "Thanks." There was that smile again.

It took them twenty minutes to get to the reef. He checked the little depth sounder for the best spot on the bottom, and idled the outboard.

He turned back to Bay. "See that anchor in front of you?"

Bay picked up the reef pick.

"That's it. Throw it overboard when I tell you."

He checked the sounder again, and when he was sure they were in the best position, he indicated for her to drop it. When he was sure that the boat was secured, he bent to bait the lines. He gave her a handline and threw his over the side.

She looked at the reel as if it were an alien being. "Do I just throw it over?"

He wasn't going to be able to fish. "See this end bit?" He lifted the end of the line where the sinker, hook and bait were tied. "You have to keep it on the bottom." He gave her the line. "Can you feel that little bump, feel the line going slack?"

She nodded.

"That's the bottom of the ocean. You have to lift the line and feel that bump all the time. If you're not on the bottom, you're not fishing." He demonstrated with his line.

She followed his directions. "How will I know if I have a fish?"

"When something starts to pull on the line. Here, come and feel mine." He gave her the line, keeping his grip back a little so he could also feel. Within seconds, a small fish had picked at the bait.

Bay turned back to him, her eyes wide. "Was that

a bite?"

"Sure was. That was a small fish. See how strong the picking is. When they all pick at it at once, we call them machine gun fish, because it feels like an assault. Here, I'll show you what to do next." He took the line back off her. On the next bite, he pulled hard at the line.

"When you feel those bites you have to strike." His attempt didn't hook up the fish, so he dropped the line back onto the bottom. "Where there are little fish, there's usually big fish. Sometimes you have to feed the little ones up in order to get the big ones interested. A big fish biting feels different. It's more like a pull or tug on the line, because a big fish will try and take the entire bait, rather than pick at it."

He set her back up with her own line and fished with his, and within seconds he had hooked a fish. He started pulling in.

She moved closer to him. "Have you got one? What is it? Is it a big one?" Her enthusiasm was overwhelming.

Having fished for most of his life he had forgotten how special the first catch was. He smiled as he reached down to pull a good size Sweetlip into the boat.

She dropped her bottom lip. "Look at it. It's sort of too pretty to eat."

Flynn smiled. "You won't say that tonight when it's crackling on the barbecue."

She looked up from over the top of her sunglasses. "You're right. Too yummy to throw back."

They fished the spot for the next hour. Bay

caught her first coral trout, although he had to give her a hand at pulling it up. After the first one she got into a rhythm and went on to catch another three on her own.

"You're a natural." She grew taller under his praise.

"I have a good teacher. How did you get so good at this?"

"My dad taught me to fish around the same time I learnt to walk. You could say I grew up on the water."

She baited her hook, cringing at the slimy pilchard she was holding. "So what did you do for a living? I mean, before you came to live on Resolution?"

"I did a lot of things. Jack-of-all-trades, master of none, you could say." He picked up the reel and pulled in the slack as he talked. "I spent some time up north after school. Then I started a mechanical apprenticeship and did two years before deciding it wasn't for me. I worked as a builder's laborer for a while in the Northern Territory. Spent a season down south, fruit picking. Some time mining, and came back up here to skipper a reef boat, then worked on a prawn trawler for a few years." It sounded like a hotchpotch of nothing, but Flynn was proud of his working past. It was the personal decisions he regretted.

She threw her line back over the side. "Sounds like you've had many adventures."

"You could say that." There was silence as they both turned their attention to fishing.

She shifted her weight a few times. "Flynn, can I

ask you something personal?" She turned to face him, waiting for the go-ahead.

"That depends on whether it's something I want known." He could only be honest. There were certain things in his past he was more than happy to leave there.

She wasn't deterred. "How old are you? I've been trying to guess, but it's hard to tell with the beard."

He contemplated for a second how much it pleased him that she had been considering something so personal about him.

"Thirty-four," he answered.

She tilted her head. "Not as old as I thought."

That got him worried. "Why, how old did you think I was?" Mock horror reflected in his tone.

"Not much older. Late thirties. Early forties." She tilted her free hand from side to side as she spoke.

"That's okay, then. So long as you didn't have me in my sixties."

"No, there's definitely no sag in your muscle tone." She looked away as soon as the words had left her mouth.

Flynn stifled a grin.

The tinny skipped effortlessly over the water as they made their way back to the islands. Bay couldn't remember a time when she had been so alive and happy. She had experienced a renewal of life the last few days she had spent on Resolution.

She recognized the feeling had a lot to do with her company. Flynn had forgotten whatever had been bothering him earlier in the day and had been attentive and happy. He taught her about fishing, explaining the assortment of creatures that lived below the water, and the dangers and beauty of the ocean.

Bay had been fascinated, not just with his stories, but with him. Flynn was different from anyone she had ever met. It was obvious he cared little about what people thought of him. This was completely new to Bay, who had grown up thinking that appearance was everything.

His sense of self and his charisma drew her like a powerful magnet. She hung on his every word, willing him to continue. Finding out more about him was like winning the lottery. As he volunteered each new piece of information, Bay added it to a list to consider later.

Then there was the strange feeling she got when he was close by. Bay had experienced physical chemistry before, but this was different. So different, so powerful, it scared her. It was more than a physical reaction—it felt as if her entire soul was being dragged towards his. It was crazy to have such a strong reaction to someone she had known for such a short time, but it was present and real, regardless of how much she tried to reason it away.

Flynn eased the engine and pointed to something in the distance. A dolphin and her baby were jumping out of the water. The mother took a huge leap, slamming her body back onto the surface and disappearing under the water. Her baby wasn't as brave, only breaking the surface of the water in gentle jumps along mother's side. She watched in amazement. She had seen pictures and documentaries about dolphins. Nothing she had seen was anywhere near this experience. They were beautiful, captivating creatures.

She pulled herself away to ask Flynn for her camera. As she turned she found him holding it out to her. He had already freed it from the case, and as he handed it to her, their hands touched, sending hot flashes down her arm.

"I thought you may want it." He grinned at her from behind his moustache.

She gave him her best smile. "Thanks."

She had been taking photos all day. Not just of the fish they had caught, but the scenery, and a turtle that had surfaced with a spit of water to float around them for a while, checking them out. Bay wished she had brought her underwater camera when a colorful reef fish swimming under the surface floated around the boat. Flynn had explained that it was a 'bat fish.' They swam beyond the reef and were quite curious, but weren't worth catching. Flynn promised to take her back out to the reef with some dive gear. He knew of some spectacular reef drop-offs that hadn't been explored extensively.

Bay looked through the lens at the dolphins. She had moments of panic when she wondered if she really belonged in this world. Nothing in her life so far had prepared her for the rough living of the island. She had lived the complete opposite, but she hadn't given the disadvantages a second thought. There were certainly some gruesome aspects, especially in fishing. There was the horrible smell of the bait, the slimy skin of the fish, the blood that slopped around the kill bin, and the salt that stuck to her skin and hair. Yet she couldn't remember when she had had such a good day.

It baffled her that she was this happy, living with none of her usual modern conveniences at her fingertips. She didn't miss the finer things in life one little bit, and was in no hurry to return to a life of luxury. She had a sense of homecoming. If only Dutch would make his appearance and complete the picture.

The dolphins moved away and they set out again, land bearing up on them.

"I just want to try this patch of reef. We've had a good catch but we could trade some fish for a few mud crabs," Flynn yelled over the noise of the motor. Bay nodded in agreement. She had tried mud crab in Cairns. It was a real delicacy.

The boat pulled up close to an island that sat across the bay from the resort. Flynn had told her it was called Turtle Island. Bay dropped the anchor at his signal. They had fallen into a routine during the afternoon.

They had been fishing for a while when another tinny rounded the corner of the island. She recognized Amos holding the outboard's tiller, but not the man in the front of the boat. He was an Islander man with similar features to Amos, but he looked younger and had longer hair than Amos. His afro blew out behind him as it caught the wind. They pulled up alongside.

"Hey, what's it like outside?" Amos nodded his head to them both, making no special reference to her presence.

"It's been good, but the weather's coming up fast. It won't be a pleasant night if you're thinking of heading out." Flynn made the introductions. "Bay, this is Neville, Amos's cousin."

Neville gave her a wide smile that she returned. His face glowed as he conveyed his pleasure at meeting her.

Flynn continued. "Looks as though the boys were wrong the other night. Bay's a freelance photographer here to take some photos around the islands. She's staying in one of the cabins."

Amos's face remained unchanged by the news.

Neville stood up to look into their boat. "How many did you get out there?"

Flynn opened the esky to count the catch. "Five nice sweeties, six trout. Bay caught her share." He smiled at her, and she grew a little taller at the pride in his voice.

Amos stood up to retrieve something from the bottom of the boat. He came to stand with two large colorful lobsters, one in each hand. Their claws were tied tight with string.

"Take these. They'll be good on the barbecue." He leaned over the side to hand them to Flynn. Neville frowned at his cousin, but said nothing.

Flynn took the creatures from him without question, dropping them on the bottom of the boat between his seat and hers. He then dug back into the esky to retrieve the two best coral trout of the day. He handed them to Neville.

"Here, we got plenty. You need to have something for your dinner." Amos gave him a lopsided grin. "But why don't you and Neville come on back to the resort for dinner? We can share this fish, and the lobsters."

Bay was slightly peeved with the idea of having to share him with others for the night, but squashed the feeling, shaking it off as ridiculous.

"We can do that." Amos pointed to the trout. "I'll clean these up and come on over."

"We'll see you back on Resolution then." Flynn started tidying up the bits of fishing gear lying in various places around the tinny.

Amos and Neville nodded, swinging the boat around and heading off. Neville gave her a big wave as they went.

Bay took out her camera to photograph the lobsters. "These are beautiful." She studied their colors, so perfectly placed it looked as if someone had decorated them with a paintbrush.

"They're painted crayfish. Beautiful eating flesh." Flynn looked up from sorting the knives. "Amos's apology." He gave her a big smile as he settled into his driving position.

Bay turned in her seat, ready for the boat to start. "You mean for making me run from imaginary crocodiles, laughing at me for falling on my butt in the mud, and dropping me in the ocean and scaring me half to death?" She rolled her eyes.

Flynn adjusted the outboard. "Yeah, for all of that."

"Apology accepted, Amos." Bay turned to settle herself against the hard aluminum as Flynn laughed.

He started the outboard and they headed back to Resolution.

CHAPTER 7

Bay finally had the photo she was after, and it was just in time. The sea eagle had been diving into the water, picking up the bait that was bubbling on the surface below, but now it disappeared into the trees. She climbed down from the ledge, perched high above the ocean. Flynn had gone to the mainland for supplies, so she had taken the opportunity to venture out alone. In the last two weeks he had taken her all over the island. It was teeming with photo opportunities, from the wildlife that called the island their home, to the huge mangrove trees and sandbars with tiny soldier crabs scuttling across the surface. She had even woken one morning to find a possum and her baby curled up high in the fork of a huge eucalypt tree outside her cabin.

Bay had spent every day on a new adventure with Flynn, but no matter how many awesome views he showed her, or how many animals they caught sight of, getting to know him had been the biggest adventure of all. She still marveled at the friendship that had developed between them, and the ease with which they communicated. Flynn looked past the outside to show a genuine interest in her thoughts, feelings, ideas, and who she was as a person. They shared their faith in Jesus and had some long and deep conversations about Him. Bay had learned so much more about some of the Biblical verses that had spoken to her. But despite the strong chemistry and connection between them. Flynn hadn't made a move on her.

Bay appreciated that, but acknowledged there were times she wished he had.

She sighed, thinking about how much she had missed him since he had left this morning. She had wanted to go with him, but it was too impractical with the weather expected to worsen. He needed every inch of spare space in the tinny for supplies, and there wasn't any room for her. Besides, she had a plan to go back up and photograph the eagle.

Flynn had pointed out the bird a few days ago from the beach below, and Bay had spotted the perfect vantage point above. She knew Flynn didn't want her climbing up there—he'd been concerned by the height of the ledge. But she couldn't resist the position, and it hadn't disappointed. She was happy with the photos she had taken.

She took her time getting down, skipping over the rocks with her camera secured so it wouldn't fall. She was back down on the beach in no time. She thought of Flynn as she made her way back to the resort. He had been careful to keep his distance physically since their fishing trip. It had been a moment she had re-lived in her mind many times since, the way he'd held her a moment longer than necessary, his grey eyes boring though her, the tingle in her stomach, and the way she held her breath, as if waiting for something more.

Although they had spent every day together since, he had been careful to keep their relationship strictly friends, which was frustrating. Bay couldn't help but want to see more of the man behind the mask of his beard. He was a hard man to read. She'd occasionally catch him giving her an intense look, usually when he thought she wasn't looking at him, like when she was concentrating on setting up a shot. When he saw her first thing in the morning he would give her a look that said he had missed her.

Lord, what is it about this man that has me so desperate to get to know him? It was a question she hoped she would learn the answer to, and soon.

Flynn had asked her several times in the last few days when she was planning on leaving the island. She had now seen most of the photo opportunities it offered. Bay kept coming up with excuses to extend the time frame as best she could. She didn't know what else to tell him, other than the truth, and that wouldn't be fair to Dutch.

Her father still hadn't returned. It was three and a half weeks since he had left, having only expected to be gone a few days. She had mentioned his extended absence several times. Flynn had a look of concern on his face that did nothing to put her nerves at ease, but he had gone on to explain that while it was unusual for him to be gone so long, it wasn't unheard of. There was an incident a few years ago when Dutch had gone missing for over a month only to turn up on a friend's reef boat. He had run into the boat while out fishing and his friend was short a deckhand. Dutch had stayed to give him a hand until they returned to port. Apparently, he had radioed in his plan, but the radio operator hadn't bothered to get the word around. He'd turned up as a search party was being considered. One of the jobs Flynn had to do while on the mainland was to ask around if anyone had heard from him.

Bay had finally managed to get her cell phone to work and filled in some time that morning making a few calls. The first one was to Braden, to fill him in on what was happening. It didn't help that he too had expressed concern for the length of Dutch's absence. But he too had reasoned her father was a man who knew the sea and there was probably a good reason for his delay. Bay wasn't convinced.

The second call was to the resort in the Daintree. James answered the phone.

"Bay, it's great to hear from you. I thought you were lost to us forever. Your mobile number went dead and we had no way to contact you." He sounded genuinely pleased to hear from her. "I've been desperate to tell you that a photography magazine called last week. They discovered the photos you took of the she-oak tree and they want to print them along with your bio. When they didn't have any luck contacting you, they called me."

He named the magazine and the contact person. Bay felt a surge of electric energy run through her. It was a highly regarded publication. "Thank you so much, James. I can hardly believe they want my photos. I hope this puts a spotlight on the area, then the resort can benefit too." She gave him her new cell phone number as well as the post office box in town where mail for the island was collected. After some conversation about James's family and staff, they signed off.

She still had several hours before Flynn was expected to return, so she had gone up to get the photo of the eagle. She was on her way back to the resort when she rounded the point and saw the tinny floating alone, anchored at its usual place in the bay. She quickened her pace and found Flynn unpacking the supplies. The bar and small dining room had become their common area during the last few weeks. They met there for meals, having set up the barbecue on the paved area outside. She had felt closer to her father here than in his cabin. There were several photos of him in various postures on the walls. Her stepfather had been right when describing Dutch—he was a male version of her. His nose was his most distinguishing feature, but his green eyes were the same color as hers, and his blonde hair was the same, although much curlier.

Bay walked in the bar. "Hey, I thought you wouldn't be back for a least another hour or two." She started to help with the unpacking.

Flynn looked up from a bag of groceries. "It didn't take me as long as I expected. Did you go up to photograph that eagle?"

Bay shook her head. How could he read her like a book after knowing her for a few weeks? "That ledge proved to be the perfect spot." She gave him a triumphant smile.

He continued unpacking. "Well, in future it may be best if you wait for me. Then if anything goes wrong, I'm there."

Bay considered his comment. At one time she would have interpreted it as a reprimand, but the concern in his voice pleased her. "I promise I won't go off on my own without you again."

He turned to face her, looking for a moment as though he was going to say something. Just as quickly, he returned to the task of unpacking. He lifted a cooler bag off the floor. "I got some dry ice, so we can have cold food for a few days. The generator parts still aren't in."

Bay was pleased for some fresh dairy products, but there was a more important question she needed answered. "Has anyone heard from Dutch?"

"No one I spoke to has heard from him, but I got the word out that anyone who does should call me immediately."

"Didn't you say the main phone line wasn't working over here?" Bay realized she hadn't even seen a landline phone anywhere.

"It isn't. I've got a mobile phone, although the service out here is terrible. Dutch may have tried to get hold of me and wasn't able to."

Bay had noticed the cell service dropped in and out with no rhyme or reason. "I called my old employer in the Daintree. James told me a top magazine has been trying to contact me. They want to publish some of my photos of the area. The last day I was there, Mick took me up the river to see this old she-oak tree. It was amazing, and the lighting was perfect. I'll have to show you."

He completed the last of the unpacking as she spoke, then turned to give her his undivided attention. "That's great news. I said your photos were good enough for publication." She beamed with the compliment, while he closed the pantry door. "So this bloke, Mick? Is he your boyfriend?" Flynn looked up as he spoke.

She wiped down the counter. "Why would you think that?"

He shrugged. "No reason. It's just that you've spoken about him before."

Bay must have looked a bit confused.

"You said he had taken you out to the reef a few times. I assumed that if he was taking you out to all these places, he must be your boyfriend." His eyes darted, and he dipped his head.

Bay smiled. Was it possible he could be jealous? The thought crossed her mind for a second to play up her friendship with Mick for that very purpose. No. Bad idea. No good could come of that. Flynn wasn't the kind of man to play games.

"We were just friends. More like acquaintances, really."

Flynn looked unconvinced. "Most men don't go to that extent to help a woman without some kind of ulterior motive." He tilted his head, waiting for further explanation.

"Yes they do. You've gone to great lengths to help me in the last few weeks." She had him in a corner, and he knew it.

A full few seconds went by while Flynn averted his eyes and played with a tin can on the bar counter. A distinct pink shade developed on the skin around his eyes, and down his neck.

He blushes! Bay was delighted with the discovery.

He finally looked up at her. "I'm not most men. Besides, it's part of my job description to ensure all guests staying here have a good time. You're not the first pretty woman I've taken fishing." He gave her the smug, satisfied smile of a man who knew his attractiveness to the opposite sex, and had the history to prove it. He also looked pleased to have put her in her place.

Bay felt a pang of hurt in her belly. She was sure he was telling the truth. Did she really think she would be special?

The smug smile on his face did nothing to dispel the slight. The pain turned quickly into indignant anger. A creeping heat covered her face and she could feel her teeth grit. *Arrogant much?* She wasn't going to let him treat her like she was just another woman.

"I'll make sure you get paid well for the inconvenience." She flashed him her best dirty look, turned on her heels and headed out the door.

Bay was a good dozen feet down the beach when she realized her whole reaction was similar to the type of scene Kate would have pulled. It stopped her in her tracks. She closed her eyes, shocked by her behavior.

Please, Lord, don't let me be like my mother. She led such a lonely life. Help me to remember I am not the measure of my past, but the potential of my future. The past is forgiven and the future is in your hands.

She reached the beach and sat down to watch a boat anchored in the bay bob up and down on the swell. How did she end up as the jealous one in that conversation? She shook her head and rolled her eyes at her passionate rampage. *How embarrassing!*

Mate came up to sit next to her. She looked sideways at him and scored a huge wet lick up her face. "Yuck. I like you too, Mate, but do you have to slobber on me?" She wiped her face on her shirt. She may be à la natural these days, but she drew the line at dog saliva.

A movement to her left startled her and she jumped as Flynn sat down on the sand next to her. It took a moment for him to talk while she sat in uncomfortable silence.

"So . . . are you rich?" A playful smile tugged the corners of his mouth under the moustache.

Bay couldn't help it. She smiled too, the humor in the exchange getting the better of her. "No."

"Then how do you propose to pay me all this money you now owe me for my services?"

She knew he was playing with her. The tone of his voice teased.

"I have friends in high places." She would never in a million years ask any of those friends to cover any of her bills, but he didn't know that.

"You're a lucky woman. Most of my friends come from low places." He smiled.

She playfully slogged him on the shoulder and laughed.

He righted himself. "Before you offered to pay me off, I was going to tell you that I ran into Patty. She works at the pub."

Bay nodded, remembering the middle-aged blonde lady who was the one semi-pleasant person she encountered at the pub that first night.

Flynn continued. "She has a spare car and she offered it to us anytime if you want to take a look around the mainland. That is, if you're staying on a bit longer."

Bay was sure there was a hint of hopefulness in his voice.

"I'd love to. That was really nice of her. How on earth did she know I was here?" Apart from the trip to pick up her luggage, Bay hadn't been off the island, and she hadn't let anyone but Braden and James know that she was staying on Resolution.

Flynn gave Mate a rub behind the ears. "Most of the locals know you're here. It didn't surprise me. I knew it wouldn't be long before everyone knew. Not once Neville had met you. He's the biggest gossip I know. Far worse than any old busybody." Flynn shook his head.

"Really?" Bay was surprised by the revelation.

"Absolutely. You want to know anything about anyone, you ask Neville. In fact, he was the first person I sought out to ask about Dutch."

Bay found it hard to believe Neville was such a talker. "That's weird. I could hardly get two words out of him when he and Amos were here that night."

Regardless of her apprehension, it had been a great night, one she'd never forget. Instead of lighting the barbecue, they had built a fire on the beach. A slight breeze blew, keeping the temperature down, and stars filled a clear sky. Amos had cooked the painted crays and fresh fish the traditional Pacific Island way, in the ground with hot coals. It was delicious. The best part of the night were the stories Amos told after they'd eaten. Stories of his youth, stories of living and working on the islands, and even some traditional stories. Bay was enthralled and wished the night hadn't ended, even though it was late and Amos and Neville had to get back to their hut around the point. Amos had done all the talking, while Neville had sat, content to listen, occasionally throwing her a big grin.

Flynn drew patterns in the sand beside her. "I

suppose he was struck dumb in the presence of such a beautiful woman." He turned to look at her, his eyes steely grey and searching hers.

Bay felt the all too familiar drop in her stomach. It happened every time he looked at her this way, with such an intense stare she was sure he could see straight into her soul.

She felt herself holding her breath as their bodies swayed towards each other. She stared at his lips, the only feature visible under the curly hair that hid the rest of his face from her.

Flynn moved in closer until their shoulders were touching and their faces were inches apart. Bay felt her heart miss a beat—Slurp!

"Mate!" Flynn pulled back, falling into the sand under the weight of the blue cattle dog. Mate had the upper hand, paws on Flynn's chest, licking his face.

Bay laughed loudly at the sight. "I'm pleased to see he found someone else to love on. At least he's leaving me alone." She giggled as Flynn got the dog under control and righted himself.

"He's annoying me because he's jealous. He's really attached himself to you. It's strange. He isn't that way with anyone apart from Dutch." Flynn tried to push the dog away.

The comment pleased her. Perhaps Mate had recognized her as family.

He got to his feet and offered her a hand up. "Let's go in for some dinner. A nice fresh salad for a change."

Bay took it and righted herself. Flynn held her hand a minute longer before giving it a squeeze and then letting go. They made their way up to the bar.

The shrill ring of the mobile phone sounded as Flynn was about to step out of the cabin. He had organized to take Bay over to the mainland to show her around the area, and he was on his way down to get the boat ready.

He searched the pockets of the pants he wore yesterday, thinking that was where the noise was coming from, but the phone wasn't there. He scratched his head and searched the kitchen table. It would stop ringing if he didn't find it soon. He finally found it under a towel lying on the cane sofa.

"Hello." He picked it up in time.

"Hey Flynn, it's Archie." The hotel owner.

"Hi Arch, what's happening?" Flynn didn't get many calls from the man, only when Archie wanted to go fishing, which was not that often.

"I thought you'd want to know. They found a tinny. Looks a lot like Dutch's. That useless ranger towed it into the ramp this morning. It's in pretty bad condition. No sign of the owner."

"Are they sure it's Dutch's tinny?" he asked.

"That's what Ashley says." The line cracked. "I haven't seen it, but you'd know for sure."

Flynn's heart skipped a beat. He had hoped Dutch had just been waylaid, but with no word from him, as time went on it became less and less likely he was still alive. He didn't want to face that possibility.

Archie continued. "I thought you'd want to know. Bob's over there, but I didn't think he'd have phoned you." He was referring to the local policeman. Bob made no secret of his dislike for Flynn, and Flynn dating his daughter hadn't helped.

Especially not when the relationship ended badly.

"Thanks for letting me know, Arch. I'll be over as soon as I can."

"No problem. There's a group gathered at the ramp. Might be good if you can bring Amos over too."

"Will do. See you there." Flynn pressed the disconnect button, and taking a deep breath, closed his eyes. *Lord, regardless of this find, keep my friend in your hands.*

He couldn't believe that Dutch had been lost at sea. He grabbed a few essentials and raced out to let Bay know the day had been cancelled. He found her coming out of her cabin.

She gave him a big smile that made him regret having to leave her.

"Sorry, day's been cancelled. I have to go to the mainland. An unexpected turn of events."

Her smile evaporated. "Has someone heard from Dutch?"

"No. They found a tinny and they think it's his. I'm going over to take a look." Flynn explained as best he could without being alarmist.

Her eyes grew wide. "What does that mean? Is he okay? Is he lost somewhere? Do they need to send someone out to find him?" She fired the questions at him one after the other.

"Hey, hang on a minute. They aren't positive it's even his boat. I'm going there to take a look." He thought it was a little strange for her to have such a drastic reaction. She didn't even know the man.

"I'll come with you." She threw her bag down to close her cabin door.

"You can't. I've got to pick up Amos, and there'll be no room." Why did she want to come?

She looked up at him, her expression a mixture of shock and horror. "But surely you can make room for me? I can sit on the bottom." Her eyes were pleading. "My mother died a few months ago. I can't sit here on my own thinking about loss."

"I'm sorry, Bay, but it's better if you stay here." She looked like she was going to argue with him, so he took evasive action. "Look, I'll take my cell phone and call you when I get there, let you know what's going on."

She looked to say something, so he cut her off. "There's nothing you can do over there. It's better for me if you're here, then I don't have to worry about you, too."

She said nothing but her brow furrowed, and she bit her lip. Her expression was pure fear.

This is strange! She dropped her head, looking as though she was going to burst into tears. "I'd rather be over there with you than sitting here on my own thinking about death."

He touched her upper arm and turned her to look at him. "Hey, listen." He took her chin in his hand and lifted it to face him. Tears were brimming in her green eyes, and his arms ached, wanting to hold her. "Everything will be okay. I'll be as quick as I can. You won't be alone for long, I promise. I want you to go back in and wait for me to call you. Make yourself a cup of coffee and put your feet up." He emphasized his words so she understood.

He saw her swallow hard, blinking back the tears. Then she nodded her head. He gave her arm a pat and opened her cabin door to put her bag inside. She stood as if rooted to the spot.

"Go on." He gave her a slight touch on the small of her back. She walked through the doorway then turned to him.

"You promise to call me?"

"That's what I said."

She nodded again and closed the door. Flynn made his way to the tinny.

There was no doubt—the boat was Dutch's, and it was in a mess. Small patches of marine growth had started to clump on the outside, and tiny barnacles showed on the underside. The boat was larger than Flynn's, having been commissioned as a special build from boatbuilders in Cairns many years ago. It was designed to be safe in rough seas, and large enough to carry passengers. There wasn't another like it in Australia.

Flynn studied the damage to the hull. It was a strange hole, like nothing he had ever seen before. It was definitely not made by the reef. This was the explanation Ashley was insisting on and Bob, the local cop, was happy to go along with Ashley. Flynn didn't know what had caused the hole, but the absence of scratches or tears in the hull definitely ruled out a run-in with the reef.

The hole wasn't the only suspicious aspect to the boat's appearance. Flynn wondered what had happened to the extra flotation Dutch had put in the cavity between the hull and the floor of the boat. Some of it was still present, but a lot of it had been taken out, and he knew Dutch wouldn't have done that. The hole wasn't large enough to swamp the boat in seconds. Why hadn't Dutch tried to patch it, radioed for help, or set off his EPIRB, the safety beacon that sent a satellite signal marking his position and need for help? It didn't make sense, and he detailed his concerns to Bob, who dismissed him offhand.

Ashley wasn't helping. He was jumping around, muttering about how he had found the boat, and towed it in. The boat had been found semi-submerged. Something must have happened to Dutch. Dutch must have lost consciousness or suffered some sort of heart event and fallen overboard.

The more Ashley talked, the more Flynn wanted to knock him out. He was like a little mosquito, buzzing grief and negativity all over the place. He wished the ranger would either shut up or leave, preferably the latter.

Archie caught him looking at Ashley and must have read his thoughts, because he came over to Flynn and gave him a fatherly pat on the back. "Won't do you any good to take that goose out, you know." He indicated to Ashley.

"Maybe not, but it'll make me feel pretty good." Flynn raised his eyebrows. He had no intention of hitting the man. That would be foolish. But that didn't stop him from wanting to.

He turned the conversation away from violence. "What do you think of all this, Archie?"

"Well, I don't know boats real well, but I do know Dutch and knowing him . . ." He paused before continuing. ". . . It doesn't add up."

Flynn nodded. "I know how you feel."

He looked over to Amos, who hadn't stopped examining the boat since they had arrived. Now he was running his hand back and forth over the cut in the hull. He looked up to see Flynn and Archie watching him, and walked over.

"What's your take on it, Amos?" Archie asked.

Amos looked back at the tinny. "Don't know what made that hole, but I don't feel Dutch there. Don't think he's gone."

Amos had a strong spiritual faith, having an unwavering belief in God, but maintaining an indescribable connection with the land in which he was born and had lived his entire life. He had grown up literally at sea, as had all his family before him. Tradition and love for the ocean echoed in every fiber of his being, but his acknowledgment of God's power over all nature, including the ocean, transcended his ancestral spirituality. There was no doubt that Amos had a mature spiritual sense, one that wasn't often wrong.

He looked over at Bob and Ashley, their heads down in deep conversation. "Don't think that Cop's going to listen to us though, Flynn."

Flynn sighed. "No, don't think he will."

There was no way that Bob was going to take his concerns seriously. The grudge the policeman had against him meant that any opinion Flynn had would be rejected. And Amos, although recognized as a good judge, didn't have Ashley's suave sophistication. They didn't stand a chance. Archie knew there was something wrong, but didn't have the knowledge of boats or the ocean to make a difference.

Flynn hit the call button on his mobile again. The recorded voice told him Bay's cell was still out of range or not in a mobile area, meaning there was no signal on the island. He had tried several times to reach her, but with no success. The thought of her alone and distressed on Resolution concerned him.

Her overreaction to the news that a boat had been found was strange, to say the least. He put it down to the recent loss of her mother. She was clearly still grieving and oversensitive. There was no other viable explanation. He could understand her being concerned for his friend, but she didn't know Dutch. He had no time to think it through further as Ashley moved towards them. There was a frown on his face that Flynn supposed was an attempt to feign concern for the situation. Flynn wanted to wipe it off with his fist.

Ashley stood, hands on hips. "Looks like a clear-cut case of man lost at sea." He took off his wide-brimmed hat and wiped the perspiration from his forehead with a handkerchief.

Bob sauntered up next to the ranger, looking at Flynn through squinted eyes.

"You agree with that, Bob?" It was Archie who asked the question. His authority challenged the policeman to step up with his opinion.

Bob took off his police cap and rubbed his greying hair. "Looks that way to me."

"What about that flotation? That didn't jump out by itself." Flynn had gone over the missing pieces and several other suspicious features of the condition of the boat with Bob. But he knew, even as he spoke, that the old policeman wasn't going to listen to him.

Bob checked his notes. "Dutch must've taken it out for some reason."

Flynn shook his head and crossed his arms, not just as a show of displeasure—he was worried he would lose his temper.

Bob gave Flynn a cautionary glance. "Looks like we're done here. We'll put the boat in the lock-up area behind the station and let the marine surveyor take a look when they get over here. Ashley doesn't think there's any sense in mounting a search considering the time frame. There's no chance of finding anything." He shook his head. "It's a shame. Dutch was a good man."

Amos gave the policeman an intense stare. "Is a good man."

Bob frowned, then walked away with Ashley at his side.

Amos shuffled one flip-flop in the dirt. "What we going to do, Flynn?"

Flynn rubbed his beard. "We're going to have to wait until the marine surveyor takes a look. Then get in their ears about it, and hope they're sensible enough to notice the problems. Other than that, make a song and dance at the police station in Mackay." The nearest major city was about fifty kilometers away.

They didn't have much choice. He would have to take a drive into Mackay and speak to the police there. Bob wouldn't like him going over his head, but that was too bad. Dutch was his friend. First, he'd have to go back to the island and let Bay know what was going on. Then he could make it back onto the mainland and into the city before the station closed at five o'clock. If he hurried.

Archie spoke up. "I'll tell Bob we want a call if there are any further developments. If I tell him, he'll do it."

He was right. Bob certainly wasn't going to let Flynn or Amos know if anything further happened, but he would let the hotel owner know.

He turned to Archie. "Thanks, mate, we'd appreciate that. I've got to get back to the island."

Flynn took his mobile out as he spoke. Still no service. He looked across at Amos who grinned slyly. "She got you on the run already, eh?" Then he frowned and shook his head. "Something special about that girl. Don't know what it is though."

Flynn rolled his eyes. "Don't start, Amos." The two men walked back down to the tinny.

Bay checked her phone again. Still no service. "Useless piece of junk." She threw the phone into the cushion of the armchair and got up to check the window for the hundredth time. Still no sign of Flynn.

Bay could feel herself slipping into emotional exhaustion. When Flynn left, she had sat down and had a good cry, then pulled herself together enough to pray and read her Bible. Surely the Lord hadn't brought her all the way here only to abandon her?

She wanted so badly to know her father was alright, and prayed for some miraculous sign that would ease her anxiety. It hadn't come. She re-read the passage in her Bible that had spoken to her all morning. *God works all things for the good of those who love him.* Bay failed to see the good in this, but tried to calm herself down and trust in Him.

Eventually, she couldn't stand it any longer, and had taken a walk up to the point in an attempt to improve her chances of getting some phone service. The effort had been in vain. This morning's faint signal was long gone now the weather had worsened. Service was always poor to non-existent on cloudy days, and the grey clouds had rolled in after Flynn had left.

She ran her fingers through her hair and closed her eyes. The sound of Mate barking outside made her jump up and run to the window. Flynn was jumping out of the tinny and swimming in to shore.

She was out the door and down to the beach to meet him before he got out of the water. She let him secure the sand anchor that kept the boat in place before she spoke.

"What did you find out? Was it his boat? I've had no phone service since you left." She was both desperate and reluctant to know the outcome at the same time.

Flynn turned to her, water still dripping from his beard. "I know. I've been trying to call you." He flicked his head to remove some of the excess water.

"Well?" Bay felt like she was standing on a tightrope waiting for his answer to either push her off or secure her safety.

She saw Flynn take a deep breath. He slowly ran a hand over his beard before he spoke. "It was his boat. It's been in the water a while. There's no body.

It doesn't look good." His eyes were so sad.

Bay stood rooted to the spot, staring at a speck on the horizon. *No. No. No. No. No!* Silent screams echoed through her head. She could feel her heart palpitating under her ribcage, and her breathing quickened till she was hyperventilating.

"Bay . . . are you alright?"

She looked at Flynn, concern written on his face.

"But . . . I don't understand. Are they sending out a search party? Someone has to go look for him. He must be in the water somewhere. They need to get him out." She could feel herself losing control.

"They don't think it's worthwhile sending out a search party," Flynn said. "It's been too long to find anything."

"What does that mean? Is he dead?" Bay could feel tears pricking her eyes. She looked at him, willing him not to answer.

His eyes were so tender. "It looks that way. Without a body, we don't know for sure."

She heard him. She understood the words, but they didn't make any sense to her. She closed her eyes. *Oh Lord, what are you doing? You've sent me all this way, given me so much hope, only to see it all taken away again. I don't understand. Help me to understand.*

Tears rolled one after the other down her cheek, and she heard her lungs force an involuntary, ugly, labored breath. She felt faint and her body slumped.

Flynn was by her side in seconds, holding her to his chest. His wet t-shirt felt cold against her cheek. "Hey. Hey. It's okay. It's okay." He whispered the assurances to her, petting her hair as she cried into his shoulder.

She stood there, crying for a long time, letting the emotion out. She let him hold her, his strength keeping her on her feet. She thought about her father. She would never know him. Never get to see him, talk to him, and have him tell her the stories of his life. She grieved for the reunion she had envisaged so many times in her mind. She cried for the lost time not knowing him. Bay felt her heart breaking under the weight of the emotion. So much she didn't know, and would never know.

"What's going on here, Bay? I know you're still grieving for your mother but what is it that has you like this? You don't know Dutch . . . do you?" His voice was soft against her ear.

Bay knew she had to tell him. She had to share the secret she had been keeping from him. "He's my father." It felt so good to say it, to give him his place in her life, even if she would never see him again.

She felt him stiffen. "Your father?"

Bay didn't have the strength to explain.

He continued to hold her tight. She finally regained control, only allowing an occasional sob to escape. Her mind was a complete blank.

Flynn pulled away and stared at her before picking her up into his arms. He placed one arm around her back and the other supported her weight behind her knees. She allowed her head to rest against his chest and linked her arms around his neck. He carried her up to her cabin and through the door, putting her down on the bed. Bay turned on her side away from him, not wanting him to see her face. She heard his wet shirt fall to the floor with a thud. She closed her eyes and felt him lie down behind her, pulling her over and enveloping her in an all-encompassing bear hug. His wet beard prickled against the top of her head.

She looked at a spot on the wall, feeling secure and safe in his arms, and yet so numb on the inside. Closing her eyes, she wept and finally drifted into an exhausted sleep.

CHAPTER 8

Bay opened her eyes to find soft light filtering through the darkened room. How long had she been asleep? She remembered Flynn holding her, but now she was alone. Had it been a dream?

As consciousness came, so did her recollection of the last few hours. She rolled over to hug her pillow. Dutch was dead. A tear slipped untouched down her face and onto her pillow. *Where are you Lord? Why did you bring me here? Why couldn't you have let me get on the plane that day?*

In the airport, she had asked for His help, and He had given it to her. He had brought Braden into her life which had led her to the island, to her father, to Flynn.

Flynn! She sat up and groaned. She hadn't lied to him outright, but would he be mad at her for not telling him the truth? She wouldn't be able to bear it if she lost him too. She remembered how he had held her in a purely nonsexual way, just being there for her and showing her the comfort she had desperately needed.

He appeared as if on cue, stopping in the doorway when he saw she was awake. He looked at her for a moment, then smiled. Bay breathed a sigh of relief. Perhaps he wasn't angry.

"Boy, did you have a good sleep. It's six thirty. I was coming to wake you up." His eyes looked a deeper shade of grey today, the same shade as the t-shirt he was wearing.

Bay sat up. "I don't know how I managed to sleep." How had she had the peace of mind to achieve it?

Flynn moved in and sat next to her on the bed. "That happens sometimes. You went into shock and shut down. It was probably the best thing you could have done."

Bay rubbed her eyes. They felt sore and puffy. She could imagine what they looked like.

Flynn leaned against the doorway. "Will you come down to the beach with me? There's an incredible sunset." He gave her such a tender look that she got out of bed and met him at the door.

He took her hand and led her down to a blanket on the beach. A small cooler sat to the side. Bay paused to view the setting sun before sitting, recalling her long-ago memory of looking out over the bay, a large hand in hers. She closed her eyes and smiled.

"What are you thinking that's made you so happy?" Flynn asked as he took a seat next to her on the blanket.

Bay shared the memory with him. "It must have been my father who held my hand. As soon as I saw this beach, I knew it was the one in my memory. Are you mad at me for not telling you?" She needed to know.

Flynn frowned. "No, I'm not mad. A lot of things make sense now. I can see why you wanted to wait till you'd seen Dutch. He would have wanted that, too. I'm sure of it."

His answer put her mind at ease. He understood.

"I knew Dutch had a daughter, but he didn't talk about you a lot. Just once when I told him he didn't understand what it was like to lose someone." Flynn glanced sideways at her. "How old were you when you moved away from the island?"

"I didn't really move. I was taken." She explained how her mother had met Peter and ran off to LA with him and had taken her without her father's knowledge or consent. The part about her mother's deception was hard, but she forged on, wanting him to know every aspect of her past. She ended with her trip to the Daintree, meeting Braden, and the revelation of her father's existence. She also told him about her encounter with Jesus, His incredible timing with Braden, and how He had given her so much.

"But I don't understand. Did He bring me here to see me hurt again? Not only did I lose my mother, but now I've lost my father, the only family I have left." A tear escaped and traced down her cheek. It amazed Bay that she had any left.

Flynn sighed and took her hand. "Bay, I know something about losing people you love. Both my parents died in a car accident two years ago. That was before I came to live on the island. Then, after the funeral, my brother left the country. I felt like I'd lost everyone."

Bay felt his hand tighten in hers. This was the first time he had spoken about his family. The pain on his face indicated his loss was still raw.

"I blamed myself for their deaths for a long time, because I knew I had contributed to them being there. Then I blamed the truck driver who hit them. I even blamed God. That was when Dutch told me something that really made sense: God doesn't orchestrate the bad things that happen to us."

Bay thought of the verse she had read that morning. God works everything for the good of those who love Him.

Flynn continued. "He loves us through the bad times, if we let him. If we trust in Him, He can turn it around. He will forgive the wrongs. He can take our troubles, our mistakes, even our sadness, and use it for His purpose and our happiness. He does this because He loves us and wants us to be happy."

Bay nodded. "I know He didn't cause my father's death, but He could have stopped it, Flynn. He has authority over all things." It was something she couldn't grasp.

"Yes, He does, and there's a whole lot I don't understand about that. I can't tell you why He brought you here. I can only say I'm pleased He did."

He squeezed her hand. It was the first time he had expressed his pleasure at having her there.

"And you have to trust that He has a plan for your life. A plan that will make you happy, not sad or angry or lonely or fearful."

Bay thought about Richard. He had lost his family in a car accident as well, and had spent years angry with God. Wasted years, he'd told her. It was only after he let go of that anger and began to trust in God again that he had met her. He had the desire to be a father again, and she'd needed the guidance and love of a father. God had turned a loss in Richard's life around for both of them.

"I'm not telling you not to grieve, Bay, but to

grieve with Him," Flynn said. "'Come to me, all you who are weary and burdened and I will give you rest.'"

Bay recognized the passage. She had read it before, and it had given her strength. She looked out to the ocean. *Okay, Lord. I don't understand it, but I trust you have a plan. Love me through this.*

Flynn released her hand to open the cooler. "Would you like a drink? The portable bar has Dutch's homemade apple cider. I thought we could have a drink for him." He handed her a cold bottle.

Bay popped the top.

Flynn raised his bottle to the sky. "To Dutch. Father, friend, and a great bloke. We'll miss you, mate."

Bay raised her bottle in similar salute, and then followed Flynn as they both took a deep swig. Mate lay on the sand and thumped his tail as his own doggy salute.

Flynn swallowed hard and screwed his face as he looked at the label. "Blimey. That's awful." He scowled at the bottle.

Bay laughed. He was right. It was definitely something she would normally turn down.

He turned the bottle around. "But Dutch loved it. I don't know why."

They laughed together.

Bay sipped the drink, thinking of her father brewing the concoction. "What happens next?" It was a question she knew Flynn couldn't answer fully. Only the Lord knew where her life was headed. She would have to trust Him to show her the way.

Flynn took a while to answer, sipping on the

bottle, and deep in thought. She stole a glance at his profile, and her heart skipped a beat. *Please, Lord, whatever my future holds, let this man be in it. I love him so much.*

She froze with the intensity of the realization. She loved Flynn. Heat crept up her neck and onto her face and she could feel her heartbeat quicken. Prickles ran up her arm, so close to his. She straightened and held her breath for a second. Thankfully, Flynn hadn't seemed to notice her strange behavior.

"We have to go into Mackay tomorrow and see the police there." He filled her in on the scene at the boat ramp and the strange damage to the boat. Then on Amos's wise input and Bob's unwillingness to listen.

Bay rolled her eyes. "How can someone dislike you so much that they won't listen to common sense?"

"Bob and I go back a long way."

Bay looked at him for further explanation. She could tell Flynn was reluctant to reveal the extent of the relationship. He finally spoke.

"Bob's a motorcycle cop. He's always ridden one, ever since he was first posted. I was about thirteen, and a mate and I decided to play a practical joke on him. We took the bike one night and parked it in the jail cell inside the cop station. It was never occupied. The town never had any criminals to put in there."

A playful smile lit up his face. "Bob looked for that bike for days before someone tipped him off. My mate was too stupid to keep his mouth shut. I've been on his radar ever since."

Bay frowned. "But that's crazy. How can he

dislike you so much based on a practical joke you played on him when you were a teenager?" It was a complete overreaction, to dislike someone based solely on a childhood prank.

Flynn looked sheepish. "Well, that's not quite where Bob and I part company." He paused, as though he wasn't going to explain any further. "His son, Andy, and I got busted growing dope when we were fifteen."

Bay raised her eyebrows.

"We weren't dopeheads, just curious kids. We only had one plant and there was no conviction, just a slap on the wrist and a strike against our names. But Bob never forgave me. I was apparently the bad influence that led his son astray." He paused. "Then there was some other stuff. I don't want to get into it . . . let's just say that Bob doesn't like me very much."

The look in his eyes told Bay there was more to the story, but he was finished talking about it. She didn't push him. It wouldn't do any good anyway. She knew him well enough by now to recognize his reluctance to discuss something in his past. No amount of coercion would help.

She hard gulped some of the cider in an effort to get it down. "So do we go to Mackay tomorrow?"

Flynn nodded. "It'll be an early start. You know, Bay, you're Dutch's next of kin. You could force an investigation into this. It's worth a try."

"I'll do anything it takes. Do you think Dutch might've met with foul play?"

Flynn ran a hand down his beard. "I couldn't say at this stage, but the problems with the boat need to be explained." He looked out at the horizon, as if trying to spot something.

Bay looked in the same direction wondering what it was he was squinting to see. The sun had long gone and the light had almost disappeared.

"What is it?" she asked.

"Every now and then, just before dark, it looks like there's smoke on Broad Island. See over there?" He pointed towards an island a long way in the distance.

"Sorry." She shook her head. It was too dark to make anything out.

"I saw Ashley making his way over there a few days ago and thought maybe he was doing a bit of scrub burning, but I must be seeing things." He frowned and looked over at her. "Are you hungry?"

The last thing she wanted to do was eat. She shook her head.

"Better get to bed. It's going to be an early start." He leaned into her. "Are you going to be okay tonight?"

Bay bit her lip and nodded. "I'm tired again. And I don't think I have any more tears left."

He gave her a smile that reached his eyes. "Let's get you to bed then." Picking up the cooler and blanket he walked her to her cabin. They stopped at the door.

Bay turned to him. A powerful feeling of security overwhelmed her. "Thanks for everything, Flynn. For looking after me, for the shoulder to cry on, for being my friend."

She threw her arms around his neck without thinking through the action. With the blanket under his arm, and the same hand holding the cooler, he had one arm free to hold her around the waist. She held on, not wanting him to let her go. "I don't know what I would do without you." Bay could feel her heart pound in her chest. She squeezed her eyes tight and took a deep breath, filling her senses with his cologne. *I love you.*

Now that she was certain about how she felt, she wanted to say it, but her mouth wouldn't form the words. Bay knew she couldn't let him know. He cared about her—there was no doubt about that. The attention he'd given her assured her of that, but he'd never made any attempt to take their relationship to the next level. What did he feel for her?

She felt the roughness of his beard on her hair as he placed a soft kiss on the top of her head. "It'll be alright, you know. This is your home now." His words were warm against her skin, and the power of their reassurance sent a flow of heat through her body.

The dedication Richard had written in her Bible flashed into her mind- *For my Bay. May this gift help you to find your way back home. Love, Richard.* At the time it had confused her, now she realized that the Lord had indeed led her back home. And there was nowhere she would rather be.

Over a week had passed since they had found Dutch's tinny, and so much had happened. Bay felt caught up in a whirlwind of activity, which was a mixed blessing. The constant activity had helped to take her mind off the situation, but the curiosity and condolences of the locals had kept her mind firmly on her loss.

The trip to the police station in Mackay had gone well. They had started an investigation into Dutch's disappearance, including a full forensic detail of the boat. She and Flynn had also visited Bob. Bay had gone in to the police station to see him alone, to let him know who she was, and inform him that she had involved the police in Mackay. Initially he had looked slighted, but quickly reassured her he would do everything he could to help.

Word that she was Dutch's long-lost daughter had spread quickly. She had been inundated with phone calls from people she didn't know. Locals who had known Dutch had been to see her, passing on their condolences and concerns over the situation. Most were genuine, but there were a few who were simply curious to meet Dutch's daughter. It was nice to have people care, but it was emotionally draining, and Bay wished they would all go away and leave her alone. Flynn had started screening her calls to give her a break.

She longed for the days when it was her and Flynn on their island together, no visitors.

Ashley had visited four times, saying he was concerned for her wellbeing. The last time he had tried to convince her to come back onto the mainland to stay, stressing how much more comfortable she would be in a hotel room. Bay found him annoying, and assured him she was well taken care of on Resolution. Flynn displayed outright dislike for the man. When Bay commented on it, he said it was a personality clash and not to worry. It was his problem.

The bright point of the week was the email she received from Richard. He made reference to her search for her father and filled her in on his experiences. Bay enjoyed his stories behind the photos he had taken and the people he had come across. She got the distinct feeling he was keeping any unpleasant aspects of his life in a war zone from her. Good. She wouldn't be able to cope, worrying about him as well.

In a strange turn of events, she'd received a call from a legal firm in Mackay. The secretary had explained that they needed to see her immediately and she had made an appointment. Bay had asked Flynn to come with her, and now sat in the waiting room with him. The last thing she needed was bad news to handle on her own.

The secretary looked up at them and motioned for her to follow.

Flynn shifted in his seat but didn't make any effort to get up. "Are you sure you want me to come?"

She looked down at him. "Positive." She was tired of facing all these things on her own, and Flynn was the only constant in her life. She trusted him, and as crazy as she knew it was, she loved him.

He took some time getting to his feet. It was obvious he was uncomfortable. This made her appreciate his presence even more.

The solicitor introduced himself as soon as they walked into the room. Bay recognized him as the suited man who was so intent on playing the poker machines in the bar her first night at Kiisay Point.

"Hi, we haven't formally met. I'm Jack Turvill."

His handshake was firm.

An elderly man entered. Turvill's posturing made it apparent that the older man was the superior.

"This is Mitch Bloomberg. He's asked to sit in on the meeting." Turvill introduced his boss, and he shook both Bay and Flynn's hands. Bay recognized the surname from the titles of the firm, Bloomberg, Roberts and Austin.

They all took the appropriate seating.

Turvill looked at Flynn. "There are things I need to discuss with Bay that are of a personal nature." He turned to face her. "You may want to be alone."

Bay frowned. She was sure Dutch wouldn't have minded Flynn sitting in on this meeting. "You can proceed. I have no problem with you disclosing any personal information."

She wanted to involve Flynn in every aspect of her life. Thankfully he hadn't picked up on her motives for clinging to him, although Bay suspected his support was more due to her being Dutch's daughter than any reciprocal feelings.

The suited man sat back in his chair. "As you wish. Thanks for coming to see me at such short notice. It was a bit of shock to hear you were in town. As soon as I did, I found out how I could get in touch with you. There are a couple of things we need to discuss." He sank into his high-backed leather chair as he spoke. "Firstly, I'm sorry to hear of your father's disappearance. Dutch was well-liked in the community. Unfortunately, no formal death certificate has been issued yet, and most likely won't be until the investigation into his disappearance has concluded. However, I am authorized to tell you that we hold his will, and it names you as the sole beneficiary of the estate." He paused, as if waiting for the information to sink in.

"Do you mean Resolution?" Bay hadn't given her father's estate a lot of thought.

Turvill played with a pen on his desk. "Yes, the island, and the remainder of Dutch's possessions."

It was a shock. Dutch hadn't even known her, and certainly didn't have an inkling she would be returning into his life. It touched her that he wanted to leave this legacy, his most precious possession, his home, to her.

"That can all be finalized when we have the death certificate. The other matter is about your mother's will." Turvill dropped the pen.

Bay could feel her forehead furrow as she grabbed the chair armrests. "Kate's will was read in LA." She recalled the pain at having been told that her mother had left her nothing. Not even a keepsake to remember her by.

Turvill adjusted his thick-rimmed glasses. "Yes, but there were provisions in the will that upon notice of her death, the LA firm handling her estate was to contact us. It took them a while to do that." He stopped to clear his throat. "We made an attempt to get in touch with you, but we had no luck. It was a complete shock to hear you had turned up here. We had been chasing a Jane Anders, you see. We didn't realize you had changed your name."

"I haven't. I'm still legally Jane, but I've always gone by Bay. What was the problem with my mother's will? I was in LA for months after her death." She was hanging in anticipation, keen to know what Kate had been up to.

The older man had been sitting quietly all this time. He now sat forward, placing his forearms on the desk. "We want to issue our formal apology to you for the length of time it has taken us to track you down. The notice from the LA firm came in the week following your mother's death. For some reason we cannot explain, the notice was lost." Bloomberg's eyes pleaded forgiveness. "When I heard of your return to the island I looked into it, as I was the one who spoke to your mother all those years ago."

Bay was confused. The older lawyer had just contradicted what Turvill had said. He had told them that it was the LA firm that had taken their time getting in touch, when it was in fact their firm had delayed in contacting her.

She was diverted from thinking further on the matter as Turvill continued. "Many years ago Kate set up a trust for you that we maintained until her death. At that time it was to be released to you."

He passed her a document. Bay looked it over while Turvill went on explaining. "It was originally a large sum of money. At that time, anyway. She directed us to invest in mining shares. As you can see, they are worth quite a bit today. The . . . ah . . . full sum is …. here." He flipped through the document and found the page, pointing to the figure at the bottom.

Bay felt her mouth drop. "What!" She couldn't believe her eyes. "Are you kidding me?" The amount was over thirty million dollars.

Turvill pulled the paper back. "That is what the

trust is worth. We're happy to continue looking after the trust for you, if you are unable to take possession of it today." He fiddled with the papers.

Bay was in shock. She couldn't even string a sentence together. She shook her head and closed her eyes tight before gaining some level of sanity. She looked over at Bloomberg. "Can I have the paper again, please?"

Bloomberg nodded at Turvill, who took his time flipping through the papers, then inched the papers back over the table to her.

Bay handed the document to Flynn, and pointed to the spot where the total was detailed.

He lifted his eyebrows and gave a resounding, "Wow."

Bloomberg sat forward in his chair to address her. "Jack here has been in charge of looking after the trust. We've prepared it to be transferred to you at any time. Let us know when you're ready."

Bay weighed up her options, and realized she had no idea what she needed to do. "I don't have a bank account or anything."

"That's not a problem. We'll continue to maintain it." Turvill spoke fast and clicked his computer mouse.

Bloomberg stood up. "I have another appointment to get to. Bay, if you would like us to set everything up for you to receive the inheritance we can do that."

Bay look at Flynn. He was giving Turvill an undisguised scowl. Bay knew he had picked up on the same weird vibes she had. She wasn't at all keen on having any further contact with the strange man.

She turned back to Bloomberg. "It would be convenient for you to handle everything for me, but . . ." How could she say she didn't want Turvill in charge?

Bloomberg raised his grey eyebrows, and looked down at Turvill. "I'll organize the transfer for Miss Anders, Jack. I started this process all those years ago, so I'll enjoy the chance to see it to completion. You can continue to handle the trust until I have everything in place for the transfer."

Bay breathed a sigh of relief. The older man had picked up on her reluctance to engage his underling. Turvill, however, was clearly not happy about the change. His furrowed forehead, open mouth, and direct gaze spoke volumes.

Bloomberg didn't give him a chance to respond, handing Bay his card. "I'll be in touch soon. If there's anything else you need, give me a call." He started to walk out the door, then turned back. "Oh, you may not be aware that we also hold your original birth certificate and change of name, if you are ever in need of it."

So that's what Kate did with it. Perhaps in some warped way her mother had intended that she have contact with her father—just after her death, not before.

The older man said his goodbyes, and Bay and Flynn got up to follow him out. Jack Turvill stood behind his desk. His face still had a pink hue.

"Ah . . . for interest's sake, what do you think you will do with the island?"

Bay felt Flynn stiffen beside her. "Why do you ask?" She wanted to be clear on his motives.

"We've had contact from an interested party who is willing to pay an excellent price for the freehold title." Turvill backed away a little when he saw Flynn straighten up.

Bay squinted at the man. "You can tell your interested party that Resolution isn't for sale. Not at any price." Her voice was clear and strong and, she hoped, left the lawyer in no uncertain terms.

They walked out of the office.

Finally Flynn broke their mutual stunned silence. "I guess you're rich enough to pay me off now." It was evidently meant as a joke, but there was a strange unease in his voice.

"Flynn, I'm certain my mother stole that money from Dutch. Peter told me she cleared out his bank accounts when she left. Every cent he had worked for in his life."

It was a complete conflict of emotions. On one hand, how could she be happy her mother had fleeced her father of his life's savings? It didn't seem right to accept the money. On the other hand, her mother had finally come through for her. She had seen to her future after all.

But not in the same way Dutch did. Bay recognized the distinction. She had grown up with her mother, knowing Kate her entire life, but Kate had left her nothing but a legacy of deceit. Her father had a very short time in her life but left her his whole world. She knew which she valued the most, which one would contribute to the peace in her life.

Flynn looked behind at the closed office door. "Jack Turvill is out to get a kickback if he can sell the island. You know that don't you?" His eyes conveyed his displeasure. "It's probably why he stressed the urgency of getting you in here today."

She had thought exactly the same thing. "Like I said, the island isn't for sale. And now I have the money to fight to keep it if I need to." Bay smiled, hoping her words reassured him of her intentions. "Resolution is our home. Mine and yours, for as long as you want to be there."

She looked up at him. His eyebrows sat in a low frown. Bay hoped he would want to stay there and be with her as much as she wanted to be with him.

He ran a hand over his beard and shook his head. "I don't think you understand, Bay. That's a lot of money. It's going to change your life."

Bay lifted one eyebrow. "You're wrong. It can't change who I am. Not inside." She rolled her eyes. "Don't you understand? I've had money, privilege, and every luxury in the world in LA. Not one of those things made me happy. I watched my mother die surrounded by nothing but her things. Giving me this money is not going to turn me into her. It's too late for that. I know better."

Flynn looked away and walked a few paces down the hall towards the reception. Bay caught up and touched his arm. "Flynn?" He looked over his shoulder. "I grew up with money. A lot of it. A lot more than that." She pointed back down the hall. "This money is perfect timing. We can use it to fight off anyone wanting to take Resolution away from us. But as for me? I've discovered who I am, and I've finally found my way home. I'm not giving that up. Not for any amount of money."

She felt the decision reverberate through her

being. Flynn lifted one side of his mouth and gave her a smile that made his eyes brighten.

The next week passed in a blur. The investigation had unearthed several discrepancies in the theory that Dutch had fallen overboard, or that the boat had incurred damage to the hull from a run-in on the reef.

The police had informed her that they hadn't ruled out foul play. But if her father had been murdered, who was the guilty party? It was apparent Dutch didn't have any significant enemies. Everyone involved in the recovery and salvage of the boat had been checked out and cleared. Even though there was pressure on Dutch to sell Resolution, the developer had tight alibis for himself and all his employees. He'd also phoned Bay to offer his condolences and to let her know that if she ever changed her mind about selling the island, he would be happy to talk to her.

She had made it clear that the island would not be sold. Not now or in the future. She intended to live on the island permanently.

The highlight of the week was when Braden sailed in for a short trip. Bay had let him know about Dutch's disappearance as soon as she was able, and he had sailed down from the Whitsundays to see her.

She had spent some time with him on his luxury yacht. It was great to see him and he completely spoiled her. He took her out for a day on the reef and had his cook whip up five-star dinners for both her and Flynn, who, regardless of an obvious liking for the Texan, looked at times like a fish out of water.

Bay enjoyed the comforts of the yacht, but it wasn't her island. When Braden offered to leave the vessel in the bay for her to use, she told him that although she appreciated the offer, it wouldn't be necessary.

Braden had winked at her, and Bay felt certain he had discerned the connection she had with the island and its other inhabitant. He had left yesterday, making her promise to contact him if there was anything he could do to help her. Bay considered that he had done so much already. It was clear he would always be a part of her life. He had become a friend.

She now sat on the beach, Mate by her side, looking out over the bay. The day had been her most peaceful since Dutch's boat had been found. She wondered where Flynn was. He had remained close since confirmation of Dutch's disappearance. She usually only had to walk the length of the resort to find him, but in the last week he'd distanced himself from her and she didn't know why.

Bay had thought it was due to Braden's presence, but she had been back on the island since yesterday and had only seen him once for dinner last night. He had barely spoken two words to her. Now he had disappeared again.

She missed him.

A tinny rounded the point that led into the bay — Amos and Neville, travelling full speed towards the resort. She waved from her position on the beach and Neville waved back with a big smile. Amos drove over to the rocks to drop off his cousin, then threw out the anchor and dived over the side.

She had seen them both several times in the last

week and both had offered their sympathy, which she had also returned. Amos had known Dutch since before she had been born and could vaguely remember her as a child. He had lived on a smaller island in the group at the time but came over to Resolution occasionally to visit his friend.

Amos and Neville reached her at the same time. Neville juggled two large boxes as he walked.

"Hey there, Bay. How you going?" They had forged a friendship in the last few weeks and he was much more relaxed in her presence.

"Not too bad thanks, Neville." She gave him her best smile.

Amos motioned to the boxes. "Is Flynn about? The generator parts have arrived, so we brought them back out with us."

Bay breathed a huge sigh. "That's great. I've almost forgotten what it's like to have electricity."

She was happy to see the parts. As much as she loved her home, it was going to be a great convenience to have the power back on.

She lifted her hand to shade her eyes from the sun that was streaming down. "I don't know where Flynn is. He's been AWOL all day." She must have looked upset because Amos gave her a reassuring smile.

"I'm sure he's around here somewhere. I'll go find him." Amos ambled off in search of his mate.

Bay turned to Neville. "I guess you can put them up in the dining area for now."

Neville's face lit up. "Maybe have a coffee while we wait for them?" He didn't wait for her answer.

Bay smiled to herself. Neville would take any

opportunity for a chat. They both got a coffee and sat outside to wait, discussing the police investigation.

"Just think, if they had taken Bob's advice and refused to look into it, nothing would have been done." Bay shook her head thinking how close the investigation had come to being closed early.

Neville huffed. "Nah, Bob knew something fishy was going on. He hates Flynn enough to stick it to him."

Bay took a sip of her coffee. "I can't say I fully understand why Bob carries such an intense grudge."

Neville peered over the rim of his cup. "Bob never liked him much, but that whole business with Samara and that other bloke really sealed it."

Bay's ears pricked up. Flynn had never mentioned any Samara. She decided to push Neville a bit further. "Yeah?" She shrugged. "I don't know the full story."

Neville didn't need further encouragement. "Well, you know Flynn hadn't been with her for long. 'Bout six months I think. He was away at sea most of the time."

Bay nodded her head. He obviously thought she knew more than she did.

"He was out on the trawler a lot, and she was staying in the flat at Kiisay Point. Old Bob, he never did like his daughter going out with Flynn, but when they moved in together . . . well, Bob was pretty mad." Neville paused to take a drink then continued. "She was a good-looking girl and it must have been hard for her, with him gone so much of the time. Word was she eventually scored herself another bloke, but I don't think they were ever together. He was a bad egg, always down the pub, brawling and causing trouble. I couldn't see her taking up with the likes of him. If you ask me, Bob should have been thankful Sam was with a good bloke like Flynn."

He paused and Bay thought he had finished the story, so she sat back to digest what he had told her.

But Neville was just getting started. "Then when Flynn found out about them, he kicked Samara out of the house. The boyfriend went down to the trawler to see Flynn about it and he said Flynn attacked him. He ended up knocked out in the water and Flynn went to the slammer for assault." Neville shook his head. "Everyone knew Flynn had a temper, but most of us knew it was the other bloke that started the trouble. Flynn was just the better man."

Bay was shocked. Why hadn't he told her any of this? She framed her next question in her mind, so it sounded as though she knew about the conviction, but not the term length. "So how long did he spend in jail, exactly?"

"Six months, including the time before the trial. He was on probation for a year after. That was when he come to live on the island." Neville looked like he was enjoying her attention.

"So, he left to get away from the trouble?"

"Yeah, that, and most people thought Sam had broken him. I don't know about that though. Never seen Flynn nursing a broken heart. Then he took up with that Pommy backpacker soon after he got here."

What? She took a breath and composed herself, choosing her words with care. "Yeah, the Pommy backpacker. What was her name?"

Neville screwed up his face. "Jean, or Joan, or . . . Jill. That's it. Jill. Nice little thing. Made great French fries."

Bay looked towards the beach so Neville couldn't see her face. He must assume there was nothing romantic between herself and Flynn to be so honest about Flynn's past love life. Ultimately, they were no more than friends. The thought of Flynn carrying a broken heart for some other woman hurt her more than anything else Neville had said. Why couldn't he see how much she cared about him? Why couldn't he see her as more than a friend? Wasn't she good enough? Maybe she just wasn't the girl he wanted to be with.

Neville continued his story. "He was pretty busy that year, between her and that French chick. No, now I think of it, I don't think Samara put a dint in him."

Neville finished his coffee. Bay sat stunned, wondering what these women had meant to him. If he had had relationships with girls who lived on the island before, what was wrong with her? Wasn't she his type?

"You telling tales again, Neville?" A stern voice sounded behind her as Amos stepped onto the paved area. "One day someone might just cut your tongue out!"

Neville looked sheepish under the glare of the older man. He turned to Bay. "Mind if I get a water?" He motioned towards the empty mug in his hand.

"Sure. Help yourself," she said. He got up and high-tailed it into the kitchen.

Amos took a seat next to her. "Don't you listen to

a word that old woman tells you. Gossips got nothing to do with the truth."

She gave him a closed-lip smile. "You didn't find Flynn?"

"He's doing some fishing around the point. Not ready to come back yet." Amos gestured towards the far end of the beach.

Bay wondered if Flynn had stayed away because he knew she would be there. She looked down at the mug in her hand.

"Big changes take time." Amos patted her hand, and then called to his cousin. Neville appeared at the door.

"We're going, Neville."

Neville walked past her, swigging on the bottle of water. "See you later, Bay."

Amos nodded to her as they strode off down to the beach.

Flynn looked out to the horizon. The sun was setting and the mosquitoes had found him. He ignored their assault and continued to cast his rod.

He hadn't caught a thing in the last two hours, although he had to admit that fishing wasn't his purpose for being there. The rhythmic motion of the cast and reel helped him think. Ever since he was a child, when he needed time to think, he would escape to cast a lure. Sitting by the ocean was calming.

His thoughts, as always, were on Bay. The trip to the solicitor had thrown him completely. She was a multimillionaire now, and she was naïve to think she wouldn't be changed by that newfound status. She'd told him she'd had grown up with money but having so much of her own changed things. He didn't know how to be around her.

Money changed people. He had known women before who had turned into monsters where money was concerned. Samara had changed from a nice small-town girl into a narcissistic villain who stopped at nothing in the pursuit of money to furnish her lifestyle. She lied, cheated, and broke the law in an effort to acquire quick cash, then spent it on junk—jewelry, handbags, clothes and anything and everything that the magazines told her was fashionable. Sam was always chasing the next 'must have.' In her wake she left people angry, and her father heartbroken. But Flynn had paid the heaviest price, and Samara disappeared.

Flynn had forgiven her years ago. He never thought he would, but it had been a natural progression to forgive those who'd wronged him after he'd found God's forgiveness in his own life.

In the last week, he had been toying with the idea of leaving Resolution. He knew Bay wasn't the same person as Samara, but the inheritance would buy her all the help she needed. It also gave her incredible opportunities. She could travel the world with her photography. There was no doubt she had a great talent. So many possibilities were open to her.

The magnetic attraction he felt for her was growing, so much so that she was seldom far from his mind. Every aspect of his day, every thought, he wanted to share with her. He couldn't see any good coming from him staying. Either she would chain herself to the island for him, not willing to spread her wings and reach her potential, or she would eventually leave. Who knows what mess he would be in if that happened. By then, he wouldn't know what to do without her.

It was better to leave now and make a clean break before the situation broke both their hearts. He knew the way he felt about her was different from the way he had felt about any woman in his past. This was dangerous territory. He couldn't take the risk.

He looked up to see night falling. A smidgen of light still remained in the day. He squinted at the horizon. A fine wispy trail rose in the air above Broad Island again. That was the fourth time he'd seen what looked like faint smoke. He'd have to take a run over when the weather was good and have a look around. No matter that Ashely said it was nothing to worry about. If someone was setting fires on the islands, there was a chance one could take hold and devastate the native wildlife.

He walked back to the resort, hoping Bay had already gone into her cabin. He worried that one look at her would kill his resolve to keep his distance. During the week he had sought to put up a barrier between them. It was proving a lot harder than he expected. It was as though being away from her physically hurt him. He found himself having to push through the feeling to keep a level of controlled indifference.

The appearance of Braden Ewing helped. She had spent a lot of time with him on his yacht. He liked the man, but his presence drove home to him the differences between himself and Bay. She truly did have friends in high places, while he inhabited the lower levels of life. The distinction between himself and Braden was so obvious that it confirmed his thoughts. He had nothing to offer her.

CHAPTER 9

The sun had broken the horizon. Flynn had been up before dawn, not able to sleep, so he had set out for a bushwalk. He ran into Amos as he rounded the point. "You see that smoke out on Broad again last night?"

Amos looked out to the horizon. "Yeah, I saw it. What do you think it is?"

"At first I thought a lightning strike may have started a small bush fire, but it's gone this morning. Besides, that couldn't have happened four nights running."

His friend shrugged. "Don't know. Probably nothing. I saw that ranger heading out there a few times. Maybe he's over there."

"Doing what? There's nothing on that island. And it's rough water between here and there. He wouldn't go over that ocean trough, not without a decent size boat." Flynn sighed and shifted his weight, resting one foot on a large rock. "You're right. It's probably nothing. Anyway, weather's supposed to come good this week. I'll take a run over and have a look around. It's a rotten place to get to if a major fire broke out."

"I'd come with you, but I've got to go up to Cairns today. My sister's crook again. It's looking real bad." Amos frowned.

Flynn knew Amos's sister had been ill for some

time. "That's no good. I hope it all works out for you, mate." He gave his friend a pat on the shoulder.

"Me too. She's too young yet. Neville's supposed to be looking after the place for me. His work on the mainland's dried up for a few weeks, so I've got him doing repairs to my roof. Give him something to do."

Amos's place was nothing more than a tin shack he and Dutch had erected years ago. Flynn had offered numerous times to help him construct something better. Amos always thanked him for the offer but insisted that he was happy with his place in the world the way it was. Flynn suspected Amos had given Neville the job simply to keep him occupied.

Amos moved from side to side, as though he wanted to say something, but didn't know how to start. He finally spoke up. "You might want to know, Neville's been talking tales to Bay."

Flynn's stomach lurched. "What kind of tales?"

He knew Neville had trouble keeping his mouth shut, although it usually didn't worry him. In spite of the gossip, Neville didn't have a forked tongue. But talking about him, in particular to Bay, was a different story.

Amos shrugged. "Didn't hear much of it. Just a comment about Samara."

Flynn wondered how much Neville had said. Not that the story was a secret, but if Bay was going to hear about his past—especially his mistakes—he wanted to be the one telling her.

"Thanks Amos. I'll have a talk to Neville."

"Might be a good idea. Don't know when I'll be back. Few days maybe."

"No worries, mate. See you then." Flynn gave

him a wave as they parted company.

He took his time getting back to the resort, hoping Bay had already had breakfast so he didn't have to see her. He had the best distraction planned for the day—fixing the generators. It would keep him busy.

Flynn had decided to tell her he was leaving the island. It was the best option. The fact that he hadn't asked the Lord what He thought bothered him, but he didn't see that there was any other choice. Leaving was the best thing for both of them, although he couldn't shake the feeling of ill-ease inside, the thought that he might be wrong.

There was no sign of Bay as he collected the generator parts and got started on fixing the oldest, most frustrating pieces of machinery he had ever come across. They were long overdue to be replaced, but Dutch didn't have the money to buy new ones. They were forever patching up Gyrtle and Myrtle, as the generators were affectionately known.

Before he had left, Dutch had contacted two groups of fishermen booked into the resort cabins to cancel their accommodation. They couldn't charge for amenities without electricity. Flynn had to cancel a further four bookings in the last weeks due to the parts not arriving. Gyrtle and Myrtle were buckets of junk that were costing the resort customers.

Flynn had been hard at it for about two hours when he looked up to see Bay walking his way. The girl had legs up to her armpits, and it didn't do any good that all she was wearing was a pair of short cut-off jeans and a bikini top. She had a couple of bottles of water in her hands. She flashed him a smile that lit up her face as she came to stand next to him.

"Here you are, I was wondering what you were doing." Her voice was so sweet to his ears, but he didn't look up as she spoke, continuing his work on Myrtle.

"Well, these girls won't fix themselves, you know." His answer had come out short, mostly because he was trying to keep himself in check.

She said nothing for a few moments, her perfume catching on the breeze. His senses tingled.

"I thought you might need a drink."

Out of the corner of his eye he saw her extend a bottle to him. Her presence was so strong next to him that his resolve to remain aloof was slipping into oblivion. He had to force her to leave.

"I'm a bit busy right now. Leave it there and I'll get it later." He pointed to the sand with his screwdriver. He didn't dare to look up at her.

She placed the bottle on the sand next to Gyrtle and paused for a moment before talking.

"Flynn, have I done something to upset you?" Her voice was so hurt that he almost threw the screwdriver aside and moved to comfort her. Instead, he stopped and took a deep breath in an effort to gain some composure.

"What makes you think that?"

"It feels like you've been avoiding me this last week, and when I do see you, you can't get away from me fast enough."

Flynn hid his face behind Myrtle's girth. He closed his eyes for a second and sighed. Now was as good a time as any to let her know he would be leaving. *May as well get it over with.*

"You haven't done anything. I've just been busy getting this place running for you. I've decided to leave next week. I've been offered a job back down south and it's too good to turn down. Besides, you've got plenty of cash now. You can hire someone else." It was a lie. No job existed, although he was confident he could pick up work anywhere he went.

Bay was silent, and still. So still, that if Flynn hadn't been able to see her out of the corner of his eye he would have thought that she had gone.

"Is this about the money? Because I told you, it doesn't matter to me." There was a distinct edge in her voice.

He sighed. It was going to be harder than he anticipated. "Not everything is about you, Bay. I have a life of my own to lead."

As soon as he said it he realized that any life he led without her would be empty. The thought sent his spirits plummeting. He saw her move her hands to her hips. He didn't dare look up for what he might find in her eyes.

"Will you put that screwdriver down and look at me?" Yep, she was mad.

Better her anger than her affection. "I can't stop. I've got too much to do. Not all of us can laze around the beach all day." Flynn knew he was adding insult to injury, but he needed her to go before he changed his mind.

"Fine. Leave then, Flynn McKenna. I hope you have a nice life." She spat the words down at him and turned on her heels.

When he was certain that she was far enough away he looked up, watching her back as she strode down the beach, away from him.

Flynn didn't take a break for the next two hours. Concentrating on getting the generators going kept him from thinking. It was only when he felt faint that he stopped and sat down to drink the bottle of water Bay had left him. It was incredibly hot. He wiped the sweat from his brow and shook his head in an attempt to get some air onto his face.

It was times like these he wanted to get rid of the beard, but something always stopped him. He knew it was less a fashion choice and more a way to hide from people. He had grown it over a year ago, when being attractive to the opposite sex was a lower priority than hiding away from the world. It had been a convenient barrier. Now it felt like a burden he was carrying, and he itched to get out from underneath it, especially in the heat.

It was now eleven o'clock and he looked out to see Bay on the beach, talking to someone. He moved his head a little to the right to see around a coconut tree that blocked the other person from his view. There was no mistaking the khaki uniform and blonde hair. Ashley Chambers. Flynn narrowed his eyes. *What does he want?*

The man was as slippery as a snake, and arrogant to boot. There was something not quite right about him. He had gone out of his way to make life hard for Dutch, and it was obvious he wanted to secure the island for his employer. Then there was the unusual activity at Broad. Where might Ashley fit into that picture?

Flynn was also suspicious of Ashley's story of how he had come across Dutch's boat and towed it in. He had said that he found it semi-submerged on one of the northern island beaches, but Dutch was heading in the opposite direction. The prevailing currents running from Dutch's destination didn't go anywhere near the island Ashley claimed to have found the boat on. But when the police questioned him, he had an answer for everything. Flynn didn't trust him one inch.

Besides, he had been hanging around Bay since finding out she was Dutch's daughter. There was something amiss about the whole thing, and Flynn questioned the man's motives. Even if his sole motivation was to spend time with a pretty girl, Flynn resented his intrusion.

He moved to get a better view of them. They were deep in conversation, obviously discussing something important. Ashley moved in to extract a piece of leaf from Bay's hair. Bay pulled back at first, and then smiled as he showed her the leaf.

Flynn sat fuming. *How dare he touch her!* He got to his feet, ready to go down there when he remembered she was angry with him. It wouldn't do to go racing off and punch out Ashley in a jealous rage, not when he had gone to so much trouble to put distance between them. Besides, he was leaving soon. Didn't he just relinquish his right to care who she saw romantically?

She turned around and made her way up to her cabin. He reluctantly resumed his work on the generators.

Minutes later, Bay appeared at the door of the generator shed. She had changed into some three-quarter length pants and a t-shirt, with her hat on her head and camera case strapped over her shoulder.

"I'm going with Ashley to have a look at some volcanic caves on the island behind Resolution. Do you know them?" She sounded a little unsure, as though she wanted his reassurance.

He did know them and tended to stay away from them. If you didn't know where you were going it was easy to get into trouble. Ashley should be familiar with the area, but the thought of her going off with him anywhere made his stomach churn. He had to stop her. "The weather's coming up. Might be best to leave it today." It was a lie—the weather was perfect, but she didn't know that.

She pulled at the strap on her bag. "Ashley checked the weather and the forecast is perfect for the rest of the week."

There goes that excuse. He racked his brain for another one. "Do you think it's a good idea to go off exploring places you don't know?" He was reaching, but he hoped she remembered her promise not to go anywhere without him. Besides what was he going to say? I don't want you to go anywhere with that man?

Bay gave him a steely look that bore holes through him. It was obvious she was still mad at him. "I didn't ask for your permission. I'm telling you out of courtesy in case you were wondering where I was. Not that you would come looking for me anyway." She turned to go.

He got to his feet and called to her. "Bay." She turned around, the steely look still prominent in her eyes.

"Be careful." He knew voicing his concern for her

didn't coincide with his policy of distance, but he couldn't help it.

"What do you care?" She turned and strode away.

More than you know. He clenched his fist as he watched her get into Ashley's boat.

A heavy feeling of loss swirled with a fever pitched rage inside him. He wanted to go after her. He wanted to force her to stay on Resolution. He wanted to keep her safe. He wanted her with him, and he wanted to tell her that he loved her more than he had loved anyone in his life.

The realization stunned him. It was too late to take it back. He loved her. So much that it was screaming at him from the inside, and now he had pushed her away into the company of a fool. He shouted out in frustration, throwing the spanner he was holding against the tin wall of the shed. It ricocheted back off to hit Myrtle.

He closed his eyes, taking deep breaths and concentrating on gaining control of himself. He rubbed his hands over his face and sighed. What was he going to do now? There was no one to blame but himself. He thought he had known best, and had pushed her away so he could execute his plan for her life and his. He was as guilty of arrogance as Ashley.

Forgive me Lord, for thinking I know better than you. As usual, I've stuffed the whole thing up. Please show me your way out of this mess.

He looked down at the generators and tapped into the frustration he had suppressed to pull the starter cable on Myrtle. She flew to life in a flash, not giving him enough time to get out of the way. It was so quick that he almost got his beard caught in the belt as it sprang into action. He jumped back in shock, thankful for his lucky escape. He could have given himself a serious injury.

He fingered the useless mass. "Stupid hair."

With determination, he strode off to his cabin and searched around the drawers of the kitchen, finally coming across what he was looking for. He moved into the bathroom and, checking that the scissors worked, started cutting.

Bay couldn't believe her entire world had stopped in one day. If she wasn't so angry she would sit down and have a good cry. As it was, she was on a boat headed to a secluded location with a poor substitute for the man she wished she was with.

Why had Flynn tried to tell her the weather would be bad? There couldn't be a more perfect day. The water was like glass. They raced across it without a bump, gliding on the surface like they were on ice. The sun beat down on her arms as they went, and she thought of Flynn working in that little shed. The heat would be intense.

Serves him right. No, that was a horrible attitude. Something had to be going on inside his head, something he wasn't sharing with her. A fear or hurt that had come between them, ruining their friendship, and destroying any chance they had for a future together.

Bay moved the thoughts aside. It wouldn't be any good if she burst into tears in front of Ashley. He wasn't the kind of person she'd choose to share her thoughts and feelings with. She had little faith in his ability to sympathize with others.

In the short time she had known the man she had picked him as self-centered, arrogant and narcissistic—his view of the world was similar to her mother's. She had only taken him up on his offer to get away from Flynn. There was also the added benefit that Flynn couldn't stand Ashley. She hoped it had annoyed him.

Bay had picked up that Ashley would like to get to know her better. He gave her all the signals, working overtime to impress and compliment her. Leading him on wasn't wise. She'd have to do her best to keep him at arms' length.

They drew the boat into the shore so Ashley could let her off without getting her camera wet. He then took the boat out a little further to anchor it. He waded into shore, his khaki shorts getting wet at the top of the legs.

He looked down at the hemline and screwed up his face. "I hate getting wet."

Bay almost laughed. It was such a contradiction to Flynn, who spent most of his day getting wet.

He pointed to the top of a hill. "The caves are up here. It's a bit of a walk, but you'll find it's worth it."

"After you." Bay gestured for him take the lead.

They had little conversation on the way up the hill as the going was steep in places. Most of the time Ashley whined about the scrub getting in their way. Why did he take the ranger job if he didn't like the area?

But the journey was worth it. Ashley was right—the caves were incredible. They fell into the cliff from the top of the rocks, inaccessible without rock climbing and rappelling gear.

Ashley pointed to one of the smaller holes in the rock. "Most of them fill up with water at high tide. You're lucky you know me, because I'm one of the few people authorized to be here. The area is permanently closed to the public."

Bay kept snapping photos as the sun moved behind a cloud. "Well, I appreciate it. This place is amazing."

"Like I said, I'm doing you a huge favor."

Bay turned so he couldn't see her roll her eyes.

The one cave they could get into was huge. The opening cast shadows and an eerie light filtered through smaller holes in the volcanic rock. There were so many different shots, and angles to choose from. Ashley followed her around trying to get her attention, but she managed to ignore him most of the time by concentrating on the job.

"It amazes me that more people don't appeal to the National Parks for access to these." She took one last shot as they were leaving.

"They don't let anyone here. There's the danger aspect, but also because it's a culturally sensitive area." Ashley talked over his shoulder at her.

Bay had heard of sacred sites—areas of the country where Aboriginal or Island people held sacred rituals, or burials. There were a few in the Daintree, and access to those sites was prohibited out of respect for the culture.

She frowned. "How will they feel about us being here then? If I had known the site was sacred I never would have come." She made a mental note to locate the appropriate authority to apologize and inquire as to whether she could use the pictures she had taken or to destroy them.

Ashley turned to her. "It's not scared, just sensitive. And this particular area isn't either. North of here is the sensitive area. We can still come here. Anyway, nobody will ever know." He gave her a sly grin then turned to progress back down the hill.

Bay raised one eyebrow to his retreating back. The man was painful, and much worse, dishonoring. But she was relieved to know she hadn't unintentionally made a cultural misstep. She was looking forward to getting back to Resolution, even if it did mean facing up to the situation with Flynn. The reminder of his decision to leave the island permanently brought a lump to her throat.

He isn't gone yet. There's still time. She sent up a silent prayer for guidance. *Please, Lord, tell me what to do. I don't know how to turn this around on my own.*

Bay considered how much her faith had grown since the day she discovered Dutch was missing. What Flynn had told her that afternoon on the beach made a lot of sense. Trusting in God and leaning on His strength to see her though this time in her life, even though she didn't understand His plan, had strengthened her faith. She wondered now how happy she would be with Flynn gone. The physical connection she had with him was only one part. She would miss his friendship the most.

They moved back onto the beach and Ashley swore in frustration when he saw that the tide had come in. The boat was now floating well offshore.

"One of us will have to swim for it." He looked

at her as if he expected her to dive in.

Is he kidding me? "Sorry, I can't get the camera wet."

She gave him a mock apologetic look. It wasn't that she didn't want to swim, more her reaction to his complete lack of chivalry. He huffed his way down to the water and dived in, reaching the boat in no time.

This can't end soon enough.

The sun set as they made their way back to Resolution. Ashley killed the engine around the point and turned to her. "I packed a hamper we didn't get to eat. Perhaps we can set it up on the beach when we get back?"

Bay gave him another closed-lipped smile. She was getting good at faking it. "That was really nice of you Ashley, but I'm pretty beat. It was a big day. All that walking." She sighed, feigning exhaustion.

"Come on. It's the least you could do after all the trouble I went to. Remember, I was the one who swam for the boat?" His tone was teasing, but underlying was an all-too-familiar manipulative whine.

Bay knew he wouldn't play nice if she didn't comply, and he did still have her out in the ocean quite a way offshore. She couldn't swim for it if he got nasty. "Okay, but I warn you. I'm used to going to bed early these days." She faked a smile.

He revved the engine and they took off towards the island. As they entered the bay she scanned the resort. Something was different. In a second she realized what it was. The whole main building was lit up. Light streamed through the windows and colorful party lights lit up the whole outdoor area.

Bay sucked in her breath at the sight. Flynn had the generators going. She couldn't believe the transformation. The old stone walls of the building glowed in a variety of colors. The contrast between the dusk of the day and the color of the light formed a pretty hue in the outdoor areas.

Ashley pulled up on the rocks. She scrambled to get out of the boat.

He held out a hand to her as she placed one foot onto the rocky wall. "Looks like the hired help earned his keep today."

Bay squinted back at him. If she wasn't so eager to get out she would have told him off for being the arrogant pig that he was, but she was too intent on getting to shore.

"I'll set up the blanket on the beach," he called, as she picked her way over the rocks in record speed.

She ran into the bar, but found it empty. Flynn must be in his cabin—it was the only other building that was lit up. In her excitement she ignored their argument and his announcement that he was leaving, and ran over to his cabin. She was too thrilled to even knock on his door before yelling.

"Flynn. Flynn. You got the generators going."

She stopped at the door as it opened. For a second she didn't recognize the man who stood in front of her. It was only when her heart skipped a beat that she did a double take, realizing who it was.

She had always wondered what he would look like without the beard, but not even in her dreams had she pictured him like this. His strong jaw and rugged features transformed his whole face. He had cut his hair as well. Where his hair was once a mess of curls, now short brown-red rings sat on his head.

Bay froze, taking in his whole face for a moment, before meeting his eyes. They pierced through hers with more intensity than she had ever seen before. She felt as though she was seeing him for the first time. Her heart threatened to jump out of her chest. She was aware of a great compulsion to touch him. To feel, not just see, who he really was. She couldn't help it. She touched her hand to his clean-shaven cheek. It was soft. Bolts of electrical current streamed down her arm. Bay could feel her chest heave.

"It's you," she whispered. She rubbed her hand down his cheek and felt the softness of his face.

Flynn closed his eyes for a second, allowing her to touch him. Then he took her hand and placed his lips in her palm. His grey eyes flashed open to lock with hers once more.

Bay could hear her pulse hammer in her ears as his free hand reached for her. He found her waist, pulling her to him. Their bodies collided and his lips met hers, soft and slow at first, then deepening the kiss with desperation.

She felt her body give way under the passion, melting into his as the kiss eased and softened again. As he began to pull away a soft moan sounded in her throat and she felt him respond, pulling her back against his body and kissing her again.

A distant voice sounded behind her. Someone calling in the distance. The noise got louder and closer and Flynn broke away, gently pushing her from him. Bay opened her eyes to see Ashley appear next to her.

"Here you are. I've been looking everywhere for you. You should really do something about that dog. It was going to attack me." He looked Flynn up and down. "I see you cleaned yourself up." Then he looked back and forth between them, finally gauging that something was amiss.

Bay could feel the heat rise on her neck and crawl up to burn her face.

"Have I interrupted something?" Ashley frowned. His eyes scanned both of them as they stood silently, rooted to the spot.

"No."

"Yes."

They both answered him at the same time. Her 'no' was a casual attempt to cover up her embarrassing blush. Flynn's 'yes' was more an undisguised insult to Ashley.

Bay rubbed her cheeks in an attempt to stem the fire. "Um . . . I . . . ah . . . was . . . ah . . . just asking Flynn if he wanted to join us."

"Really?" Ashley didn't sound convinced. His bottom lip bulged in a defiant pout. "Well, I'm sorry that's not possible. I didn't bring enough food for three. Unfortunately." He stared at Flynn, lifting one corner of his mouth in an arrogant, satisfied way.

Flynn gave him a smirk, but his eyes threw daggers at the man. "I've already eaten, thanks. And it was very . . . very good." A slow, satisfied grin spread over his face. He shot a knowing look in her direction.

Bay felt the heat returning with a vengeance. Ashley didn't need an interpretation to know what Flynn was referring to, and he straightened up and huffed.

Bay remained silent, not trusting herself to speak.

Ashley swept one hand towards the beach. "Great. That's sorted then. Let's go, Bay." He stood to the side for her to pass.

Bay ducked her head so she didn't have to look at Flynn, and made her way down to the beach. She felt unsteady on her feet.

Ashley had set up a picnic blanket, and the hamper was the fancy kind. All the plates and cutlery were placed neatly in the designated sections. Bay thought back to the best meal she had ever had, sitting on the sand with Flynn, Amos, and Neville, with not a fork or a plate in sight.

He waited until they were both sitting. "I don't know if you're aware but I feel the need to tell you that your hired help is a bit of bad news." He retrieved the plates and a packet of muffins from the basket.

Bay felt the heat rise again, but this time it was due to the arrogance of Ashley's words. Not only did she object to Flynn being called the hired help, but the implication that he was bad news was enough to make her blood boil.

Ashley didn't stop there. "I don't know if Dutch would have approved of his daughter consorting with criminals." He passed her a muffin.

Bay wanted to throw it at him, but remained calm. "I'll have you know that I am fully informed about Flynn's past. As to my father's disapproval, you forget that Flynn and Dutch were close friends. They've lived here together for two years. Besides, my relationships are none of your business." *Who does he think he is?* Bay could literally feel the fumes evaporate over her head.

Ashley gritted his teeth, but continued to arrange the food. "While we're on the subject, what are you going to do with the island? Wouldn't it be better to sell it? It looks like a lot of work, and surely you won't want the hassle, not with your newfound riches." He sat back taking a bite of his muffin while he talked.

Bay was stunned at the man's audacity. Then it occurred to her that no one but Flynn knew about the money from her mother, and she was positive he wouldn't have told Ashley.

She stared at him with the same intensity as Flynn had moments before. "What do you know about my so-called newfound riches, Ashley?"

His posture deflated, and he was looking anywhere but at her. "I . . . I heard somewhere that you'd come into some money."

"I see. So who was it that told you that? Because I haven't made that anyone's business but my own." She got to her feet and dusted the sand off her knees. "I think it's time for you to leave."

Ashley stared up at her. "Fine." He threw the picnic stuff into the basket and shook the blanket. "You know, when I met you in the pub that night, I thought you were a sophisticated lawyer here to sort out Dutch's estate. But now I see you're as low-class as your father." He looked at her with such revulsion that Bay recoiled under his gaze.

A noise from the top of the beach broke them both out of the moment. Bay looked up to see Flynn striding down to them, purpose in his step.

Ashley threw the blanket and basket back onto the sand. "I'll be back to pick these up." He took off at high speed into the water, forging a stunning freestyle to the boat.

Flynn reached her side as he pulled himself up onto the duckboard. "Did I interrupt something?"

The way he mimicked Ashley made Bay giggle. "How did you know I needed a knight in shining armor? You didn't happen to be watching us, Flynn McKenna?"

He gave her a big smile. Bay's heart skipped a beat. Seeing his whole face would take some getting used to. He looked years younger.

He wiggled his eyebrows. "I was watching you." He then glanced out to Ashley's boat as it tore off around the point. He turned to her then, his grey eyes locking with hers. "Baby Jane."

Hearing him refer to the nickname her father had given her warmed her inside. She gave him her best smile. There had been a change in him since that morning. The tension she had felt then had disappeared. Whatever it was that had been troubling him was gone. Flynn was back, and he had kissed her. Bay decided she needed to find out where she stood considering the new development in their relationship.

She shuffled her feet in the sand, working up the courage to ask him about their future. "Is there any chance you might reconsider leaving Resolution? Perhaps if I commission the purchase of two new generators?"

Flynn laughed. "Get rid of Gyrtle and Myrtle?

No way. I won't have anything to do but take you fishing." His tone was teasing.

"Sounds good to me," she said, as Mate sidled up next to her and nudged her hand for a pat.

She turned her attention to the dog. "May I say, Mate, that you are an excellent judge of character." She gave the dog a pat and squatted down to rub his face with both her hands. He lapped up the attention, rewarding her with a big lick to the face.

"Looks like he's a sucker for a pretty face as well."

"He knows a soft touch when he sees it. Don't you boy?" The dog woofed in happy agreement.

"I'm taking a run over to Broad tomorrow to have a look at the island. Would you like to accompany me, Miss Anders?" Flynn asked in mock formality.

"I believe I would very much enjoy an outing with you, Mr. McKenna," she replied, playing along.

"I'm warning you, I'll be early."

"I can handle an early morning." Bay had turned into an early morning person since living on Resolution.

They walked up to her cabin, turning to look at each other as they reached the door.

He paused, not making any move towards her. "Till tomorrow then?"

The light coming from the bar threw enough to illuminate the area. Bay wanted him to kiss her again, but didn't have the confidence to instigate it herself.

"Tomorrow." She bit her bottom lip.

Flynn swayed toward her for a second, then did a pivot towards his cabin.

"Flynn," she called after him. He stopped and turned around. "Thank you."

He was barely visible. She could only make out his outline in the shadows.

"For what?"

She took a deep breath. "For being here for me."

He took a step back towards her and then stopped.

"That's alright, Bay." Then he turned around and went back to his cabin.

Thank you Lord. You have given me what I asked. You have brought me to people who care about me.

Bay went into her cabin and flicked the switch, and watched as the fluorescent tube lit up the room.

CHAPTER 10

Bay was awake before dawn. She lay in the darkness, contemplating the events of the last few days, reliving the kiss with Flynn over and over in her mind, and praying that today would be a new beginning for them—the beginning of a life together.

She knew Resolution was her home, the place God had for her. She hadn't known Dutch, but she missed him all the same. Missed what could have been.

All the stories of those who knew him were filled with tales of his courage, strength and vibrant personality. The ringing of a telephone startled her. It wasn't her cell. Bay followed the sound into the kitchen. It was the landline. The return of the electricity must have restored the landline connected to the cordless phone.

Bay picked up the receiver. "Hello?"

"Oh, um, my name is Yvette. I'm calling from Western Australia. I'm a friend of Dutch's. I heard he was missing and . . . I . . . I wanted to know if it's true that he's passed?"

Bay stretched one side of her neck before answering. "They found his boat, but there's no body." Saying it out loud was still hard.

A heavy sigh sounded over the line. "Oh . . . Well, there's still hope then."

Bay took a sharp breath. Was there hope? She

filled Yvette in on the details of the find and investigation—as she and Flynn had done with all of Dutch's friends. "How did you know Dutch?"

"I spent four months on Resolution last year. I'm a marine biologist and I've been researching dugong habitats. The estuary around the islands has a significant dugong population. Dutch was so helpful during my stay. He ferried me around in his boat, and was invaluable to my work." She gave a little giggle. "At times I felt like he knew more about the animals than I did. I would still be there if it weren't for my baby granddaughter falling ill. I had to come home to help, but she's recovered now so I've been planning to come back." She gave a deep sigh. "I do hope they find Dutch. The island won't be the same without him."

Bay smiled, wishing for the millionth time that she had reached the island sooner and had the reunion with her father she had dreamed of.

"Are you looking after the resort?" Yvette's question broke through her sadness.

"No. I'm Bay. Dutch's daughter." She went on to give the gently spoken woman on the end of the line the short version of her journey back to Resolution.

"Oh, Bay. He always knew you would find your way home. He told me all about you. If he is indeed gone, like they think he is, I know he would still be so happy and thanking the Lord right now for your return."

Yvette's words brought tears to her eyes, and Bay let them roll down her face.

They went on to talk about the situation. Bay offloaded many of her feelings. It was cathartic to get it all out, and Yvette had a motherly knack of gentle coaxing that made Bay feel safe, even over all the miles that separated them. They finished their call with the promise to talk again soon.

Bay sat for a moment and thought about her father and Yvette's relationship. Dutch must have been close to her to have revealed so much of his life. She decided that their relationship must have been more than friendship.

Bay picked the landline receiver back up and listened for the dial tone. It rang out clear. The newfound freedom of the electricity was a great relief. She loved Resolution, but hoped to put in more modern amenities in the near future to bring the resort up to a higher standard. Perhaps something similar to the eco resort in the Daintree, so that the natural environment could be preserved as much as possible. All her plans included Flynn. She pictured them working together to build something special.

She grabbed her cell and checked her email messages. She had sent a collection of Resolution Island photos to several magazines in the hope that she could draw some attention to the beauty of the area. Most tourists bypassed these islands in favor of the popular Whitsunday Islands, but this area had so much to offer.

No replies for the photos, only a series of social media notifications that highlighted her old life in LA. She smiled and thought about how different it had been to her life now, and the life she envisaged in her future. There was no doubt she had felt lost in L.A. She realized that, although she was lucky not to have to worry about money or where her next meal was coming from, spending so much time amongst the privileged of the world had revealed a distressing truth—they had all the things, all the toys, but they weren't happy.

Like Tasha, who modelled her life after meaningless things, and wasteful people. She was obsessed with the continual 'reinvention' of her life. She even had a three-year plan to go on a reality TV show to gain her five minutes of fame and bag a millionaire husband. She sacrificed who she was, put up with cheating boyfriends because they were rich, associated with people she didn't like, then worked like crazy to afford all the things that made her feel valued.

Bay remembered when the LA lawyers had read her mother's will and she discovered she had been left nothing. At the time she would never have believed that being cut off was a positive, but now she marveled at God's timing. He had a plan for her even back then when she didn't know Him. She would have stayed in LA if she had the means, and would probably have wasted her life chasing meaningless things, never coming to know who she really was. She was so lost amongst all the 'stuff' and He had given her a way out, even if she didn't recognize it at the time.

Her resolve to her newfound inheritance was a reaction to who she had become since arriving on Resolution. The freedom the island offered from the constraints and expectations of society was a touch of heaven on earth. A place to breathe and be herself. A place to be liked for who she was, with no pressure to perform, no new dresses, no social obligations and no leering men out to get what they wanted. Just her, the island, and a man so different from any she had ever known. Now it looked as though he had finally put aside whatever reservations he had about having a relationship with her. The thought of seeing him that morning excited her.

She reached over to check the time — it was later than she thought. She raced to get dressed and was ready to go in no time. For breakfast she grabbed one of the muffins Ashley had left behind, and found a change of clothes. She grabbed her bag and flew out the door to meet Flynn.

He was down on the beach waiting for her. His hair was wet, dripping in ringlets. He had already retrieved the tinny from the bay. The water was so calm he could leave it sit on the beach. The water gently lapped in tiny waves on the sand.

Bay swallowed hard. He looked so good. It had taken ages for her to fall asleep last night, thinking about his physical transformation, the rugged good looks he'd been hiding. It was hard not to stare at him. Even though it was him she had fallen in love with, not his looks.

He shook his head, extracting the excess water. "Good morning. Sleep well?"

Bay wondered for a minute if she should answer honestly and tell him that she had lain awake thinking of him, but decided to keep that to herself. They had a trip to Broad Island, and if they allowed themselves to get as intense as yesterday they might not get off Resolution at all.

She fiddled with her ponytail. "Fairly well. You?"

He grabbed a clean t-shirt from the tinny. "Horrible. I lay awake thinking of you most of the night."

Seemed Flynn either didn't have her ability to lie, or he didn't mind if they never left Resolution. Bay couldn't help the smile that spread across her face.

He looked back at her and grinned. "Come on. Get in the boat." He held the tinny stable while she climbed in.

It took under forty minutes to get out to Broad Island, the last and most remote island in the group. It was all open sea after Broad, and Flynn explained that in rough weather it was a long and bumpy trip. The island was smaller than Resolution, but the same trees and bushes marked the rocky surface.

Flynn stopped the boat in a small bay on the sheltered side of the island, and moved the tinny into the shore to let Bay out. He also threw out a bag with a change of clothes and sneakers for himself, as well as a cooler containing some drinks and snacks. Then he took the tinny back out to anchor.

Flynn scanned the island terrain. "I guess we'll have a walk around the island and cover as much of it as possible. I don't even know what I'm supposed to be looking for. Signs of bushfires, maybe?" He shook his head.

If he didn't know what he was looking for she certainly didn't. She was just happy to be there with him.

They spent the morning walking the goat tracks around one half of the island. Flynn explained that nineteenth-century sailors had placed goats on the islands throughout North Queensland so that in the event of a shipwreck the survivors would have a food source. The National Parks had killed off the goat populations on the majority of the islands due to the impact on the environment. As so few people went to Broad, it was one of the few islands left where the creatures roamed free.

The trails were hard in places and Flynn would reach down to offer her a hand up a rocky patch. When they had reached as far around the island as they could go, they tracked up over the top, and back down to the little beach.

Flynn took one of the towels she had retrieved from her bag. "Well, there wasn't a sign of anything out of place. Strange we didn't see any goats. Usually you see at least one."

Bay pulled her shirt away from her sweaty body. "I might change before we eat. I'm so hot in this." The t-shirt had been a bad choice. It was made from a heavy cotton and polyester blend that didn't breathe. She had mentally planned during the walk back to change into whatever she had thrown into her bag that morning.

"No worries. You go this way." He pointed to the bushes on the left. "I'll go that way." He indicated the trees on the right. "And we'll meet back here." His smile held a hint of mischief.

"Okay." She grabbed her duffle bag.

Bay discovered that she had not only worn the wrong shirt, but that she had grabbed the wrong one too. All she had were her bikini top and a see-through cheesecloth cover that would be hopeless at keeping out the sun's harmful UV rays. Unfortunately, they would have to do. She made the change and stuffed her bag, walking back to where they had set up under the shade at the top of the beach.

She pulled out her ponytail and ran her fingers through her hair, as she took a seat next to Flynn on the towel. "All done. Boy, do I feel better." He had also removed his shirt and hung it on a branch of a tree.

He glanced at her, then jolted back a few inches. "Don't you have anything else to wear?"

His voice and look was so insulting that she frowned at him and screwed up her face. "I'll have you know I think I look pretty good in a bikini, thank you very much." It wasn't as though she was wearing a potato sack.

Flynn let out a deep breath. "I don't know how you expect me to keep my hands off you when you constantly wear next to nothing." His squinted eyes and pursed mouth gave away his frustration.

Bay bit her bottom lip. His admission that he wanted her sent thrills coursing through her body, but considering his disgruntled tone, she decided to play it cool. "Well, I'm sorry my supposed inappropriate dress is affecting your self-control. This is all I have." She gave his arm a playful push. "Hey, it's not like swimwear falls under the banner of inappropriate beach wear."

Flynn frowned at her attempt to pacify him, then jumped to his feet and started to walk away.

She got up too. "Flynn, I'm sorry. I'll change back into the other shirt if you want. Where are you going?" she called to his retreating back.

All that was ahead of him was bush. He must

have realized that too, because he turned back around. He stared at her, shifting his weight from one foot to the other. "I'm just a man, Bay. I don't have unlimited self-control, you know."

He then put a hand up to stroke his beard, an action Bay had seen him do a hundred times before, except it wasn't there anymore. He threw his hand back down in frustration. Bay couldn't help herself. She giggled at his antics.

He looked up, shooting her such an intense stare, that Bay stopped laughing and held her breath, expecting him to explode at any moment. Instead he came towards her, covering the distance between them in seconds.

He grabbed her to him and kissed her so hard that Bay thought she might bruise. His fingers dug into her hips, holding her to him as his mouth forced down on hers. As she wrapped her arms around his neck he softened, kissing her with such passion that she allowed her body to melt into him. His chest was hard and warm, only the thin layer of her shirt separating their skin.

They moved down to lie on the towels in one swift motion, his lips never leaving hers. As he lay on top of her Bay realized their bodies fit together perfectly, like two pieces of a puzzle. He traced a path of soft kisses down her neck and along her collarbone. One of his hands trailed up the length of her body, moving up from her thigh and lingering at her breast. Bay felt as though her entire body was on fire. She reciprocated, rubbing her hands down his back, and feeling the muscles move and contract under her hands. She could feel her heart beating in sync with his. Her breath labored. Her body arched towards him and a faint sigh escaped. He responded, his lips meeting hers.

Flynn stopped and lifted his head to look at her. His grey eyes were so full of emotion that she touched his face. It was still so new to her. "I love you." The words were out before she had though them through, and relief flowed through her at having finally let him know.

He smiled, and then moved to kiss her again. This time he was so tender and slow that she was the one who escalated the passion, kissing him back with everything she had. In a flash she was broken from the moment by a sharp pain on the top of her head, then another and another in quick succession.

What is that? She broke from Flynn to hold her head back and look up behind her to see what was causing it.

Flynn, realizing there was a problem, looked up too. "Go on, get away." He waved his hands.

Bay could see a creature retreating from them. "What is it?"

Flynn kept his eyes on the intruder. "A curlew."

Bay knew the bird with the long stilt legs and piercing cry was shy and nocturnal. What was it doing pecking her out here in the middle of the day? She giggled at the humor of the intrusion. So did Flynn, smoothing out her hair where the bird had pecked.

The tenderness of his petting made Bay stop giggling and she held her breath, looking at his face inches from hers, so soft and new. He stopped and looked at her, taking in her whole face before his eyes connected with hers.

"I love you, too," he whispered, his voice deep and husky.

Bay arched for him again, lifting her head to touch her lips to his. He returned her kiss for a moment then whipped his head away from hers. "God, will you leave us alone." He flipped his hand at something she assumed was the curlew again.

She froze. It wasn't his tone—she knew he was talking to the bird. It was his choice of words that had her immobilized body and soul. She felt his body stiffen as well, picking up on the same vibes. Each time they gave reign to the physical attraction, they had been interrupted. Was God trying to tell them something?

Flynn looked at her for a moment, then seeing her concern, rolled over onto the towel next to her. They lay in silence for a while, lost in their own thoughts.

Bay knew where they were heading before the curlew intruded. Neither of them would have stopped. It was what she wanted, what her body screamed for. The passion she felt for this man was so real and strong, but was it the right time? *Lord, you're telling us it's too soon, aren't you?*

She felt in her soul she was right. He wanted them to wait for His timing. Would she have come to know Flynn the way she had—would she have built such an intense friendship with him—had they consummated their relationship sooner? She knew the answer. The physical chemistry would have eventually faded, and they would have gone their separate ways, never realizing their love and trust for each other. The physical attraction was strong, but God had fostered so much more between them. They looked at each other, both reaching the same conclusion.

Flynn spoke first. "I love you, Bay Anders, so I can wait until this is right." He looked at her and grinned. "But you can't wear that bikini in my presence until then. Get yourself a tank top and a pair of board shorts. A one-piece at least." The grin reached his eyes as he looked over at her.

Bay grinned back. "It would be a little easier if we weren't the only two people on a deserted island."

Flynn raised his eyebrows. "Well, the return of the electricity will put an end to that. There's a group of fisherman coming in next week. I'll have to make it clear to them who you belong to." He gave her a wink.

Rather than feel affronted by his manly claim to her, Bay found herself smiling. She relished the thought of belonging to him.

His face morphed into a frown. "Actually, considering they're coming, you'd better make that swimwear long-legged board shorts and a t-shirt. Loose. Not a fitted one, and not white."

Bay gave him what she hoped was an incredulous look. "Would you have me in a potato sack?"

Flynn looked to the sky. "No . . . you'd probably make it look too good."

He sat up, reached into the cooler, passing her a drink and sandwich. They sat eating their lunch in silence.

"So which direction do we go now?" Bay asked as they packed up.

Flynn looked up onto the hill behind them. "Not sure." He reached again to finger his beard, dropping his hand when he found his chin instead. "You know, Amos told me once about a cave on this side of the island. He said the entrance was hidden under the bluff. Want to see if we can find it?"

She felt excitement bubbling. She wished she had brought her camera. "Absolutely. Um . . . give me a second to change."

She pulled the other shirt out of her bag. He shook his head, saying nothing as she slipped behind the bush.

They walked as far as they could, then the climb got so rough Bay felt her footing slip with each step.

Flynn kept hold of her hand. "Perhaps this wasn't the best idea. It's a lot rougher than I expected."

Bay looked down at the steep drop beside them. The rocks fell away into the ocean below. "How much further, do you think?"

Flynn pointed ahead of them. "See that big section of scrub up there? I'm hoping that's it."

They scrambled over the last section of rock and picked their way through the bushes. The scrub was thick and prickly. Bay managed to score a few scrapes on her arms for the effort. They finally broke through and saw the entrance to the cave. As they came to the opening they looked back, taking in the magnificent view of the ocean. The endless blue horizon pushed out as far as their eyes could see.

Flynn peered into the cave. Bay could see that the

cavity wasn't deep. The light that streamed in revealed the back wall. Several huge boulders also lined the walls of the cave. Flynn squatted to pick at the remains of a campfire at the entry.

"This is fresh. Someone's been lighting fires here." As he got, up a noise sounded behind one of the boulders. Flynn moved like lightning over to her and put his body between her and the noise, placing one arm across her in defense.

The noise sounded again and the shadow of a man moved out from behind the boulder, taking several steps towards them. Flynn stiffened his defensive stance, and formed a fist with one hand as the shape continued to move towards them.

"Flynn. You took your sweet time finding me. I could have died here waiting for you." The voice was low and gruff, a slight accent in the inflection.

Flynn let out an uproarious laugh and sped towards the man, who met him halfway. They embraced, thwacking each other's backs in manly affection.

Bay stood at the cave entrance, transfixed by the scene. When the older man broke away, Flynn looked her way. As the older man turned too, Bay could see his features in the light. His greying hair hung in dirty strands around his face, where several months' growth prickled his chin. There were big rips on both the t-shirt he was wearing, and down the front of his shorts. Even under the dirt and hair there was no doubt.

It was Dutch.

They stood, rooted to the spot, staring at each other. He moved first, taking two steps towards her before stopping.

"Janie?" His tone was low with disbelief.

Bay couldn't find her voice. She felt like she was in a coma where she could hear and see, but not move or talk.

He walked closer. "Baby Jane, is that you?"

"Yes, it's me." It was all she could get out. Her eyes filled with tears that clouded her vision.

His face broke out in a great smile. "You've come back then." It wasn't a question but a statement.

Bay couldn't stand it any longer. She ran to him, and he caught her in such a safe embrace that she never wanted it to end. They stood for a long time holding each other, letting tears of joy fall down their faces. It was strange, but she felt as though she had never left, that somehow she had always known him.

She rubbed her eyes as they came apart. "We all thought you were dead."

Dutch ran his forearm over his face. "I was close a few times, but thank God, I'm still here. And here you are!" He put both hands up to cup her face. "My little Bay." His voice was so loving she almost burst into tears again.

Flynn came to stand next to them. "Let's get you out of here, old man. You can fill us in on how this happened later. Bet you could do with a good meal right now." He thumped his friend on the back.

"You bet I could," Dutch skipped a merry dance past the cave entrance where he stopped and looked back for a second. Then, without a word, he led them both down an easier route back to the beach.

They decided to get straight back to the island. There wasn't much chance to talk in the boat, but as soon as they got back to Resolution, Dutch let out a raucous, "Woo hoo!" as the resort came into sight.

As they came closer to the island it was clear something wasn't right. Mate wasn't on the shore to greet them, and what looked like rubbish was strewn throughout the outdoor area.

Dutch lifted a hand to shade his eyes and scanned the shoreline. "What's going on? Where's my old Mate?"

Flynn maneuvered the boat towards the rocks. "I don't know." His eyes widened as he spotted something.

Bay looked up in the direction of the bar. The glass in the windows was shattered and the door swung wide open.

They wasted no time disembarking, racing up to the main building in minutes. The rubbish outside revealed itself to be broken bottles and glasses, as well as pieces of damaged furniture.

Bay called for Mate as they went, but the dog didn't answer. When she reached the open door the state inside the building forced her to let out a gasp.

The bar was a mess. Tables were upturned and broken chairs littered the dining area. Every bottle and glass in the bar had been broken and crunched several layers deep on the floor. There was damage everywhere. Not one piece of furniture was left untouched. Flynn took off into the kitchen area to check for further damage.

He returned shaking his head. "The kitchen's worse." His jaw twitched and chest heaved. "When I find the person who did this I'm going to . . ." Flynn didn't finish the threat but the intensity of his rage was clear.

Dutch stood amongst it and sighed. "I can see that the vultures have been circling in my absence."

Flynn let out a sharp breath. Bay watched the rapid rise and fall of his chest as he struggled to control himself. He was livid.

"You could say that." He looked over at her. "Half a dozen people have approached Bay to buy the island. I'm guessing one of them decided to get serious." He kicked a damaged chair, trying to release some of the anger.

Bay stood, incredulous. "But who would go to these lengths?" She considered the extent of the damage.

Dutch sighed deep and long. "The same person who would commit murder." They both looked at him for further explanation. Dutch rubbed the stubble on his chin. "I'll fill you in later. Right now, let's check the rest of the island."

A shiver of fear traveled up her spine. It was obvious whoever did this would go to any lengths to acquire the island. They were playing for keeps.

The cabins were a mess. Every door had been kicked open and the windows broken. Both Bay and Dutch's cabins had been ransacked. After sifting through the mess she finally found her camera on the floor. It had been taken apart and several pieces crushed, but nothing that couldn't be replaced. Fury took the place of shock, and she had to stop to take a few deep breaths in order to continue. The other cabins weren't much better. They had been pulled apart and every piece of furniture was broken. The worst was Flynn's cabin. It was unrecognizable under the mess.

Dutch looked up at Flynn from underneath bushy eyebrows. "Looks like someone particularly dislikes you."

Flynn sifted through the mess, occasionally picking something up, then tossing it back down again. "Looks that way, doesn't it?"

The stench of the stale food that was strewn from one end of the cabin to the other filled Bay's nostrils. She tried to take shallow breaths. "I need some fresh air."

After receiving a nod from both men, she headed down to the beach. She was at the edge of the sand when a shape under a large coconut tree caught her attention. Heading over to investigate, she quickly recognized the blue hair.

It was Mate, and he wasn't moving.

Bay ran the rest of the way. "Mate. Here, boy," she yelled, but had no response. She fell to her knees and patted him. One look at his body revealed that he had been shot in the head. There was the prominent red, round mark of an entry wound below his ear.

A heavy blanket of grief overcame her. She sat with her head in her hands and wept. She had never had a pet. Her mother had forbidden her to have anything to do with dirty, smelly animals. She had realized how much she had missed after she had met Mate. He was such a joy. He was always happy to see her, his tail wagging so hard she thought it might wag right off. He was protective, always a guarding presence at her side. He was comforting. She thought back to all the times they had sat together, his head in her lap and eyes looking lovingly at her while she cried, mourning the losses in her life. She thought of the first night they had met. He had shown her where to find shelter and had guarded her door since. Mate had truly been her mate, her friend. She sat, mourning the loss of that friendship.

A noise behind her, and a hand on her shoulder forced her to look up. Dutch squatted down, his eyes filling with tears at the sight of his dog. Bay wrapped her arms around her father's body to comfort him.

Tears streamed down his cheeks. "He was a good friend."

"The best." Bay hiccupped with emotion as she spoke. She buried her face in Dutch's shoulder.

They stayed that way for a long time before the sound of Flynn approaching forced them apart. They both got to their feet as he reached them. Flynn stooped down, touching the bullet entry point. Bay could see his shoulders heave.

He looked up at them, then without a word, took her in his arms. The action renewed fresh tears. Flynn stroked her hair and whispered into her ear. "It's alright. I'll find who did this." He kissed her head before releasing her and turning to Dutch.

"I'm sorry, Dutch. He was a good friend." Flynn patted his friend on the back.

Her father looked at her and smiled. "My best mate."

They took their time, burying Mate exactly where he fell. Dutch said a few words about his dog, happy that he would have liked his final resting place under the biggest coconut tree.

Dutch stared out across the water of the bay.

"Not exactly the homecoming I imagined, but home just the same." He turned to give Bay the biggest smile. "I have my life, my girl, and my island. What are a few bottles of grog and some squeaky chairs, hey?" He threw an arm around her shoulders.

Bay tilted her head against his shoulder. "We can go over to my cabin and try to forage some food. I think I saw some that was still good."

Dutch sighed. "I could go some decent tucker and a shower."

Bay knew she would feel the loss of the dog, but she looked at her father, amazed yet again that he was here.

Lord, you have truly given me all I have asked for. Thank you for his return.

They found a packet of sausages still intact, so Flynn cooked a barbecue dinner in front of the cabin. Dutch savored every bite, sinking his teeth into the food with gusto and moaning over every morsel. Bay and Flynn laughed, happy to watch his enjoyment, and every now and then snuck a longing look at each other from across the table.

She occasionally had to blink hard to make sure both men were still there. Flynn, his love for her evident as his eyes locked with hers. Her father, alive and well beside her. The best meal she ever had wasn't that night on the beach with Flynn, Amos and Neville. It was this night, with the man she loved, and her father returned alive and well.

After they finished eating, Dutch stretched out in his seat and rubbed his stomach. "That's got to go down as the best meal I've ever had. Sure beats bush tucker and goat."

Bay laughed. It was exactly what she had been thinking.

Flynn gave his friend a slap on the shoulder. "Couldn't you catch a mud crab, old man?"

Dutch sat up and frowned at Flynn's teasing. "I caught plenty, but as gourmet as that meal is, you get pretty sick of it if you eat it for a full week. Besides, I couldn't really eat anything the first few days. My head was too sore." He took a sip of cider. "I guess I'd better fill you in on what happened."

Bay pushed her plate aside. "Yes, please."

Dutch rubbed the growth on his face and nodded to Flynn. "After you saw me off, I came across this little tinny in the middle of that deep trough. They were a long way off, and waving at me, so I went over to see what was wrong. As I came alongside, one was ducked down so I couldn't see who they were, and the other hit me over the head with a mallet."

Bay covered her mouth with one hand.

"Next thing I know I'm lying on the floor of their tinny, falling in and out of consciousness, and the two of them are arguing over where they're going to dump me. One of them wanted to go further out to sea, the other wanted to tip me out where we were. The second man was hurling as he was talking. I reckon he was sick as a dog from the motion. Meanwhile, I'm bleeding all over the place." He lifted his fringe to show them the gash on his hairline.

Bay gasped at the length of the cut, but it had healed cleanly.

Flynn winced. "They got you a beauty."

Dutch lifted one eyebrow. "Hurt a mighty lot, that's for sure. Anyway, they argued for a while before the first man agreed to dump me there. I played dead while they threw me over. I had no chance of fighting them in my condition. I could barely keep my eyes open." He took a moment to yawn before continuing. "You wouldn't believe it, but that water was cold. I've never known the temperature to be so low this time of year. It woke me up completely. Thankfully, the fools didn't hang around to make sure they finished the job."

He paused to take a swig of his apple cider. "I was relieved when I saw how close I was to Broad. I swam for it, but I must have still felt woozy because it was hard going. I almost gave up several times, but the good Lord gave me strength and I made it in."

He cocked his head to the side and glanced up at the stars. "I've been living on bush tucker, fish and goats. I was relieved that Amos taught me to spear a few years ago." He gestured around the area. "I'm lucky I've lived here for as long as I have, so I know what's good to eat. Broad has some natural springs, so I had drinking water, but I can tell you those goats were a bugger to catch. I did myself several injuries chasing the rotten things."

Bay grinned at the mental picture. Dutch had changed into clean clothes. It was obvious that he had lost a lot of weight. But his skin had a good color, and the sparkle in his eyes revealed his body hadn't suffered too much.

He turned and gave Flynn a direct stare. "By the way, what took you so long to find me? I've been sending you smoke signals since I got there."

Flynn lifted his eyebrows. "Is that what you were doing? Signaling me? Why didn't you light a bushfire? Someone would have probably come to investigate."

Dutch huffed. "I was worried whoever tried to kill me would see it and come back to finish the job. Why do you think I was hiding behind the rocks in that cave? You pair sounded like the cavalry coming up that hill. It scared me half to death." He laughed a deep rolling chuckle.

Flynn adjusted the stick holding the damaged table up. "Did you get a look at the two men?"

"No, I wouldn't be able to place either of them. I've never seen the boat they were in before, either."

"I thought I saw the ranger heading over to Broad a few times. You didn't see him?"

Dutch shook his head. "I kept mostly to my cave, unless I needed food. I didn't see a single soul while I was there. Who do you think's responsible for today's effort? Maybe the same person had something to do with what happened to me."

"Not sure." Flynn frowned. "The ranger's been here, stirring things up, but I don't know that he's capable of this sort of thing. He's too much of a sook."

Dutch looked at her. "He's been giving you a hard time?"

It was Flynn who replied. "You could say he's shown quite an interest in your daughter, but I think he's been set right." He wiggled his eyebrows at her.

Bay felt the heat return to her face. She avoided eye contact with either of them. When she finally looked up it was to see Dutch frown. He was clearly picking up on the vibes between the two of them.

"Did you hurt him?" he asked Flynn.

Flynn pointed at her. "It was your daughter who showed him to his boat, not me. Looks like the apple doesn't fall far from the tree."

"That's my girl." Dutch gave her hand a pat. "I suppose his pride was mightily wounded?"

"Surely not enough to warrant trashing the place." Flynn got up from his seat. "I'll leave Bay to fill you in on the happenings since you've been gone. No doubt you pair have some catching up to do from way before that. I'll see you both in the morning."

Flynn gave Dutch's arm a slap as he walked past. "Good to have you back, old man."

Dutch looked behind at him. "We'll take a run into town in the morning to see Bob, hey?"

Flynn nodded his confirmation, then looked at her. "G'night all." He smiled and winked at her, then turned and headed off to his cabin.

"He's a good man," Dutch said, as they watched him disappear into the night.

"Yes, he is."

"You two have been getting on, then?" Dutch dipped his head in a knowing nod.

"You could say that." Her father was observant, but Bay still felt a little nervous being so open with him, especially about her feelings for Flynn.

Dutch took her hand from across the table and stared at her. "If it's worth having, it's worth getting God's way, Bay." He squeezed her hand.

Bay felt a hot blush burn her cheeks. She was pleased for the fading twilight. "I think we've worked that out. But he still keeps his past from me, and I don't understand why."

"What do you mean?"

"Neville told me he had an assault conviction, although there were extenuating circumstances, and I can see he's not that person any more. The conviction doesn't bother me. But Flynn not telling me about it does."

"He'll fill you in when he's ready," Dutch said. "He was a bit of a mess when he came to live on Resolution. It took him a long time before he could put it behind him. I can't imagine it's a time of his life he wants to relive. Besides, I suspect your opinion is important to him. He may need a bit of time."

He let go of her hand to slap the table. "But enough of that. Tell me about your life. I want to get to know you again."

She took her time. Her childhood growing up in LA. Her relationship with her mother and her early death, not yet a year ago. Her internship and job with Richard, and the influence he'd had on her. Her experience in the Daintree, and the discovery of her faith in Jesus.

When she got to the part about Braden, Dutch burst out in a rambunctious chuckle. "That mad American tracked you down."

Bay went on to fill him in on all the happenings at Resolution—finding his tinny and assumption of his death. The pursuit of the developer; the revelation about her mother's bequest. Her throat was sore by the end of it.

Dutch looked out over the black water of the bay. "So that's what she did with the money. I wouldn't have believed it."

Bay knew how he felt. She wasn't any less amazed, and she had known Kate much better than he did. "It's your money, Dutch. I know she stole it from you."

He tilted his head. "That's true, but she gave it to you, and that's fine by me. Besides, I forgave her long ago."

Bay thought about her mismatched parents, steeling herself to ask her next question. "Dutch, how did the two of you get together? You were complete opposites." She hoped he wouldn't interpret the question as presumptuous.

He fiddled with the glass cover of the lamp that lighted their table. "We weren't so different back then, Bay. We both had a lot of ambition. Kate wanted to get out of the small town and become someone. I wanted to build my dream holiday destination. It wasn't enough for your mother. Her aspirations were greater than I could afford. We met, I fell in love with her, and she fell in love with what I could do for her."

Dutch set his gaze on the flickering lamp. "I had a bit of money back then, and I had the island. She thought I was her ticket out of oblivion, but she was never happy living on Resolution. It was even smaller than the town she was so desperate to get out of. We hadn't been together long before we discovered she was pregnant with you."

He paused and sighed.

"She stayed a while, trying to get me to agree to sell the place and move to the city, but I loved my island. She was so unhappy that I didn't argue when she insisted on taking trips up to Cairns. She worked up there on and off for some time, and then one day she was gone, taking you with her. That was the hardest time of my life. My little girl was gone and, Kate had emptied the bank account. I had no means to track you down."

He looked at her and patted her hand. "It took me years to save enough to travel over to the States, only to realize you weren't there. Kate had taken off again, and I ended up on the street with nothing but my return ticket. An old priest working with the homeless took me in for a while. He worked hard on me, and I finally realized there was a God and He did love me. I'd always known He existed. My mother had a strong faith, but I had always felt that I didn't need Him in my life. I boasted I was a self-made man."

He sniffed, and huffed before continuing. "I was left with no options. The situation was totally beyond my control, so I trusted you to Him and boarded a plane back to Australia."

He took her hand in his. "Trusting you to the Lord and leaving you behind was the hardest thing I ever had to do in my life, but I knew without a doubt that one day you'd be back. He would show you the way home, and I would see you again."

Bay felt her eyes fill with tears and wondered how many she had shed that day, and for so many different reasons.

Dutch cocked his head to the side and gave her a big grin. He was certainly a character full of charisma and personality. "And here you are." He dropped her hand to do a melodious slap on the table top.

Bay smiled and looked out into the darkness, trying to digest his story. She knew Kate was more than capable of bald-faced lies. She had seen them trip off her tongue whenever it suited her. But she had always hoped Kate would have only ever stretched the truth with her, not told her outright lies. Now she was convinced that Kate didn't have the ability to be honest with anyone, including her own daughter. The old wound of betrayal opened up for a moment before she put it back in its place. She had had no control over how her mother treated her, but she did have control over how it affected her life, and she had placed all the hurt and anger directly in God's hands.

Something occurred to her, another aspect of her mother's life she had most probably lied about. "Did my mother have any other family? She always told me her parents had died and she had no siblings."

Dutch nodded. "Both her parents are dead. They were hard people, Bay. If you had known them, you would've understood a little about why Kate was so difficult. Her father was a severe man, intent on over-discipline, and her mother was a small nondescript woman who never showed love. Kate was expected to work in the family business, a coffee shop, and she was overworked and constantly criticized. She was desperate to get out from under their control."

Dutch rubbed his now smooth chin. "Kate has a sister, Wendy. She lives in New Zealand with her family—her husband Ray and three children, Sam, Becky and Zoe. Sam would be about nineteen, Becky sixteen, and little Zoe would be about twelve, I think."

Bay felt a flood of warmth spread through her at this revelation. She couldn't believe she had family other than Dutch. "I have cousins?"

"They come over for a holiday on Resolution at least once a year. Last year I was lucky to see them twice," he said.

Bay shook her head. "Nobody told me." Why hadn't Flynn said something?

"That would probably be because nobody knows the connection I have with them. I was devastated when Kate took you away. Wendy was a support and help, but we came to a kind of unspoken understanding not to mention Kate, or you. I suppose we both knew it was unfinished business. That one day we would all be able to pick up where we left off with you. Besides, everyone calls me Dutch. I'm not the kids' uncle. Kate and I never married."

"I remember Peter telling me you had asked her." Bay recalled their conversation on the day of her mother's funeral.

"Oh, I asked her. Many times. But Kate was determined to make a fortune first. She even promised to marry me if I sold the island and moved to the city with her."

Bay rolled her eyes at the thought. It was typical Kate, manipulating the situation to her own ends.

"Wendy will be over the moon to see you, Bay. She was the one who saw to you when you were a baby. Kate didn't grasp motherhood. She hated the sleepless nights and didn't take to motherhood. I guess she was too young and selfish at the time."

Dutch tried to make excuses for Kate, but Bay

knew her mother was never selfless enough to put anyone else first. Not at any age.

"Wendy had turned seventeen, but she came over here and took care of you. You were three-and-a-half when she met Ray, but she only left when I forced her out. The girl had to have a life of her own, and you were my responsibility. It took her a while to leave. She loved you like you were her own." Dutch smiled.

A bubble of excitement surfaced at the thought of her extended family, and she couldn't wait to meet them.

"I have no doubt they'll want to come over as soon as they hear about your return to Resolution, and my return from the dead." He laughed, but then became serious as he looked around him. "Unfortunately, there's a bit of work to do here before we can entertain guests again."

Bay considered the strange mix of destruction and beauty around her and she knew what she needed to do. "I want to use the money Kate left me to rebuild this place, with proper timber cabins. And new generators, and all the modern ecologically sound building materials."

Dutch frowned. "That's mighty generous of you, love, but have you thought about your future? You may want to do some travelling, and there's your career to think about. Rebuilding this place to that standard is going to take up most of that money."

Bay thought about his question for a moment. She knew in her heart she didn't want to leave Resolution. "There's plenty to keep me occupied right here. I've done my roaming and I'm home. This is where I'm supposed to be. This is where my heart is." It was the truth in more ways than one.

Dutch picked up on her meaning and rolled his eyes. "I suppose I'll have to get used to sharing my girl with another fella."

She felt the heat rise to her face again.

CHAPTER II

Bay could feel the sun hot on her arms as she sat on the beach with Neville. Dutch and Flynn had insisted that she stay with Neville at his cabin while they went into Kiisay Point to report the miraculous return of her father, his attack, and the vandalism of the resort.

Like them, Neville hadn't been on the island yesterday. He had left for a fishing trip early in the morning and didn't return until after dusk. He was unable to give them any clue as to who had done the damage.

Bay giggled when she recalled his reaction at seeing Dutch that morning. If it was possible for dark skin to go pale, Neville achieved it. His face had dropped and eyes popped as though he were seeing a ghost. Dutch had played up the reaction by placing his hands on each side of his face and yelling a loud "Boo!" Neville physically jumped in the air before they all broke out in roaring laughter.

Neville had recovered from his shock, and now sat next to her, shelling fresh oysters he had gathered that morning. He handed every second one to her.

"You're doing pretty good here now, hey." He nodded at her.

She looked down at her cut-off jeans and t-shirt, dirty from the clean-up she had started on the resort that morning. With her hair pulled back in a ponytail, and Flynn's cap on her head, she must have looked a sight.

"You could say that, Neville." She laughed at herself.

"Nobody would think you'd be a flash lawyer from the city now." His big cheeky grin filled his face.

Bay thought back to that night in the pub. She recalled the dirty looks she was getting from the locals, and the vague answers to her questions about Dutch. The only person to take an interest in her was Ashley. She remembered the way he winked at her as if they shared a secret. Her memory piqued.

What did he say? That he took me for a sophisticated city lawyer come to sort out Dutch's estate. Bay jumped up straight as a shot of adrenaline surged through her.

Dutch's tinny hadn't even been found then. How did he know Dutch was missing, unless he had something to do with it?

Bay also remembered what he had said about Mate trying to bite him, and how angry he was when she told him the island wasn't for sale. Flynn may think Ashely wasn't capable of destroying the resort, but perhaps he was a party to it.

Bay scrambled to her feet, feeling inside her pockets. "Neville, I just thought of something. I've got to tell Flynn right away." She retrieved her cellphone, but it had no service. "Oh, no."

Neville looked up at her from his place in the sand. "What is it?"

"No service. As usual." Bay stuffed the useless phone back into her pocket. "I'll have to go up to the point. I won't be long." She grabbed her bag and slung it over her shoulder.

Neville got to his feet. "But Dutch said you should stay right here."

Bay sighed, looked back towards the resort, then at Neville. "I know, but this is important. I have to tell them this so they can let Bob know. I'll go straight there and back. I promise," she said, before heading up the sand.

She ran to the point only to find the service was still non-existent. The other spot capable of catching the cell tower signal was the pergola on the rocks at the other side of the bay. She thought for a second about going back to Neville and waiting for Flynn and Dutch to get back, but this was important. She'd try her luck.

She walked past the resort, still a mess with broken bottles and furniture littering the once grassy areas. How could anyone be so driven by greed that they would try to kill someone and destroy a home to acquire a piece of land?

She reached the pergola and looked at her phone. Still no service. She moved it around in the air hoping a signal would appear as if by magic. A movement out of the corner of her eye drew her attention and she peered down the rocks jutting out from the other side of the pergola. A tinny lay at anchor. The logo on the side was unmistakable: National Parks and Wildlife. Ashley's boat.

Bay felt her stomach drop and adrenaline run through her.

Ashley was here.

On the island.

She had to warn Neville.

Bay ran back down the rocks and through the

resort, getting to the point in record time. She passed the stone cabin. Bay willed her legs to go faster. She heard a crack and a sharp pain coursed through her head. The ground was coming up fast.

Everything went black.

"Get her up there." The voice was Ashley's.

Bay struggled, trying to open her heavy eyelids. Pain vibrated through her head. It was almost too much and she closed her eyes again and concentrated on regaining full consciousness.

"She's coming to."

The other voice was vaguely familiar but she couldn't place it.

Bay realized she was being carried. Her hands were tied behind her back and her ankles were secured. She swung back and forth between the two people carrying her. Ashley was holding her feet and the other man was holding her under the arms. They were trying to get her up a steep slope, judging from her almost-vertical angle.

"Keep going. She won't be able to fight us," Ashley said.

It took them a few more minutes to get to the top, dumping her when they finally made it to level ground.

Bay could feel sticky wetness on her head running down a clump of hair that fell across her face. Blood. She blinked hard in an attempt to focus.

Ashley was sitting on the ground, head between his knees, trying to catch his breath. The other man was slumped over, hands on knees panting. He looked up and Bay caught her breath.

It was Jack Turvill, the solicitor she had seen concerning Dutch's estate. *What has he got to do with this?* She struggled to get her head out of the fog.

She pulled herself to a sitting position. "What are you doing?" Bay could feel the pain in her legs, and her back was wet. They must have brought her here by boat.

"What does it look like we're doing? We need that island and you won't sell it to us so we have to engineer its' sale." Ashley sneered at her.

Bay turned to the solicitor for an answer. "Jack?"

His eyes were wide and his head was the color of beetroot. "Don't talk." He turned to Ashley. "Maybe it would be better if we knocked her out again."

Bay took a deep breath to counteract the fear that consumed her. Whatever they had planned for her didn't look good. *Dear Lord, please help me. Don't let their plan succeed. Don't let them take my life. Not when I've finally found it.*

The best way to prolong their plan was to try and engage them in some way. "You won't get away with this, Ashley," she said.

He scoffed. "Won't I? I've done it before. Besides, I let everyone know you wanted me to take you back up to the caves. I'll say I dropped you off and left you to explore. Then you fell into one and couldn't get back out. The tide came in, and bye bye, Bay." His lips curled as he unveiled his plan to end her life.

It was only then that Bay looked around. They were indeed up at the volcanic caves. They planned to drop her in one and leave her there. She looked at Jack. Where did he fit into this picture?

"Why Jack? Why are you doing this?"

He looked everywhere but at her.

It was Ashley who answered for him. "Money is a motivating factor. Isn't it, Jack?" He tilted his head at his accomplice.

"I don't understand." Bay said. "Who's paying?"

"You could say we have a mutual friend who has agreed to pay us both a generous commission if we can secure Resolution for him," Ashley said. "It's my ticket out of this dump and into the life I was meant to have. Jack here is in a bit of trouble, money-wise. He gambles it quicker than he makes it."

Jack didn't answer, and Ashely continued speaking.

"If it's any consolation, he didn't want to kill you off at first, but it became the only option. With you dead, we can orchestrate the purchase of Resolution, and there's an added problem for Jack. You see, he's been siphoning off money from that trust account of yours for years, and it wouldn't do for you to stay alive long enough to find out. With you gone, he can continue to take the cream off the top of the fund."

Bay recalled the intensity in which Jack played the poker machines in the pub her first night here. It all fell into place. Ashley was greedy, Jack was broke, and the developer had bought them to do his dirty work.

"Shut up, Ashley. I told you not to talk." Jack almost spat the words.

"What does it matter if she knows about your gambling debts if she's dead? Idiot." Ashley glared at him then pointed at her. "We never would have had to do this if you had agreed to sell the island. You don't need it, not with all that other money. You've obviously sunk to a lower class by getting involved with that grubby fisherman. Well, I fixed his little kingdom." Ashley lifted his eyebrows in a knowing way.

It was now apparent that Ashley was the one who vandalized the resort and killed Mate. Bay couldn't believe two grown men could be so foolish, so greedy, so evil. A wave of shock overcame her. "You tried to kill my father for the island and now me. This is crazy."

"We did kill your father." They looked from one to the other. Oh. They didn't know Dutch had survived their attack. This was the chance she had been waiting for.

"Dutch is alive. We picked him up off Broad Island yesterday."

Jack's mouth dropped. Ashley squinted in clear disbelief.

"He was unconscious when we dropped him in," Ashley said. "There's no way he could have survived."

"I should have let you take him out further. I was just so sick." Jack's voice was shaky.

"He's not alive, you fool, and she's lying to us. Trying to save herself."

The features she once thought boyish were in fact the mark of a spoiled child. Jack was the one to work on, the weaker one.

"He's alive, Jack, and at Kiisay talking to Bob right now. Trust me, you'll gain nothing by killing me. It will only make things worse for you." Bay tried to get through to the solicitor. She had a chance if she could get him to doubt the plan.

Jack's mouth drooped, as the sweat dripped down his face. "What if he did survive? We're done for." His eyes portrayed his fear.

Ashley shook his head and rolled his eyes. "Don't be so gullible, Jack. She's lying to us." He moved towards the scared man. "Look. Let's get her in the hole and then it's done. The more we talk about it the worse it gets."

He moved towards Bay and grabbed her under the arms. Jack was planted firmly to the spot. Bay felt the throbbing of the strain Ashley's hold created on her body. Her armpits felt as though they were on fire and her legs were cramping under the constraints. She had to keep talking.

"Think about it, Jack, if you kill me, it's murder. At the moment, it's kidnapping and attempted murder. You could be out of jail in no time. This story you've concocted is so flawed—Flynn will never believe I went with Ashley willingly, and you don't even have my camera. What would I have come up here for without it?"

"Shut up!" Ashley yelled down at her. "Get her feet, Jack."

Jack snapped out of his stupor and ran over to grab her feet. She tried one last time to reason with him.

"Don't do this, Jack. You know it's not right. You'll never get away with it."

They stood at the edge of the largest hole. "Cut that tie." Ashley motioned towards the plastic tie around her ankles. "We can't have her body found with feet and hands tied."

"Jack, you know about crime scenes," she said. "The marks on my skin will show I was tied up. Just like the Dutch's boat showed his disappearance wasn't an accident."

Jack had retrieved a pocket knife and moved to cut the tie, then stopped and looked up at Ashley. His face was sullen. "She's right. We're not going to get away with this. I should never have let you talk me into it. I can't be a party to it." He sounded pathetically scared. He stood up and put the knife back into his pocket.

"Too late." Ashley shoved Jack away with one hand, holding Bay with the other. The solicitor stumbled backwards, landing hard on the rock. Ashley cut both ties and pushed Bay backwards.

In seconds Bay felt the cool water of the ocean. The hole was deep but the water at the bottom had broken her fall.

She bobbed in the water. It was dark all round with light coming down the entry hole above her.

She heard a rustling echo. Two heads floated over the hole, casting shadows in the light. One of them—Ashley?—lifted a hand and waved before they both disappeared. The light from the hole beamed down again.

Bay scrambled for the side and grabbed the rock wall, trying to get a foothold, only to sink back into the water.

Lord, please help me. Send me a miracle.

Time passed, and the water level rose as she tried again and again to climb out of the hole. Bay knew that once the tide reached its peak, and started to go back out again, the pull from the ocean would eventually suck her out, drowning her in the process.

She prayed unstopping, for strength, for help, and for that miracle that would free her. Every now and then she would call for help, hoping someone was looking for her and would hear her. Perhaps Neville had seen her or realized she had been taken.

Time passed and Bay felt every aching second. Her strength was waning. She had managed to pull herself up onto a slight ledge. It wasn't large enough for her to sit on, but it bore her weight as she rested her arms and torso on it. The water was up to her waist. As the water level inched up below her, moving up her chest, she clutched to the ledge. Her arms and fingers throbbed in pain from hanging on. Her body was already weak and sore from the abduction, and her head swam with fatigue.

She estimated at least thirty minutes had passed. She was slowly drifting in and out of consciousness, when she thought she heard her name being called. It sounded so far away that at first she thought she must be dreaming, but as it got louder she realized it was coming from above her.

"I'm here!" she yelled with as much strength as she could muster. She managed to pull her head away from the rock to call out again. There was no answer. Perhaps she had dreamed the voice?

She tried one more time. "Help!" This time a reply sounded from above.

"Bay?" She recognized the voice.

"Flynn! Help."

"Hang on. We're going to get you out," he yelled back down.

Thank you, Lord. Thank you. Bay closed her eyes

for a moment.

"I'm going to throw you a rope." His voice echoed in the chasm. "Put it around your waist and we can hoist you up."

Bay did as she was told. The rope came up under her armpits, which hurt, but she helped her ascent as much as she could. She used her feet to grab at the wall of the cave as she was pulled up.

Flynn let go of the rope and reached in to grab her as she neared the opening of the hole. He held her to him as she slumped against his body. Every fiber of her being was fatigued. She sank into him like a rag doll, his strength keeping her up.

"Oh, Bay. Thank God. Are you hurt? Did they hurt you?" Flynn stroked her hair and placed gentle, relieved kisses on her head.

"I'm okay. Nothing broken. Just a bit sore. My head."

Flynn fingered the gash gently. Then he pulled her away from him, checking she had no obvious sign of injury. He took her hands in his and saw the state of her fingers, red raw and bleeding from hanging on to the rocks.

He hugged her to him again before asking his next question. "Nothing else? They didn't hurt you in any other way?" The love and concern in his eyes warmed her.

She knew what he was asking. "No, no other way."

He wrapped her in his arms again. "Thank God." He said it with so much emotion Bay could physically feel his relief.

"How about a cuddle for your old Dad?"

Bay looked up to see Dutch standing close by, his arms stretched out for her. Bay fell into them and he hugged her with the ferocity of a bear. She broke into tears, letting all of the fear and relief out.

"My little Bay. It's okay, you're safe now." His soothing voice calmed her.

She pulled away to see Neville, his big grin indicating he was pleased to see her.

"How did you know where I was?" she asked.

Neville explained. "When you didn't come back right away I went looking for you, but didn't find you anywhere. Found your phone though, so I thought maybe something happened to you. Then, when I saw Ashley and that other bloke going fast in his boat, I knew something was up. I got in the tinny and followed them. I saw them come here and drag you out of the boat. I knew they were up to no good, so I got to where there was some service and used your mobile to ring Flynn and Dutch. They came straight away."

Flynn gave Neville a pat on the back. "Looks like Neville's a bit of a hero. This'll be a good story to tell at the pub."

Neville smiled.

The humidity hit with full force as Flynn stepped out into the hospital garden. The intensity of the northern Australian autumn didn't drop, even late in the afternoon. The waiting room had been crowded and he'd had trouble finding somewhere to sit, but there was plenty of room out here. None of the other people in the waiting room were desperate enough for space to venture out of the air conditioning. He had been here two hours already, waiting on the doctors to run their tests. Both Bay and Dutch were in separate cubicles, each getting a complete physical.

Bob had been their first stop. He called in reinforcements, and the entire local police force had been mobilized in an attempt to capture Ashley and Jack. Flynn had no doubt they would catch up with them sooner rather than later. He hoped they would be in custody by the end of the day.

Thoughts of 'what if' surfaced again. He couldn't contemplate losing Bay. He thanked God again for her safe return and tried to steer his mind away from the disaster that could have been.

The door opened and Dutch came into the garden, taking a place next to him on the concrete seat.

"Got the all clear?" Flynn asked his friend.

"Yep. The doc says I'm in good shape. Apart from losing a bit of weight, it seems fish and goat isn't such a bad diet." He smiled.

"You're lucky those two chose to dump you close to Broad. Its natural springs and food source was perfect for a marooned sailor."

Dutch nodded in agreement. "I saw Bay on the way out. They were taking her down to x-ray to check out that gash on her head. They want to make sure it's not dangerous."

Flynn frowned. "Did she want someone to go with her?" It would be good to feel useful.

"She said to tell you she'd be okay."

Dutch gave him a look he had seen all too often.

He was gearing up for a serious talk about something. Flynn braced himself as Dutch collected his thoughts.

"I guess there's no perfect time or easy way to say this so I'll ask you straight out." Dutch shifted towards him. "What are your intentions with my daughter?"

His friend wasn't one to mince words and Flynn was surprised he had needed the build up to the question. He supposed fatherly concern was a relatively new role for him.

Flynn decided honesty was the best policy. "I love your daughter," he said, with conviction.

Dutch lifted his eyebrows. "Well, I'd gathered that much already, mate. What I want to know is what you're going to do about it?" He gave Flynn a steely look.

He sighed. *What am I going to do about it?* "I honestly don't know. She's a beautiful young heiress with the world at her fingertips. I'm a busted-up fisherman with a criminal record. I've got nothing to offer her. All I own in the world is a tinny, a garbage bag full of old clothes and a few handlines. Even if she stays for a while, eventually she'll realize what she had to give up, and I don't want it to be for me."

Loving her didn't change his position. He still wondered how they could make a life together. Even if there was nothing in the world he wanted more.

Dutch laughed and slapped him on the back. "You're right. It doesn't look good on paper," he said. Then he sighed. "You know, God doesn't put people together based on material compatibility. The material things in this life don't interest Him. Neither does it matter to Him what you look like, your past, your age, or whether the rest of the world thinks you're a good match. God places a couple together mind, body and soul. He knows who's going to make the best team. You're a fool if you think you're not good enough for her. Especially if God thinks you are."

Flynn rubbed a callus on his hand. He knew what his friend said was true, but could he embrace it? "But does He? Think I'm good enough?"

Dutch looked up at him. "Have you asked Him? Nothing is ever a coincidence where God's concerned. He brought Bay to the island in His time, His way, and from what I can see, He's put the two of you together for His purpose." He stopped to scratch his head. "I don't believe Bay's going anywhere. Her mother left, but looking back, I have to admit I always knew she would. This girl is not her mother. She's had it all, but found everything she wanted here with you. I wouldn't be concerned about her leaving. You don't give her enough credit for knowing her own mind. So I'll ask you again. What do you intend to do about it?"

Flynn took a moment to digest what Dutch had said. Did God think he was good enough for her? He had certainly given him a love for her so intense that he couldn't think of living one more day without her. She was constantly in his thoughts. He had never wanted anything more than he wanted to be with her, and Dutch was right about her love for Resolution. Besides, who was he to predict the future? He knew from his own experiences in life that the future was in God's hands.

He knew without doubt what he wanted to do. "I want to marry her. That is, if she'll have me."

Dutch gave him a smile and got to his feet. "Well, looks like I won't have to beat some sense into you after all." He laughed. "Flynn, I can't speak for Bay, but I'd be mighty happy to have you for a son-in-law."

Flynn smiled and looked up at his friend. Little did he know all those years ago how important a part Dutch would play in his life.

Dutch looked towards the waiting area. "Now we've got that sorted, shall we go and see how far along this x-ray is? Before all this sentiment destroys our manhood." With a grunt, he walked to the door, holding it open for him.

Flynn got up to follow him. As he passed he gave Dutch a smirk. "Speak for yourself . . . Dad."

Dutch threw him a disconcerted look.

Flynn laughed.

CHAPTER 12

Flynn couldn't believe how nervous he was. His hands were sweating, and his pulse raced. He was sure his face shone red like a beacon now he had no beard to hide behind. The weather had turned cooler in the last few days, as winter began to take over. Pastel pink and blue bands marked the horizon. The ocean was dead flat and the neighboring is-land reflections shimmered on its surface. Bay sat next to him on the blanket that he had set up for them on the sand. Her hair hung in thick curls down her back, and her perfume clouded his senses.

Flynn knew what he had to do, but it was hard to talk to Bay about his past. Trust wasn't the issue—he trusted her implicitly—but he realized he had been harboring an unnatural fear that she would think less of him because of his past mistakes. The Lord had shown him the bad decisions he had made in his past had sabotaged his confidence. He had grown a beard to hide behind, and his life on Resolution had allowed him to withdraw from humanity.

Yes, the time had done him good. It had allowed him to heal and grow, but now that season in his life had passed. He had to come out of hiding and embrace this new season.

So much had happened in the past month, it was hard to believe they finally had some peace. Ashley and Jack had been apprehended quickly. Both were still in custody, with no chance of getting bail. Bay and Dutch had both made official statements, and the developer, Greg Neilson, had also been taken in for questioning. He claimed he had no idea Ashley and Jack had taken his bid to get the island so far, but there was enough evidence to charge him as an accessory. The police had found the tinny the two men used to dump Dutch in Greg Nielson's holiday home in the Whitsundays, proof he was aware of part of their plan.

Dutch and Flynn had arranged a clean-up of the resort a few days ago, and were inundated with people wanting to help. So many locals turned up that they had cleaned up the island in no time, patching up the buildings so they were livable again. Thankfully, most of the damage was to the furniture and stock. The structures themselves were able to be fixed with limited effort.

Amos had also returned. He'd received a call from Neville, who happily filled him in on the goings-on at Resolution. He was quite a bit peeved at having missed out on all the action, and feigned exasperation at the fact that Neville had enough ammunition to gossip forever. Flynn had never seen Amos so happy as when he laid his eyes on his old friend. He flung his arms around Dutch, crushing him with the impact of his affection, his smile going on forever.

Dutch had become a media star. Every major television network and newspaper wanted his story. He had enjoyed playing up to them, and got Resolution a good deal of publicity in the process. The National Parks had also sent a representative to assure them they had no idea what Ashley was doing, and in fact had fired him a month ago—he was taking advantage of the fact that the replacement ranger couldn't start immediately and was masquerading as their representative without their knowledge. It explained why he was in such a hurry to get the money the developer had promised. They also offered any assistance for the future, assuring them they would work as closely as necessary to help with the rebuilding of the resort once the new ranger arrived.

Flynn sighed deep as he dwelled on the goings-on of the last month.

"That was a big sigh. What are you thinking?" Bay turned towards him.

"Just about all that's happened."

Bay leaned into him so their arms were touching and slowly placed her head on his shoulder. Flynn felt the familiar yearning to pull her to him, and moved to hang his arm over her shoulders, cuddling her.

"Bay, I need to talk to you about something." He didn't know how to open up the conversation.

"Is it about your past?" she asked.

"Yes." He stopped short. How was he going to proceed?

Bay picked up on his hesitation and she pulled out of his embrace to look at him. "If it's about the assault conviction, we don't have to talk about it if you don't want to. Neville told me about it and I don't care what you did or didn't do in your past."

Flynn shook his head at the thought of Neville's interference. He knew he would have to forgive him for his loose tongue. After all, he did save Bay's life. "You don't understand. A lot of it changed me. It contributed to who I am. That's why I need to tell you."

Flynn felt Bay stiffen beside him.

"Is it about Samara?" she asked him, keeping her head down.

Flynn realized she had the wrong impression about his past relationship, and that she had probably jumped to the wrong conclusion as well. "Some of it's about her, but it's not what you think."

Bay bit her lip.

"Look," he said, then sighed before making a start. "I had been away some time, and when I came back to Kiisay Point, I took up with Samara. Bob's daughter. It was nothing more than a convenient relationship for me. I was away fishing for most of the time, and she was good company when I came back to port. A relationship with me was her ticket out of her father's house because she lived in my flat."

"Flat?"

"Apartment. She didn't want to work, and I was silly enough to give her access to my bank account." He shook his head at his stupidity. "Sam had been a model and she wanted to maintain the image. Over the course of a year, she spent all my savings on junk. Everything she purchased had to be the best and latest. Clothes, handbags, shoes, mobile phones . . . it was never-ending. The relationship soon became inconvenient and I told her we were through. The mistake I made was giving her time to get out of the flat." He paused, remembering what that mistake had cost him.

"I went to sea, and when I got back I found out she hadn't made any attempt to get out. She also had accounts all over town in my name, and her friend was using the flat to deal drugs. I told them both to get out or I'd report them to Bob. Samara was terrified. She knew I'd carry through with the threat." Flynn wished he had done just that.

"They got out, but the friend held a grudge. A few months later, he came down onto the trawler in an attempt to get his revenge. He pulled a knife on me." He paused, remembering the night his whole world stopped.

"I only hit him once, but he fell back into the water, hitting his head on the pontoon as he went. I fished him out and saved him, but he reported me for assault. The thing was, Bay, I almost killed him. He spent several weeks in hospital and it was touch-and-go for a while. I never recovered from the thought that I almost took a life. It did my head in." Flynn shook his head as he remembered the feeling, and thanked God again for his forgiveness.

Bay frowned at him. "But if it was self-defense, why did you get charged?"

"Partly because Bob hated me. He blamed me for Sam's problems—she disappeared without a trace after I kicked her out of the flat—and because it was his word against mine. The knife fell into the water so there was no evidence to contradict his story. It didn't help that I already had a strike against my name, and he was clean."

Flynn remembered the mixed feelings of injustice and self-loathing. At the time he truly believed that he had deserved the punishment, however great. He had almost killed the man, so doing the time, justified or not, made him feel that he had paid his debt.

But there was more to his story, the main reason he fell apart. "Having to spend a few months in jail and another year on probation was nothing compared to the flow-on effect."

Bay gave him her full attention, waiting for him to explain.

"My parents believed me without question, but Kiisay Point is a small town and there was a lot of nasty talk. My mother bore the brunt of the gossip. She couldn't stand the character assassination of her son. She and Dad had purchased an old camper and were preparing to take a trip around Australia, so they decided to leave early to escape the talk." He stopped to swallow the lump that had formed in his throat. "They had travelled three hundred kilometers away from Kiisay when a truck hit them. They were killed on impact." It was still raw, hard to talk about, and Flynn had to take a few deep breaths.

Bay took his hand in hers. "Oh, Flynn, but you know their death wasn't your fault."

"I know that now, but for a long time I felt that if I hadn't made those mistakes, they'd still be here. They wouldn't have left when they did. They wouldn't have been killed. All the possibilities drove me mad." The memory of that time was hard to bear.

"I also felt that my brother blamed me for their deaths. You could say I was the black sheep of the family. Jed never put a foot wrong. He was a happy kid, worked hard, and all but put himself through medical school. He was the good, reliable son. We had always been close, but after Mum and Dad died, he distanced himself from me. He joined a medical charity and took off overseas a week after we buried my parents. I think his way of dealing with it all was to escape, but it left me in a huge hole. I was a mess."

Flynn remembered the retreat he made to the trawler. His days consisted of working and drinking himself to sleep.

"It was a good thing Dutch stepped in when he did. I would have turned myself into an alcoholic," he said. "He gave me a job over here and slowly worked on me until I realized that there was a God and His love and forgiveness was more powerful than the hatred, self-loathing and grief I was suppressing."

"So . . . ?" Bay stopped short, as if she wanted to ask him something but wasn't quite sure how to continue.

"What is it?" he said. "You can ask me anything."

She gave him a hesitant look that prompted him to raise his eyebrows.

"Well … I was under the impression that Samara broke your heart."

Flynn could tell it was a difficult question for her to ask. "How did you get that idea?" Then he answered his own question. "Neville."

He smiled at her, wondering how on earth she could have any insecurity where his feelings for her were concerned. "Samara didn't break my heart. Nor did any of the girls after her."

"You mean the hundreds of backpackers?" She lifted one eyebrow.

"What did Neville tell you?" He was getting concerned with Neville's slant on the truth.

"Only that you had quite a multicultural year."

"I can assure you, none of them can hold a candle to American girls."

"Australian-American, if you don't mind."

"Well my Australian-American. You are the only multicultural girl I want, and you have nothing to be insecure about concerning my past romances. I was relieved to hear Samara had left town. And the backpackers were all happy to go on their way with a great story to tell their friends back home about a summer romance with a wild Aussie fisherman." He laughed at his self-assessment.

She pulled his arms around her. "No more summer romances for you. You can let the women of the world know you're taken."

It felt good to let her in on his past. All the anticipation and anxiety he had felt melted away and he held her tightly, trailing kisses down her neckline. "If I'd known you had such a warped opinion, I'd have had this talk with you sooner."

Bay turned to look at him. "Why didn't you?" she asked in a small voice. And then she added, "Tell me sooner, that is."

He stopped and turned her around to look at him. Her eyes were deep green against the dwindling light of the day. He knew he had to be completely truthful.

"Because I was scared, and I didn't want you to think badly of me." Now that his confession was out, it sounded crazy, even to his ears.

Bay bit her bottom lip. "I wouldn't have believed

you were scared of anything, Flynn McKenna."

Flynn smiled and shook his head. "Only of you not wanting me as much as I want you."

Bay frowned. "You never have to worry about that." The smile that followed confirmed her words.

Flynn prepared himself for the next serious question. If he didn't do it now he may lose his nerve. "I don't have much to offer you, Bay. What you see is what you get."

"I love what I see." She kissed him gently on the lips.

Flynn almost gave up and had to pull himself away from her to continue. He dug around in his pocket, finding what he was seeking and held it out to her. "This ring was my mother's. It's been in my family for generations. It's not a million carats, but it's special to me."

He paused to show her the ring. It was a princess-cut diamond surrounded with tiny sparkling diamonds. It had an 'other world' feel to its design. To his delight Bay drew a sharp breath, letting out a long, "Oh", as she looked at it in his hand.

"Will you marry me?" he asked. Even though he was sure of himself he held his breath waiting for her answer.

Thankfully, he didn't have to wait long. Bay jumped on him, throwing him off balance. He landed on the blanket with her on top of him. They both burst out in fits of giggles.

"Is that a yes?"

"Yes. Yes. Yes!" she yelled. She kissed him squarely on the lips. He returned the kiss and sat her up to place the ring on her finger. It was a perfect fit.

"I truly love it, Flynn." She fingered the jewelry, and then held it up to the sky to get a better look.

"And I truly love you."

Bay looked out of her window to see the tinny round the rocks. It was a perfect day. The afternoon shade was making its way onto her new balcony. She grabbed her hat and skipped down the stairs to meet her husband, picking her way through some building materials on the way.

She got to the edge of the sand and looked back at the resort. It would be another two months until the building was completed. Ten new ecologically sensitive cabins were nestled against the backdrop of the bush. Each one had its own unique view of the bay, and work had now started on a new bar and restaurant. Bay shook her head. She was amazed once more at the transformation of the resort. It was becoming a modern, casual, family holiday destination.

The money from the trust fund would be enough to cover the work. Thankfully, the few hundred thousand Jack Turvill had siphoned off hadn't put a dent in the capital. Even after all the work was done, they would still have a small amount left for other ventures.

Rebuilding the resort was a dream they had all put into action six months ago. Now, they were close to the fulfilment of that dream. Bay felt the anticipation for the next instalment of her life: running the resort and, perhaps, starting a family of her own.

She stood waiting for Flynn to secure the tinny onto the new floating pontoon. It had been the first addition to the island, a necessity, as they weren't able to start building without an easy way to deliver materials and workers to the island. Now it was hard to imagine their life on Resolution without the luxury.

Bay saw a tuft of red hair poking out from a bush at the end of one of the cabins. She gave a loud whistle. The red cattle dog poked her head out to see her mistress on the beach and came bounding down, red tongue flapping in the wind and tail wagging round and round like a helicopter propeller.

The dog had been a wedding gift from Flynn when they married on the beach at Resolution weeks after he had proposed. He couldn't have given her anything more precious. She bent down to scratch the puppy behind the ears.

"Have you been chasing goannas again, Sheila?" The dog sat down and lapped up the attention. "They'll get the better of a curious puppy." She got a big lick on the face for her efforts.

Bay thought back to her wedding day as she watched her husband offload a few shopping bags from the boat. The beach ceremony was short, and they had fixed up the bar sufficiently to hold the reception. She had found the perfect white silk wedding dress in a shop in Mackay. It was slim fitting and hugged her body in all the right places, formal enough to be her wedding dress, but casual enough for the tropical location. Flynn had consented to wear a dressy shirt and long pants, and

Bay had enjoyed how handsome he had looked. She wore her hair down and they both agreed to be barefoot—no heels necessary.

She'd spent more on flowers than any other part of the day, filling the island with every type of tropical flower available, as well as bunches of roses and lilies. She and Flynn had no attendants but Dutch had given her away, pride and joy written all over his face.

Amos and Neville had been in charge of the reception. They had enlisted the help of their family in Cairns, who had all come down for the event. They had spent the week fishing and crabbing, and the traditional Islander feast was like nothing Bay had ever seen before.

Amos's family were the most loving and accepting people Bay had ever met. The small event they had envisaged turned out to be a huge party once their local friends combined with Amos's extensive family. Their laughter and song set the scene for a spectacular day. Amos even had a cousin who was a pastor, and he had conducted the service for them.

Wendy and her family had come over from New Zealand for the wedding. She was every bit as pleased to see Bay as Dutch had predicted, throwing her arms around her and crying happy tears. They had promised to come back as soon as the resort was finished. Bay still had trouble coming to terms with the excitement she felt at having an extended family. It was so much more than she had dreamed.

Richard had called via satellite phone to wish them well. He also promised to take an extended visit to the resort the minute his assignment was over. Bay wasn't holding her breath. It didn't sound as though he was ready to leave Afghanistan any time soon.

Yvette had made the trip from Perth for the wedding, claiming wild dogs couldn't have kept her away. Bay suspected the joy and excitement she felt at seeing Dutch was the main motivation. It was obvious at first sight of them together that they were meant for each other, and the attraction Yvette felt for Dutch was most certainly reciprocated, so much that she had suggested Dutch visit her in Perth as soon as possible. When Yvette left, and Dutch had moped around like a man lost for three months, she and Flynn had assured him they could handle the building work and pushed him over there to see her. He was there now, spending time getting to know her again.

One disappointment for the day was that Flynn's brother, Jed, had been unable to attend the celebration. It was impossible to get a relief doctor to cover his work in order for him to fly back to Australia. His work was so vital that Flynn and Bay had no trouble forgiving his absence, although Flynn missed him.

Finally they had gone for a week on a honeymoon to Cairns, and Flynn had allowed her to book a room at a five-star hotel. He had enjoyed the experience so much that he decided they needed a trip to the city a couple of times a year, even if it was just to stay in bed all day ordering room service. As much as they enjoyed their honeymoon they were both happy to get back to Resolution. Since then, the building work had taken up most of their time.

Flynn walked down the pontoon balanced by heavy plastic bags, one in each hand, with a large envelope tucked under one arm. Bay raced forward to help him.

"Here's my beautiful wife." He smiled as he approached her. Then, unceremoniously, he dumped it all and took her in his arms to kiss her.

Bay melted into him, feeling his love for her. They still hadn't been able to stem the passion they felt for each other.

Dutch was always rolling his eyes in exasperation and saying things like, "Can't you pair keep your hands off each other for one second?" Bay thought their happiness may have been the catalyst for his embarking on a romantic pursuit of his own.

Flynn pulled away and retrieved the oversized envelope from the ground. "I checked the mailbox and found this." He handed it to her.

She turned it over. It was addressed to her, from *International Naturalist* a worldwide nature publication universally respected for its excellence in photography and journalism.

She looked up at Flynn, fearful of the contents of the envelope.

"Go on. Open it!"

Bay paused for a second then ripped it open. Inside were several copies of the latest edition of the magazine, and on the front cover was one of her photos. She looked up at Flynn and smiled with pride.

"Bay, you got the cover." His grin was as wide as hers. She flipped through the pages to find the five-page spread showcasing her photography.

The title read: *L'Australie del Espiritu Santo: The Southern Land of the Holy Spirit.* They had used two of her photos as well as the cover shot. One picture was from the Daintree showcasing the magnificence of the Daintree River. Two were from Resolution: one spectacular shot of the stone cabin, and another of the reef. The article was about remote places of Australia. It also showcased the rugged beauty of the outback, as well as the rolling hills of the Snowy Mountains, and the forests of Tasmania.

"I'm so proud of you, Bay," Flynn said, as he looked over her shoulder.

"This is only the start." She looked up at him. "I was talking to Yvette and she wants to try and photograph the dugong population in their natural habitat when she comes over here next. It will be a serious challenge as they're so shy."

Bay filled him in on their latest telephone conversation—they'd called and emailed a great deal in the past few months. She couldn't wait until Yvette moved to Resolution permanently. The lady had become a good friend, and a mother figure, giving kind and wise advice.

Flynn put an arm around her shoulders. "Dutch rang me while I was in town. Apparently he and Yvette need a lift back to Resolution from the airport this Wednesday."

Bay felt a thrill of anticipation flutter in her stomach. "Does that mean what I think?"

He jiggled his eyebrows. "Yes, he did mention an upcoming wedding."

Bay giggled and jumped up and down on the spot. Sheila got in on the action mimicking her.

Flynn steadied her before giving her a serious look. "Settle down, you two. Dutch rang me because he wanted their homecoming to be a surprise." He gave her a lopsided grin. "I just can't keep my mouth shut."

"Perhaps we should change your name to Neville."

His face fell. "Don't even joke about that, Bay." Then he winked at her. "Make sure you act surprised when you see them, or you'll get me into trouble."

She promised.

He picked up the two bags. "I'm going up to get this cold food into the fridge. When I saw that envelope, I knew we'd have something to celebrate so I went and got some fresh food. I'm going to cook us up a gourmet barbecue."

Bay slipped her arms around his neck and kissed him in appreciation.

"Then again, I may skip dinner," he said, as she pulled away.

"Would you have me starve?"

"Okay, okay, I'm going to get started." He turned to walk up to their cabin.

"I'll be there in a minute. I want to absorb this." She held up the magazine in explanation. Flynn nodded then made his way up the beach.

Bay sat on the sand and pored over the article. It was a good read and promoted Resolution and North Queensland well.

This country of her birth was incredible. She had formed a real love of the land and, as a consequence, a slight understanding about the way the Indigenous people felt about their home. It was so important to her to keep Resolution as ecologically pristine as she could. They had constantly consulted all the necessary people in the design and rebuilding of the resort. They had also surprised both Amos and Neville with new huts on their side of the island.

She skipped through the rest of the magazine, stopping to investigate further when the page fell open at an article about the plight of Afghanistan's refugees. The photo of the little girl and her mother stared back at her, so breathtakingly real she could physically feel their pain. She looked at the credits and found Richard's name as photographer. What were the chances both of them had photographs in the same magazine at the same time? How perfectly God worked things.

She looked out at the ocean. Soft white caps broke the surface, and the breeze blew in fine gusts across the beach. She couldn't have imagined the blessing God had in store for her the day she accepted Him into her life and asked Him for His help. The life He had planned for her was so far in excess of anything she could have imagined for herself. She closed her eyes and gave thanks for all He had given her.

It hadn't been an easy road. There were some major bumps along the way, but He had seen her through them all. She knew He would see her through many more to come.

She had always felt that something was missing. There had to be more to life than her experiences, more to love than what her mother had shown her, and more to faith than the limited supply she had in herself.

God had shown her a greater love, a life of fulfilment, and a faith in Him that continued to grow day by day. Bay had begun her journey a lost soul searching for a life. Now she knew—she had been found.

BEYOND RESOLUTION

Book 2 in the Resolution Series.

Available now.

Samara lifted her face to the breeze as she stepped out of the pick-up truck. The smell wafting from the louvered window of her unit was undeniable. Marijuana.

She set her jaw and pulled her shoulders back, preparing for a showdown that had been a long time coming.

The commotion in the two-bedroom duplex grew louder as she made her way to the door. The click-clacking of her stiletto heels on the concrete beat in sync with the pulsing beats inside her chest.

She glanced over to the adjoining flat before turning the knob of her own door. The unit had been vacant for over a month, a relief, as it meant there was no one to report the party den her unwanted guest had established in her unit.

The second she pulled the door open, a grey plume of smoke enveloped her. She coughed before moving further into the room.

"Here she is. The lady of the house." Ricky had made himself a nest on the two-seater sofa. One of his stocky little legs draped over the cushions, and the other was cocked up on the coffee table.

"Get your feet off my furniture." Samara threw her handbag at him, but missed.

Ricky gave his two friends seated opposite a withering glance. One scruffy young man was lolling on a recliner chair, and the other had sunken deep into a beanbag. Ricky took his time adjusting his sitting position.

Samara eyeballed the louts. They were well-known drug-affected youths in the small seaside town. "What are these two drop kicks doing here?"

The one in the chair frowned. "Hey, chill out, Sam. We're in the middle of a business meeting." He glanced over at the empty beer bottles and drug paraphernalia strewn across the coffee table. His lopsided grin said it all.

Samara turned to Ricky and gave him what she hoped was the most intense death stare in history.

His return smirk fired her anger.

"This is my home, not an office. And this is no business meeting. Get out." She pointed to the door, and kicked the shin of the lout in the beanbag.

"Yeow."

Sam squinted at the slacker, who jutted out his bottom lip in pouting response to her aggression.

Both men sought direction from Ricky, who rolled his eyes and reached for the half-empty bag of dope on the table. "Party's over, boys. Take this for your trouble."

Beanbag boy leaped from his position like a gazelle. "Hey, thanks man." He snatched the bag from Ricky and sniffed its contents. "This is the best stuff we've had in ages."

Ricky gave him a close-lipped smirk, his ungroomed, bushy eyebrows dipping over glassy blue eyes. "No worries. You know where to buy in the future, right?"

The other teen reached for a pipe on the table. "For sure. We won't go anywhere else. You got the best stuff."

Ricky rose and stumbled around the furniture. "Don't go yet. I'll get you a beer for the road."

He made his way to the kitchen. Samara followed him. He wasn't going to help himself to anything else. She could feel the fire in her gut grow, along with the overwhelming dread at the situation she found herself in. She didn't wait until they were in the kitchen to explode.

"I told you I didn't want you here if I wasn't home." She clenched her teeth at Ricky's back.

He didn't answer her until they were both in the

kitchen. "I don't care what you want. This is business. You're in business with us, so you're going to have to deal with it."

Sam could feel her breath, shallow and rapid. "My agreement was with Karl, not you, and it was for use of my landline telephone, not the entire unit."

Ricky leaned over the kitchen bench that stood between them. His lip curled. "These guys are sellers. They have a lot of buyers. I checked with Karl. He's cool about it."

Samara reached for the cordless phone on the bench. "We'll see about that." She dialed the number.

Karl answered in one ring. "Somers."

"It's me." She knew he would recognize her voice, especially after all the long flirty telephone conversations they'd had recently.

"Hi." Karl's voice was as smooth and slick.

"We've got a problem."

"Let me guess. Ricky is being difficult?"

There was just enough agitation in his voice to pacify Samara, but the situation still had to be addressed. She didn't want to squash the attraction between her and Karl, but she had to put a stop to Ricky's abuse of the limited privileges she had agreed to.

She took a breath before continuing. "The deal I made with you was payment for the use of my telephone, not full access to the unit for drug dealing. I can't be involved in that, Karl. My dad's the local cop and he knows everything that goes on here at Kiisay Point." She paused for another breath. "You've never been here. You don't know how small this place is."

"Well, that's about to change, because I'm an hour away."

Sam bit her lip and lifted her long dark hair off the back of her neck. How did she feel about seeing Karl again? When he and Ricky had taken a table next to her at a cafe in the nearby town over a month ago, she had been both instantly attracted to, and wary of Karl. As interesting as he was, she had judged that the suave, sophisticated city man wasn't someone she could fully trust. She had encountered his type in her modelling days. They were after a trophy girl, fun with no substance. Maybe her attraction to him was because he was so different from her last boyfriend.

Her still fresh uncoupling fiasco pricked her conscience, and sent a rush of fear through her. "If Flynn comes back and finds out what's been going on in his unit, he's going to freak out."

BUY NOW at Amazon or www.rosedee.com

ABOUT THE AUTHOR

Rose, who holds a Bachelor of Arts Degree, was born in North Queensland, Australia. Her childhood experiences growing up in a small beach community would later provide inspiration for her first novel, *Back to Resolution*. *Beyond Resolution* and *A New Resolution* are the second and third books in the Resolution series.

Back to Resolution won the Bookseller's Choice award at the 2012 CALEB Awards, while *A New Resolution* won the 2013 CALEB Prize for Fiction. She has also released *The Greenfield Legacy*, a collaborative novel, written in conjunction with three other outstanding Australian authors, and has recently released the standalone novel, *Ehvah After*.

Her novels are inspired by the love of her coastal home and desire to produce exciting and contemporary stories of faith for women. Rose resides in Mackay, North Queensland.

279

BOOKS BY ROSE

The Resolution Series:
Book 1: Back to Resolution
Book 2: Beyond Resolution
Book 3: A New Resolution
A Resolution Novella: A Christmas Resolution

Other books by Rose Dee
Ehvah After
The Greenfield Legacy (A conjunction novel).

Visit Rose at:
www.rosedee.com
https://www.facebook.com/Rose-Dee-Author-172886062810998/

9 780099 440114 4